BLACK SHEEP COTTAGE

To my daughter, Felicity Dawe,

for never giving up

Chapter 1
December 2012

On Christmas Eve, Deborah greeted her son and Erica at the front door and Erica let out a gasp. Dave gripped her hand.

'Excuse this old thing,' said Deborah, 'but what with all the preparations and everything, I've been feeling a bit weak. It's just easier sometimes to use the chair.'

'But I could have helped you with...'

'Nonsense, Erica. No, please, it is in no way your fault, heavens no. Now, come in, come in. Phyllis has been telling me all about when she first met you. I must say, I'd have loved to have seen old Gertrude's face.'

In spite of herself, Erica sniggered. 'It was quite terrifying.'

'Oh, she's nothing to worry about; all growl and no bite, that one.'

Standing in the living room, with her back to the door, Erica admired the decorations. The tree touched the ceiling, its tip bent over; the angel with her twisted halo dangled at a precarious angle; one wing pointing up and the other down.

'It's much too big, I know, but Dave, my husband Dave, always insists that if you're going to have a tree you might as well have a tree.'

From behind them came a booming, avuncular voice. 'Ah, I thought I heard the doorbell,' followed by an audible gasp. 'Melissa?'

Deborah swung her chair round. 'Dave! This is Erica.'

'Of course, of course; silly of me.' He bounded across the room and shook Erica's hand vigorously. 'Lovely to meet you at last, it was just that split second when I first

5

caught sight of your back, the hair, but now, looking at you, I see, well there you are; Erica. Welcome.'

The moment of tension passed. Drinks were consumed, and they made their way to the dining room situated at the back of the house. It overlooked a large mature garden with a raised bank. Erica could see two ponds; the one on the top bank had a waterfall that cascaded down into the pond below. 'You have a beautiful garden,' she said. 'Were those ponds already here when you moved in?'

'There's another one at the side of the property too, you know,' said Deborah. 'And they are all the creations of my dear and wonderfully talented husband.'

Dave gave a theatrical bow. 'Guilty as charged.'

'You have a very good eye; they look so natural; like they've been there for ever.'

'Well, thank you most kindly,' said Dave as he reached across the table to place a butterfly kiss on the back of her hand.

'Will you give over, Dad,' exclaimed Dave.

The meal, when it arrived, was served by staff. Erica watched, mouth slightly open, as her soup was ladled into a bowl by a stiff-looking gentleman in a penguin outfit. Coughing and spluttering, she grabbed her pristine white linen napkin to cover her mouth. Dave gave her a warning glance. Phyllis asked if she was alright, and Dave's father dashed over to thump her firmly on her back. With tears streaming down her face, she caught Deborah's eye. Deborah looked away quickly and nodded towards the penguin-suited staff. 'Thank you. I'll ring when we're ready for the next course.'

As the last of the staff waddled out, Deborah snorted loudly and Erica collapsed into giggles.

The two men shrugged and Phyllis, with an indulgent smile, remarked, 'Honestly, Deborah, will you never grow up?'

6

Wiping her eyes, Deborah said, 'Sorry Mum, but you have to admit it's all a bit farcical.' She turned to her husband. 'Honestly, love, I know you said that you were getting help in, but I hadn't realised quite how formal they were going to be. Poor Erica, I'm sure she must think we're all quite mad.'

'No, not at all,' hiccupped Erica.

Deborah cocked her head to one side.

'Oh, alright,' confessed Erica. 'Maybe just a little mad.'

The following day started well. They ate their Christmas lunch at one o'clock, and the moment they'd finished Dave's father stood and declared, 'Let the games commence!'

Phyllis clapped her hands. 'Erica, would you be a dear and bring the trolley through. It's just outside in the hall,' she said. 'And no peeking!'

Erica frowned.

'It's best just to do it,' said Dave with a grin.

'Right then,' said Phyllis, revealing a small garden tub filled with water. 'Who's got the oranges?'

'They're in the kitchen, Mum.'

Dave jumped up. 'I'll get them.'

'The rules are very simple,' said Phyllis. 'Everyone will get 20 seconds and the person who grabs an orange in the fastest time is the winner.'

'We are, as you surmised last night, Erica, just a little mad; I hope you don't mind getting wet,' said Deborah.

Erica's shoulders began to shake.

'Are you alright, dear?'

'Yes, yes, Phyllis, I'm fine,' she spluttered. 'I'm just imagining my mother's reaction—she'd, she'd have a fit; I can hear her now: 'what a ridiculous notion, orange bobbing indoors; the floor will be ruined,' and then, and then she'd add, 'besides, shouldn't it be apples?''

Deborah went first. Lifting her head after just a few seconds and dripping water from her nose, she said, 'It's no good, I can't get any purchase on the damn things. You have a go, Mum.'

Phyllis came up spluttering and giggling. 'I used to be so good at this; come on, Erica, your turn.'

'Don't forget; hands behind your back.'

'She knows the rules, Dad; go on, Erica, you can do it.'

Lifting her head up as time was called, she spat out a leaf. 'It's a lot harder than it looks.'

'It's all down to control,' said Dave.

'Oh, listen to the expert; go on then, Dad; show us how it's done.'

Dave knelt in front of the tub, put his hands behind his back, and dunked. After just 15 seconds he came up coughing and spluttering. Phyllis thumped him hard. 'Swallowed a gallon of water,' he gasped.

'Come on Son, your turn, and remember, the family honour is resting on your shoulders,' said Deborah.

Dave stepped forward. He whipped off his glasses, handed them to Erica, and plunged his head completely into the water, coming up almost immediately, hair plastered across his face and an orange clenched between his teeth. He shook his head, soaking everyone, snatched the orange from his mouth, kissed Erica and said, 'Easypeasy, orange squeezy.'

Once everyone had dried off, Dave's father announced the next game. He held up some cards. 'Here are a few I prepared earlier,' he said with a broad grin, handing Erica one. 'As our guest, Erica, you go first.'

She turned over her card. Her eyes widened as she slowly took centre stage.

'I hope you haven't made them too rude this year, darling,' said Deborah.

'Who, me?'

Erica held up one finger and then tapped three fingers on her arm.

'One word; three syllables,' said Dave.

Erica nodded, took a deep breath and started.

'Can?' said Phyllis.

'Can-can?' said Deborah.

'Can suck?' suggested Dave.

Erica giggled and shook her head.

'Can spaghetti?'

She furiously tapped three fingers on her forearm again.

Dave glanced across at his father, raised his eyebrows and declared, 'Can noodle!'

'Yes; oh, well done,' exclaimed Erica.

'Your turn,' said Phyllis.

Dave snatched a card from his father and turned it over. 'Oh, for pity's sake, Dad, really?'

'Too difficult?'

'No, Dad, just, oh, never mind.' He marched to the front and began.

'One word; three syllables; the whole thing,' said Deborah.

'Bottom?' said Deborah.

'Bottomless?' suggested Erica.

'Arsehole!' cried Phyllis.

'Mother!' exclaimed Deborah.

'It's a word, dear.'

'Well obviously it's a word but…'

'It only has two syllables though,' said Erica.

'Yes, there you are, Mother,' said Deborah, throwing a stern look towards her husband.

'Bottomlessly,' declared Phyllis.

Deborah snorted. 'That's not even a word, Mum.'

Phyllis folded her arms across her chest. 'That may be so, dear, but it's got three syllables.'

'Actually I think bottomlessly has four syllables,' said Erica.

Phyllis frowned. 'Oh yes, so it has. Go on then, dear; you have another guess.'

'Um, um, oh, what about endlessly!'

Phyllis turned to Dave.

He shook his head.

Hysteria set in as the guessing became more and more ridiculous, until eventually Deborah wiped her eyes and said, 'It's no good, we give up; what is it?'

Erica threw her hand up. 'No, hang on, I think I've got it,' she cried as she winked at Dave's father. 'Is it Uranus?'

Dave chucked the card back towards his father, rushed over to Erica and planted a kiss on her lips. 'You wonderful creature,' he gushed. 'You've saved me from further humiliation.'

'Well done, dear,' said Phyllis. 'It's your go again.'

Erica glanced at her watch. 'Actually, would it be alright if I rang my parents?'

'Of course,' said Deborah. 'The phone's in the hall.'

Erica's mother answered the phone. 'Darling, is everything alright?'

'Yes, of course it is; I'm just ringing to wish you a happy Christmas.'

'Yes, right; fine. Happy Christmas darling,' she said as she yelled, 'William, William! It's Erica, ringing to say happy Christmas.'

Erica heard a chorus of happy Christmas wishes. 'Having a party?'

'No, dear; your father just invited the neighbours over, Margaret and Harold, remember them?'

'Of course I remember them, Mum; I only left home a couple of years ago, for goodness sake.'

'Alright dear; don't take on. Anyway, did you like your present; it's from both of us obviously but as usual your father left all the present shopping to me; I doubt very much if he'll even remember what we gave you.'

10

'We haven't opened any presents yet.'

'Don't be ridiculous; the Queen has already given her speech. Not opened them yet; I've never heard the like.'

'So, let me guess,' said Erica. 'You're all in the living room, eating turkey sandwiches and watching *It's a Wonderful Life*.'

'Well, oh, hold on; your father wants a word.'

'Happy Christmas, sweetheart; we're missing you and guess what we're doing now.'

Erica heard her mother snap. 'We've already covered that and listen to this; they haven't opened their presents yet.'

'What's wrong with that, Audrey?' said William. 'Lots of people don't open their presents until after the Queen…'

'Like who?'

'Well, um, well…'

'Erica; are you still there?'

'Yes, Mother, but I've got to go now; we're playing Charades.'

'Charades,' exclaimed Audrey. 'Such a silly game; I can't be doing with it. Anyway, it's a children's game.'

'Not with the words we're using.'

'I see,' said Audrey in that disapproving tone that Erica recognised from her childhood. 'Right; well, you'd better get back; here's your father again.'

'Is everything alright, Dad?'

'All perfectly fine, don't worry sweetheart; you know your mother.'

'Yes, Dad, I do, hence my question.'

'Don't rise to the bait; I never do,' said William. Lowering his voice, he added, 'It drives your mother insane.'

'Love you, Dad.'

'Love you too, sweetheart; bye.'

Dave's father finally handed out the presents at four o'clock. Erica opened her small parcel under the watchful eye of an adoring Dave and was surprised to find that it contained an innocuous looking brass key attached to a comical looking black sheep key ring. There was a small card inside embossed with the words, *Black Sheep Cottage: an idyllic location; join me to welcome in the New Year.*

She held the key up and remarked, 'It's a key.'

'Well spotted,' said Dave.

'But where is the cottage?'

Before Dave could respond his father spoke. 'Um, Dave, could I have a word?'

Tearing his eyes away from Erica, Dave barked, 'What?'

'It's about your grandmother's cottage,' he said.

Phyllis glanced at Erica. 'I'm very sorry about this, dear, but I fear there is no longer a cottage in Yorkshire.'

'What *are* you talking about?' demanded Dave.

'Oh dear; this is very awkward,' said Phyllis.

'It's getting more and more difficult for me to travel,' explained Deborah. 'And you hadn't shown the slightest bit of interest in going back there ever since, well, ever since Melissa left, and so Mum felt that it would be better to sell the thing. Your father did try to dissuade her but she was adamant; she asked him to organise the sale and so, well, there we go.'

Dave went very pale. He catapulted himself out of his chair and bore down on his father. 'Sold it? Sold it? When did you bloody sell it? Jesus!'

'It's alright Dave,' said Erica. 'It was a lovely thought and…'

'Shut-up!' he screamed.

Erica's eyes brimmed with tears. She shut up.

'I ask again,' Dave yelled. 'When did you sell it?'

Deborah started to speak.

'Whatever it is that you're going to say, Mum, I'm not interested.' He returned his attention to his father. Spitting out the words like bullets, he asked, 'When did you sell it?'

'There's no need to…'

'I ask again, when?'

'Earlier this year; I think contracts were exchanged in…' he turned to Deborah.

'In February,' Deborah said. 'A lovely couple, Jason and Nicole Morgan bought it.'

'Yes, in February that's right,' agreed Phyllis. 'I appreciate that we should probably have told you, but it had become a place of such sad memories, I just thought; oh, dear.'

Dave staggered back to his chair and slumped back down. No one spoke. His father tut-tutted loudly. Deborah closed her eyes and Phyllis twiddled with the sleeve of her cardigan. Erica quietly replaced the key into its box.

'Everything's fucked,' snarled Dave. He snatched the box from Erica's hand and stormed out. The sound of the front door slamming reverberated around the house.

One more conversation about the war and the plucky spirit of the Brits would, Maggie feared, send her over the edge. She wondered how Erica was getting on and decided to ring her, not with the fake emergency call that had been discussed and rejected, but simply to speak to someone her own age.

'Happy Christmas…'

'Oh, Maggie. Thank God,' cried Erica.

'Erica? What is it; what's the matter?'

'It was all going so well, really it was, his parents are smashing and his mum, well his mum is amazing, she's got a wicked sense of humour and even though she's in a wheelchair, which was a bit of a shock I must confess, she can certainly get about, at some speed too. And Dave, he's been great, well, he was being great and then, when it turned out that the key was an empty gesture, he just went ape and he's gone.' She began to sob quietly.

'Are you still with Dave's parents?'

'Yep,' she spluttered.

'Right, no arguments, I'm coming to get you; ideal excuse to extract myself from this hell hole of geriatrics.' She glanced at her watch. 'It's five o'clock now, so I'll borrow one of Daddy's cars, should be with you by about half six. I'll grab some provisions, there's enough food and drink here to feed a bloody army, and we'll go back to the flat.'

Later, Maggie settled Erica on the settee and poured two stiff brandies. 'Here you are, get that down you, and when you're ready you can tell me all about it; your phone explanation wasn't very clear.'

After her second brandy Erica told Maggie everything.

'So, where is he now?'

'I've no idea.'

'How peculiar; and it all kicked off after he found out that his grandmother had sold the Yorkshire place, you say?'

'Yes.'

'How peculiar,' Maggie repeated.

'Oh, Maggie, it was awful; he behaved like a spoilt child.'

'I expect he was the same when he was little, throwing a tantrum if he didn't get his own way; you know, the type of kid that you would cheerfully trip up as they strutted about all cocky and full of themselves.'

'Maggie!' exclaimed Erica as a snigger escaped.

'That's more like it. Now come on, there's no point dwelling on the man. He'll doubtless turn up when he's good and ready. Let's see what we can rustle up from the goodies that I purloined from the parents.'

Chapter 2
Six Months Earlier

On the bus back to her flat, Erica Woods stared through the murky windows at the streets of London, streets that had once held promise. Her fellow passengers looked miserable; beaten down and weary. They, like her, seemed to have accepted their lot in life and just given up. The heavy dark boulder in the pit of her stomach was becoming unbearable. Her bones hurt; her head hurt, even her teeth hurt. As the bus approached her stop she rang the bell and descended the stairs; head down, she trudged along the brightly lit street. Past the ever open shops, cafes and bars, she turned down the side alley where the market stalls stood empty, bleak without their bright awnings, eerily silent in the shadows. Entering her flat, she leant heavily on the door, closed her eyes and breathed deeply. She must not cry because once started she would never be able to stop. The phone rang.

'Hello darling,' said her mother brightly.

With false bravado, Erica replied, 'Hi there.'

'What's the matter?'

'What do you mean, what's the matter? Nothing's the matter.'

'Erica, this is your mother and don't you be telling me that nothing's the matter when patently something *is* the matter.'

'It's been a hard day, Mum, that's all. I'm fine.'

Her mother's sigh must surely have been audible to the entirety of Bolton-on-Swale. 'I don't know why you insist on staying in that desolate flat, in a dead-end job. Your father and I have always said that you can come home. There's no shame in it. At least you'd be safe and secure.'

'I'm safe and secure here, Mum.'

'Well, that's a moot point dear. I have seen where you live and work and as far as I'm concerned they are neither.'

'Mum, we've been over this. Granted I'm not exactly in my dream job…'

'Hah!'

'But I'm not giving up. I've worked bloody…'

'Don't swear, dear.'

Erica gritted her teeth. 'I've worked *very* hard over the years and I'm not about to give up at the first hurdle, surely you can understand that; you and Dad were the ones who told me that failure was not an option.'

'That's your father's opinion, Erica. I, on the other hand, do not believe in beating a dead donkey.'

'Well, thanks for that Mum, I'm many things but a donkey, dead or otherwise, I am not.'

'You know what I mean. Please don't deliberately misconstrue what I say simply to make a point.'

'Anyway, Mum, you rang. Was there a particular reason or…'

'Oh, yes. That friend of yours, Marge, Matty…'

'Maggie?'

'That's it. She rang the other day to speak to you. She's back from, from, wherever it was that she went to, and wondered if you wanted to meet up.'

Erica, cheered. 'Brilliant; did you give her my number?'

'No dear.'

'Why ever not?'

'Well, I wasn't sure if you wanted to see her again, you know, considering what happened.'

'Oh, for goodness sake, Mum,' exclaimed Erica. 'That was years ago.'

'Yes, well. Anyway, she gave me her mobile number. Just a minute, I jotted it down somewhere. Ah; here it is; 0775432901.'

'Hang on, Mum. I need a pencil or something.' Erica scrabbled around in her copious handbag and located a pen. 'Shit,' she exclaimed.

'Erica, I do wish you wouldn't...'

'The blood-stupid pen has leaked. Everything's covered in ink, as are my fingers now. Right, so, what was that number again?'

Her mother repeated it. 'So, I take it that you will be ringing her.'

'Too right I will. I need cheering up,' Erica replied, immediately regretting her slip.

'So there *is* something the matter. I *knew* it.'

'Alright, alright, I give up. I'm a bit down at the moment, nothing to worry about really. As I said earlier, I've just had one of those days. Anyway, I know one thing for sure; Maggie will snap me out of it.'

'I'm sure you know best,' said her mother without conviction.

'Thanks for ringing, Mum, but I need to get on. I'll ring you soon.'

'Make sure that you do, dear. Otherwise I worry.'

'Bye, Mum.'

'Bye, dear.'

Erica put the phone down slowly. She hadn't been entirely honest with her mother. She and Maggie still had issues to resolve. They hadn't spoken since completing their finals when Maggie had swanned off with Jared and Erica had returned to her parents in North Yorkshire to contemplate her options. Her father had attempted to encourage her by leaving the morning paper outside her bedroom door with various 'situations vacant' circled. He colour-coded his circles. Green, in his opinion, was an excellent opportunity; blue, a reasonable opportunity, and red, well, red was *if you must*. Her enthusiasm dwindled day by day as rejections came from all the green and blue circled adverts until, eventually, she was reduced to the *if you must* list.

Without her grandmother's financial help Erica would have been trapped. With it she was able to rent a flat in London. It wasn't exactly a penthouse, but it was hers, all three rooms of it, including a small backyard that could be approached via the fire escape. The bathroom, such as it was, contained an unenthusiastic shower that sprinkled water slowly at a temperature that was dependent on other usage in the block. It ranged from lukewarm to icy cold. The property had been described in the estate agent's window as a self contained flat situated within an imposing and grand building, a statement designed to distract from the fact that the flat itself was not large at all. The estate agent's description had also mentioned original features, presumably referring to the bathroom's avocado coloured sink and toilet. The statement that the flat was in a thriving part of town and close to all amenities certainly covered its proximity to the market, shops, cafes and restaurants, sandwiched as it was between two alleys—Market Way at the front, and at the back an alley with no name. No name alley backed onto all the aforementioned shops, cafes and restaurants, and was therefore populated with bins as well as workers sheltering under the eaves, grabbing a smoke whenever they could. Erica looked round at her living room with its mismatched furniture covered in multicoloured throws, her Gustav Klimt prints covering the drab paintwork, and her cheese plant, which she had nurtured from a sorry-looking, three-leaved specimen bought from the market stall when she'd first moved in, two and a half years ago. She felt better; this place, for all its faults, was at least her own.

After a surprisingly warm shower and an uninspiring microwave meal, Erica poured herself a generous glass of white wine and rang the number that her mother had supplied earlier.

'Maggie Hunter-Lopez; to whom am I speaking?'

'Oo, get you. Hi, Maggie, it's me, Erica.'

The squeal emitted was such that Erica was forced to hold the phone at some distance from her ear.

'Erica! Hi there yourself. How the devil are you? Your mum says that you're living and working in London now. Well done you. So, tell me all; is it your dream job? I bet the flat is *spectacular*; where is it? Is it in Kensington, Knightsbridge, Notting Hill, or Hampstead? Tell me it's in Notting Hill, I love that place.'

'Peckham.'

'Peckham? Bloody hell Erica, Peckham?'

'It's not *that* bad.'

'Sorry, I'm sure you're right; but, Peckham, I mean, well it hasn't exactly got a good reputation has it?'

'It's not that bad,' Erica repeated. And before she had a chance to think she heard herself say, 'You must come and visit; whereabouts are you these days?'

'Back with the folks at the moment; very dreary. Anyway, I'd *love* to visit; when?'

With no way out, Erica suggested the weekend, adding quickly, in the hope that it might act as a deterrent, 'You'd have to sleep on the sofa bed though; I've only got one bedroom.'

'No problem; it'll be like the old days.'

An awkward silence fell.

'Yes,' said Erica brightly, 'just like the old days.'

'You are alright about me coming, aren't you? Because, you know, well...'

Erica took a deep breath. 'Of course I'm alright about it. I wouldn't have invited you otherwise,' she said with her fingers crossed. 'It was all a long time ago.'

There was a slight pause. 'We had such fun didn't we, before all the; well anyway, I'm looking forward to seeing you.'

'Me too,' said Erica. And as the words came out of her mouth she realised that it was true; she *was* looking forward to seeing Maggie again.

Leaning back, Erica wondered what had become of Jared. It seemed likely that he and Maggie were no longer together, otherwise why would Maggie be living with her parents? He was, of course, the cause of their fallout. The usual story; girl meets boy, they fall in love; boy meets best friend of girl, he falls in love with her; boy leaves girl and goes off with best friend. Girl and best friend fall out. Summarising it like that made Erica see how pathetic it all was, how predictable and banal, and she was ashamed to recall her rather pitiable attempt at suicide.

Having been dressed and ready for an hour, Erica was putting the finishing touches to the salad when the buzzer went. Maggie had arrived.

'I'm on the top, number seven. See you in a tick.'

At first the two women said nothing. They eyed each other up. Erica noted that Maggie, stunning, tall, and blonde, with blazing blue eyes, hadn't changed a bit. Erica, small, with mousey brown hair and dull blue eyes, felt that familiar pang of jealousy twist in her gut.

'You haven't changed a bit,' said Maggie.

'I was just thinking the same of you,' remarked Erica.

They exchanged an awkward hug. 'Come in, come in,' said Erica brightly. 'Drink?'

'I'd love some wine. Any colour, I'm not fussed.'

'So, no change there either then?'

'Nope. You?'

'Nope.'

'And don't tell me; is that lasagne I smell?'

With a little giggle Erica admitted that it was indeed lasagne.

Grinning broadly, Maggie exclaimed, 'Bloody hell, don't tell me that's still the only dish you cook.'

'It absolutely is not,' cried Erica, as she handed Maggie her white wine. 'I do a mean moussaka too.'

'That's the *same* dish, Erica; potatoes instead of pasta; oh, and a few aubergines thrown in for good measure.'

'I know,' she groaned, 'but in my defence they are both very tasty.'

Both women took a gulp of wine as the background noises from no name alley drifted into the room.

Eventually Maggie spoke. 'So, who's going to mention Jared first?'

Erica gave a wry smile. 'It looks like you already have.'

'Right; so, it will probably come as no surprise to you that Jared and I are no longer together.'

'I did wonder,' admitted Erica.

'As well you might. I was a cow, I know that and, for what it's worth, I felt awful about it, especially when I heard from Mum that you'd, you know…'

'Tried to top myself?'

'God, Erica, I couldn't believe it,' said Maggie.

'It was, as all the best books say, a pathetic cry for help. Not my sort of thing at all and frankly humiliating. A trip to hospital for a stomach pump, interviews with some nut doctors and then home to Mum and Dad feeling very sorry for myself.'

'I don't know what to say.'

'There is nothing you can say, not really. You certainly can't blame yourself. Jared was the one who dumped me, and I was insanely jealous of you,' Erica downed the last of her wine. 'If I'm honest…'

'Oh, I think that's best.'

'Well, if I'm honest, I was always a bit jealous of you.'

Genuinely shocked, Maggie asked, 'Why, for God's sake?'

'Look at you.'

Maggie looked down at herself. 'Yes; and?'

'Your silk fine hair and willowy body, for a bloody start,' exclaimed Erica.

'Well, there is that, I admit,' chuckled Maggie. 'Mind you, you stunning little pixie face you; you still look about 12, don't you ever age?'

Erica lashed out playfully and the tension was broken.

Maggie reached into her Dolce and Gabbana tote bag. 'I note that our glasses are empty. Fear not; I came bearing booze,' she cried, brandishing a bottle of red. 'Where do you keep the bottle opener?'

'Maggie! That looks like a vintage Burgundy.'

Maggie gave the bottle a cursory glance. 'I expect it is. I nicked it from Daddy's cellar. So, bottle opener?'

Erica jumped up. 'I'll get it. I need to take the lasagne out anyway.'

They ate the meal Japanese style, cross-legged at the coffee table. Gesticulating wildly with her fork, Maggie related her ill-fated trip with Jared. 'It all started so well. We trekked across Europe and made our way to Daddy's villa in Tuscany.'

Narrowing her eyes, Erica said, 'Hold on a minute; you *trekked?*'

'OK. Not exactly; we went on the Orient Express to Venice and then hired a car to drive to Tuscany.'

'Hah!'

'Anyway by the time we got to the villa I was beginning to seriously doubt my judgment. Jared was turning out to be a man of hidden shallows. He was all me, me, me, and I was beginning to feel like a brainless bimbo for giving up a perfectly good friendship for the pile of crap that was turning out to be Jared T.K. Cox.'

'He wasn't like that with me,' retorted Erica.

'Oh, I don't doubt that for one second; he was considerate, loving and charming with me too, at the beginning. But put him in radar range of breasts and lo, the transformation from a perfectly pleasant human being to dickhead was complete within nanoseconds.'

Erica's eye's widened. 'You mean like when I introduced him to you?'

'Oh, shit, um…'

'Sorry.'

'Don't you dare apologise to me,' said Maggie. 'Anyway, we were going into Empoli every day. He swanned around and flirted with every Italian woman he saw, showing off his fluent Italian among other things. He was insufferable.' Maggie took another mouthful of food, made satisfying murmuring sounds and then added, 'This is really good, very authentic.'

'Thanks. So what happened?'

'We met this equally insufferable American upstart called Chase. He'd picked up an Italian waitress who looked like she was from the cast of Carmen, called Donatella; hardly spoke a word of English. Jared and Chase thought it was hysterically funny that they could make inappropriate sexual comments to her and she would just smile sweetly. My protests simply encouraged them. One drunken session resulted in Chase being knocked to the ground by some Italian bloke who *did* speak English. Donatella stormed off, with Jared in hot pursuit.'

'What, he just abandoned you?'

'Yep. He sent me a text a short while later saying that Donatella was a bit upset, can you believe it; a bit? Anyway, he said he was taking her back to the villa and could I go with Chase to pick up her things from the hotel. A hotel, I might add that was just outside Florence, some considerable distance away. I said I'd see what I could do and that I'd be back at the villa in a few hours.'

'You went with Chase?'

'As it happens, no, I didn't. He gave me what I can only suppose he imagined was a winning smile, a sort of twisted smirk with spittle drooling down his chin, and said something to the effect of a fair exchange as he groped my arse.'

'He sounds charming; I can't think why you would turn him down.'

'No, hard to imagine isn't it? Anyway, the net result was that I got back to the villa much sooner than Jared expected, only to find him and Donatella mid fellatio on the villa steps.'

Erica snorted so violently that the wine she'd gulped down exited through her mouth and nose in a splendid arc across the coffee table. With tears in her eyes, she spluttered, 'You *are* joking?'

Dabbing ineffectively at the spray of wine, Maggie announced, 'I kid you not.'

'So,' Erica said thoughtfully, 'it seems that you saved me from a disastrous relationship.'

'Yes, I suppose I did. Obviously, it goes without saying, that wasn't actually my prime motive for going off with your man.'

'No, but still...'

'The thing is, well, the thing is, I feel, um, oh, hell!'

'You feel treacherous, disloyal and perfidious?'

'What are you; the new compiler for the Thesaurus?'

'Not exactly, no.'

Maggie bowed her head in exaggerated shame. 'Right; anyway, yes, I confess; I feel that I am all of the aforementioned adjectives. Sorry.' Slowly she bought her head up and stared appealingly into Erica's eyes. 'Are we still friends?'

Erica gave Maggie a playful slap. 'Honestly. You look like some poor lovesick puppy caught chewing the carpet. And, do you know what?'

'What?'

'Suddenly it all seems so unimportant and, from what you've just told me, the wonderful, suave and masterful Jared T.K Cox is simply an insignificant, self serving fool.'

'More wine?'

'I'd love some. I seem to have wasted the last mouthful,' said Erica with a look of innocence. 'Any idea what he's doing now?'

Pouring more wine, Maggie asked, 'Who?'

'Jared.'

'Don't know and don't care. More to the point, Erica Frances Woods, if, as you have just pointed out, you are not working on the new Thesaurus, what job *are* you doing in the great metropolis?'

'Oh, I almost forgot,' Erica slurred as she pushed herself up from the settee and made her way unsteadily to the bookcase. 'Just after I rang you I unearthed this.' She thrust a large photo album into Maggie's hand and collapsed back down. 'Oops,' she giggled.

The rest of the evening was a blur of reminiscing and wine until eventually, at three in the morning, the two women staggered into Erica's bedroom and passed out, fully clothed, on the bed.

They surfaced, bleary eyed and hung-over well after noon the next day. Neither of them could face breakfast, and after several strong coffees decided that some fresh July air was the answer. Arm in arm they made their way out onto Market Way to be confronted by the cacophony of noise and bustle that was the Saturday market. The stalls were brightly coloured and one, selling fruit, caught Maggie's eye. This was fruit like she'd never seen: the sheer quantity, the variety, the colours and, above all, the aromas. There were bananas still attached to their stems as if they had just been hacked from the tree; oranges the size of melons; melons the size of footballs. Grapes glistened in the sun, calling out to be eaten. She stared open-mouthed as the huge stall holder, a Reginald D. Hunter look-alike, wielded a large knife; the thud of this knife as it sliced through the fruits filled the air. Mid-way through this process he threw her an enormous lemon and, amazingly, she caught it. Its outer surface was waxy and very rough. The stall holder said nothing. He simply nodded his head towards an ancient looking grater. She began grating the rind, the scent rising from the lemon fresh and clean.

The stallholder shot Erica a delicious smile. 'Heavy night, Erica?' he asked.

'You could say that, Winton. I'd like you to meet my good friend, Maggie.'

Wiping his massive hands on a cloth attached to his belt, Winton extended his arm across his stall.

'Hi there,' Maggie managed to mumble.

'Are you here for a visit or…?'

'Just visiting.' Throwing Winton one of her own smiles, she added, 'I do hope my grating is up to standard.'

Picking up the wooden slab, Winton examined the lemon gratings with exaggerated concern. He scooped a pile into his hands and let them fall through his fingers back onto the board. After repeating this process three times he announced, in a sing-song voice, '*The* best lemon-rind I've ever seen.'

'You are a perfect idiot,' exclaimed Erica.

'So,' he asked, 'where are you two beauties off to?'

'Actually, Erica, seeing all this fruit has made me realise that I'm quite hungry,' announced Maggie.

'She should take you to…'

'Yes, right, thanks Winton,' interjected Erica rapidly. 'We must dash. You know, things to do, people to see and all that.' She grabbed Maggie's arm and dragged her away from Winton's stall, saying she knew of a fantastic new café that had opened up on Blenheim Grove. Twisting her body round, Maggie gave Winton another smile and a wave just before they disappeared from sight and burst out onto Peckham High Street. 'Bloody hell, Erica; what's the rush?'

'No rush,' declared Erica, 'it's just that I agree with you; we really should eat something and I've heard that this new café is really swanky.'

'Actually, I've had it up to here with swanky,' said Maggie flinging her hand above her head. 'No, I'll tell you what I fancy and that's a decent greasy spoon, and, as it happens, when I arrived yesterday I spotted a divine looking place just behind the railway station. It was called um, oh, it was a fantastic name.' As she struggled to recall the name Maggie failed to notice her friend's discomfiture. 'Lord of the Fries! That was it. Isn't it a wonderful name?'

'I'm sure you'd prefer…'

'Nope; come on, it'll be fun. A decent fry-up will do us both good.'

Erica gave up. 'OK,' she said reluctantly.

Walking through the door ten minutes later they were regaled with the delicious smell of cooked bacon and hot coffee. With her head down, Erica followed Maggie to the counter where a buxom woman with a terrifying perm was serving an equally buxom man a mug of steaming tea. 'There you go luv, get that down you and you'll feel on top of the world in minutes.' Turning to greet her new customers she exclaimed, 'Erica! Can't keep away, even on your day off; now that's what I call loyalty. What can I get for you and…?' she gave Maggie an enquiring stare.

'Maggie,' said Maggie giving Erica a wide eyed look. 'My name is Maggie, I'm um, well, I'm Erica's friend.'

'Welcome to our humble abode, luv. It looks like you've arrived not a minute too soon. You need to get something substantial down you, girl, before you waste away completely. Now, what can I get you?'

Turning to Erica, Maggie asked, 'Gosh, I'm not sure. What would *you* recommend, Erica?'

'Um, the All Day Breakfast is always good,' replied a blushing Erica.

'Right; I'll have an All Day Breakfast and a mug of coffee please.'

'I'll have the same. Thanks, Joyce.'

'Two dog's breakfasts all day, Mac,' she bellowed. Lowering her voice slightly she continued, 'Table 6 is free. I'll bring your coffees over.'

'Thanks, Joyce.'

Maggie followed Erica to table 6 and sat. 'You've got to be kidding me; *this* is where you work?'

'Yes, well, I…' Erica was saved from having to explain further as the sound of church bells filled the air. Scrambling frantically, she located her phone, which had worked its way into the furthest reaches of her bag. 'I don't believe it,' she cried.

'What?'

'It's another message for Dave.'

'Dave? Who's Dave?'

'You might well ask.'

'I just did.'

'I don't know.'

'What do you mean, you don't know?'

'I don't know who Dave is.'

'So why are you getting messages for him?'

Erica opened her mouth to reply.

'And don't say, 'you might well ask' or I will not be held responsible for my actions,' added Maggie.

'Here you are, luvs, two mugs of coffee. Food won't be long.'

'Thanks, Joyce,' said Erica as she took a sip. 'Perfect.'

'Naturally, naturally,' sang out Joyce as she made her way back to the counter.

'So, come on, tell me all,' said Maggie. She took a tentative sip from her mug and exclaimed, 'Oh Erica, you're not kidding. This really is a good coffee.'

Elbows on the table and leaning forward, Erica began to tell Maggie about the many text messages that she'd received. 'It's really weird,' she said. 'It all started soon after I moved into the flat. So I've been receiving these things for over two years now.'

'But haven't you told whoever it is that you're not this Dave person?'

'Oh, it isn't just one person. I must have received texts from dozens of different people and, to answer your question, yes, I have told them, well most of them, that I'm not Dave but, as you can see,' she said, flashing the phone in front of Maggie's nose, 'I'm still getting them.'

Grabbing the phone, Maggie said, 'So, what does this one say?' She quickly scanned the message. 'Reminding him of a doctor's appointment; intriguing. I wonder who he is.'

'I get a lot of those; I hope he's not seriously ill or anything,' remarked Erica. 'The thing is, given all the different messages from all these people, I actually know quite a lot about him, whoever he is.'

Before Erica could continue, Joyce plonked their food in front of them. 'The sauces are on the—oh, Erica knows. Enjoy.'

'This looks delish,' cried Maggie. 'I'm ravenous.'

Once they'd finished their food and ordered another coffee, Maggie extracted a notebook and pen from her handbag. 'So, what do you know about this bloke, Dave?' she asked, eyes glistening with anticipation.

Erica tut-tutted; scrolled back through her messages and read them out to Maggie who made a list. 'This is quite extensive,' she said, handing her notebook to Erica. 'Look.'

Erica looked. 'Good grief, you're not wrong.'

Under the heading, *what we know about Dave*, Maggie had listed twelve pieces of information, including that he played golf at various posh golf clubs, attended parties in the West End, and had a Paypal account. This last piece of information also revealed his surname.

'I bet we could track him down, you know,' said Maggie. 'We even know that he most likely lives in London.'

'And we know his age,' declared Erica.

Maggie grabbed her notebook back and scanned the list. 'How?'

'A voicemail from his grandmother last week, wishing him a happy 30th.'

'Perfect; so, what do you say; shall we go on a Dave Hunt?'

'Don't be ridiculous!'

'Why is that ridiculous? Come on. It'll be fun,' cajoled Maggie as she looked around, 'And, let's face it; if this is where you work it seems to me that you could do with a bit of fun.'

Reluctantly, Erica was forced to agree.

'And while we're on the subject; why *are* you working here? I was under the impression that your sights had been a *little* higher. Wasn't it journalism or something of that ilk?'

'I am still writing,' Erica wailed, 'but none of the papers or magazines are exactly breaking down doors to offer me a job. I've had a few pieces published; just not enough to keep me fed and watered; hence this job. I'm so knackered when I get back home that all I want to do is collapse into bed; I certainly don't have the energy to be creative. Anyway, it isn't that bad here. The staff are lovely and the customers, well, the customers are interesting.'

'Such a useful word, 'interesting;' it covers so many sins,' remarked Maggie with a broad grin. 'Oh, do say we can investigate this Dave chap. I'm at an impasse with my research...'

'Something to do with the rise of Mary Seacole to a heroic black role model, wasn't that it?'

'Yes, that's exactly it. There's been loads written comparing her nursing skills to those of Florence Nightingale; the problem is verifying it. I'm waiting on some paperwork from Jamaica but it seems to be taking forever. Your phone call came just in time; I was going insane at my parents' place. This would be a fun interlude...'

'Maggie, I haven't got the time. Did you not hear a word of what I was saying?'

'Listen, if it's a question of money...'

Erica threw Maggie a look of thunder as she thumped the table. 'Jesus, Maggie, what am I, your new charity case?'

'I'm just saying...'

'I know what you're *just saying*, you're saying that you've got money and I haven't,' Erica screamed.

Holding up her hands, Maggie shouted, 'Yes, but that's hardly my fault is it?'

The general hubbub within the café ceased as all eyes turned towards the two women. Joyce came bustling over. 'Whatever's the matter?'

'Nothing, really,' said Erica, 'just my friend, making ludicrous suggestions.'

Two teenagers sitting at the next table cried, 'We'll have some of that.'

Joyce clipped them round the ear.

'Ow! That's physical assault that is!'

Joe Reed, an off duty policeman, strode over to their table, flashed his badge and rejoined, 'And *your* comment was sexual harassment. So why don't you be good little boys and shut up.'

They shut up.

Erica shot him a grateful smile.

'No problem, Erica; as long as you two ladies are alright, I'll get back to my coffee.'

'We're fine, Joe,' said Erica. 'Thanks.'

'Right then,' said Joyce. 'Can I get you anything else?'

'No thanks, just the bill,' said Erica as she leaned back and stared out at the street.

Maggie, watching the retreating back of Joe, cleared her throat. 'Sorry.'

Erica turned back to face her friend. 'No, I'm sorry; I over-reacted.'

Maggie waited until Joe had sat back down and then muttered, sotto voice, 'Who was *that*; he's bloody gorgeous.'

'Joe? He's our local copper.'

'I bet he looks fantastic in his uniform.'

'Give over, Maggie, honestly. Anyway, he's an Inspector; he doesn't wear a uniform.'

'No matter; an Inspector—even better: a man with power.'

Erica scowled and gave Maggie a playful thump.

Chapter 3

Two weeks later Maggie had moved in with Erica and they were enjoying a celebratory drink in The Goose and Hounds.

'I have to confess I'm looking forward to playing private detective,' said Erica. 'So, where do we start?'

Reaching into her copious bag, Maggie extracted her laptop. 'We start by doing a name search.' She switched on and logged in. 'Why don't you get us another drink and by the time you get back I'll have all the information we need,' she added confidently.

A few moments later they were staring at the screen. There were just eight listings.

'How did you do that?'

'The wonder of 192.com,' explained Maggie.

'Yes, but don't you have to be registered or something?'

'Yep.'

'So, why are you registered with them? Do you make a habit of this sort of thing then?'

Maggie cleared her throat and flushed red. 'Um, not exactly.'

'You tried to find out where Jared ended up, didn't you!' exclaimed Erica triumphantly.

'You've got me,' admitted Maggie. 'Pathetic, isn't it?'

Extending her hand across the table, Erica said, 'Actually, Maggie, no, not really, especially considering my response to the loss of that particular bêtenoire.'

They exchanged a look of empathy.

'Anyway, this is brilliant. We've only got eight addresses to check out and then we've got him.' said Maggie gleefully.

'Yes, but then what are we going to do?'

'Haven't a clue,' confessed Maggie. 'So, I suggest we finish our drinks, get back to the flat and research these addresses.'

'How do you mean?' Erica asked as she took a swig of wine.

'We'll need a map of London…'

'Got one.'

'Excellent. So we'll mark the addresses on the map…'

'What, with little flags or something, like in some detective drama,' said Erica.

'You may well mock,' grumbled Maggie, 'but that way we'll be able to cross reference the addresses to locations where we know he goes; you know, pubs and the like.'

To stop her mouth from twitching, Erica held her breath and kept her lips clamped firmly together; she nodded her head so rapidly that her earrings clashed against her neck.

'So, do you have any little pin flags?'

Erica stared at Maggie. 'You're serious, aren't you?'

'I am.'

'OK, right,' said Erica, taking a deep breath. 'No, I do not own a single pin flag. I do, however, have some transparent dot stickers that might do.'

'Terrific.' Maggie downed the last of her wine. 'Come on then. Oh, this is so exciting!'

Back at the flat Erica shoved the coffee table to one side, spread the London map out on the floor, and weighted it down with a set of decorative rocks that she normally kept in the bathroom.

'What the hell are these?' exclaimed Maggie.

'I know! Awful, aren't they? Mum gave them to me as a moving-in gift. In her defence, sort of, they are from Harrods.'

'Oh well, that's alright then; we wouldn't want just any old rocks now, would we?'

'Absolutely not. Gracious, what a thought.'

They sat, cross-legged, on the floor on either side of the map. 'Come on then; read out the addresses and I'll mark their positions with these cute stickers that you originally intended for…?'

'No actual reason,' confessed Erica. 'It's just I thought, like you, that they were cute. I'm afraid I'm a bit of a sucker when it comes to stationary, especially notebooks; I've got dozens of the things, all with very attractive covers.'

'Fetch one immediately,' demanded Maggie with a huge grin. 'We're going to need to take notes, especially when we go out on surveillance.'

'Are you serious?'

'Absolutely.'

Erica retrieved one of her notebooks from the bookcase and placed it on the floor next to the map.

Maggie said, 'Pass me the laptop and let's take a look at those addresses.' She quickly scanned the list. 'OK, we can immediately eliminate two of these; the Daves in residence are too old. That leaves us with just six. Grab the notebook and jot these down.'

Erica saluted. 'Ready; read out the first address.'

After a short while she'd written down the six addresses, and between them they had the stickers in position. 'Well, these Daves can't be short of a penny or two,' remarked Maggie. 'We've got two in W11, two in W14, one in W3, and one in NW8. So let's find out exactly where they are *and* what these places cost. I bet they'll be in the bloody millions.'

'So, where shall we start?' Erica asked.

'Didn't you say something about receiving texts from the Brook Green Medical Centre reminding our Dave of appointments?'

'That's right,' cried Erica. 'And the Brook Green Medical Centre is in W6,' she continued, slapping a sticker in place. 'Right here, near W14.'

'The two in W14 then,' said Maggie. She checked the notebook. 'That's Auriol Road, West Kensington: a top floor, two bed flat, one occupant, Dave Mardle, age 30-35, cheap at half a million, nearest tube station, Baron's Court or Hammersmith; and then Aynhoe Road, Brook Green, a massive six bed property, three occupants, Dave Mardle, age, a bit more vague this one, 30-60, Deborah Mardle and Phyllis Adams; a cool two and a half million, nearest tube station, Hammersmith.'

As Maggie was speaking, Erica began frantically flapping her arms about.

'Are you alright? Do you need the loo or something?' enquired Maggie.

'No, listen; remember you said about the pubs?'

'Yes; and?'

'Well, our Dave goes to one called The Bird in the Hand and another called Distillers, and guess where they are.'

'W14?'

'Yes,' Erica exclaimed. 'So, they're both within walking distance of Auriol Road and Aynhoe Road.'

'Well, I suppose it's got to be one of those two properties then,' whined Maggie.

'What's the matter with you? I thought you'd be pleased.'

'Oh, I don't know; I was looking forward to a complex investigation; it's all been a bit easy, that's all.'

'We haven't found him yet.'

'I know, but…'

'And, as a matter of interest, how will we know if we have found him? I haven't a clue what he looks like or anything.'

'Shit, that's true,' agreed Maggie. 'Um, well, we obviously need a plan.'

'Yes, and?'

'And?'

'What is the plan?'

'Haven't the faintest,' said Maggie. 'Why don't we case these two properties first and see what develops.'

'We'll probably end up being arrested.'

*

For their foray into investigative detective work they dressed as neutrally as possible. Maggie wore a plain linen beige pinafore dress, designer but discrete, and Erica wore a light brown skirt and cream t-shirt, Dorothy Perkins sale, two years ago. They both wore dark glasses, reasonable given the weather, but they also, for reasons that escaped them, carried umbrellas. They scurried through the market, heads low, trying to make it through to the high street without being seen, but were spotted by Winton. 'And where are you two off to? Spy school?'

Whipping her glasses off, Erica smiled sweetly. 'I don't know what you mean. We are simply going about our normal business.' Waving the glasses above her head, pointing in the general direction of the sun, she went on. 'I don't know if you've noticed, dear friend, but it is quite bright out here.'

'That it is, that it is,' remarked Winton as he looked skyward, shielding his eyes with his broad hands. 'Not a cloud in the sky.' He looked pointedly at the two umbrellas. 'So, if your intention is to meld into the background while um, going about your normal business, then I'm afraid you have both failed miserably.'

Erica and Maggie looked each other up and down and collapsed into hysterics. 'He's right, you know,' said Maggie. 'We look decidedly suspicious. We need to think again. Come on.' They dashed back inside and emerged a short while later looking casual and summery, and minus the umbrellas.

'Better,' remarked Winton. 'Now you just look like two beautiful English girls out for a stroll.' He gave them both a wink. 'Remember now, you two: be careful out there on those mean streets.'

'Hah! Have a good day; see you later,' Erica called out.

Having researched the area, they decided to travel to Hammersmith tube station. They would then wander down the Hammersmith Road to Auriol Road, have a look at the half- million property first, and then cross over into Brook Green towards Aynhoe Road. They had also located two convenient cafes: Paradiso, some fifty yards from the Auriol Road turning, and Betty Blythe, opposite the turning into Aynhoe Road.

Their initial survey complete, they entered Betty Blythe's, which was all 1920's chic and fine bone china, with cupcakes served on silver tiered platters.

'OK,' said Erica, 'so we've seen the properties. What now?'

'Not sure. Do you know if he's married or not?'

Erica frowned. 'How is that going to help?'

'I despair sometimes; just think for a moment: we know from our search that the Dave who lives at Aynhoe Road lives with two women, one with the same bloody surname as him for goodness sake, so it's possible that she's his wife…'

'Or his mother,' countered Erica.

'True, and since we don't know the woman's age, or indeed that particular Dave's age except to say that he's somewhere between, what was it?'

'Between 30 and 60.'

'Right; so, either scenario is possible,' agreed Maggie. 'The point is, there seem to be two women living with him, whereas the Dave at the Auriol Road property lives alone.'

'I see,' conceded Erica. 'The thing is I'm not sure; I don't *think* he's married. I mean there has never been a mention of any female in the texts.'

'Did you want that last cupcake?' Maggie asked.

'No, I'm fine. You have it,' replied Erica and, before she had a chance to change her mind, it was gone.

'Mmm, delicious.'

'How the hell do you stay so slim?'

'Daddy says it's because of my nervous energy. Anyway, you're not exactly massive, are you?'

'True, but I don't eat like you.'

Erica ducked, skilfully avoiding the balled up cupcake paper that Maggie threw. Unfortunately the sweet old lady sitting a couple of tables away, unaware of the approaching missile, didn't duck; it struck her mid forehead, causing her to spill her tea so that it dripped down onto her dress. Her companion, a severe, grey haired Miss Haversham type, stood and marched over to Maggie.

'Have you lost your senses? You could have caused a major injury to my friend...'

The sweet-faced friend began to protest. 'It's alright Gertrude, there's...'

'Nonsense, you could have suffered major burns.'

'The tea was cold, Gertrude.'

'And your dress...'

'Gertrude, please don't fuss,' she looked down at her damp, tea stained dress. 'I never liked this dress much anyway.'

Erica kept her head down.

'I am so, so sorry,' pleaded Maggie. 'I'll pay for the dry cleaning, whatever is needed; I'm really sorry.'

Eyes twinkling, the sweet old lady replied, 'It isn't a problem. I, unlike Gertrude, can remember being your age, my dear. It was an accident.'

'At least let me get you both another pot of tea,' Maggie pleaded.

Gertrude began to protest, muttering threats of talking to the manager.

'That would be lovely. Do sit down Gertrude; remember your blood pressure.'

With a final death stare directed solely at Maggie, Gertrude harrumphed and sat back down heavily.

Outside the café, Maggie and Erica began giggling like schoolgirls. 'I thought I was done for,' gasped Maggie. 'My investigative career cut short by the wrath of that ghastly Gertrude.'

'Honestly Maggie, I nearly died. The woman was *massive*.'

'She was like an enormous bird of prey,' squealed Maggie. 'Did you see the talons on her?'

'Stop it,' protested Erica weakly. 'My sides are aching.'

Pulling herself together, Maggie said, 'Anyway, I think we've done all that we can for now; how about a spot of retail therapy?'

'With what?' Erica moaned.

'My treat. I spotted a very interesting looking shop selling lingerie back near Auriol Road. Come on, no arguing, you really could do with some new bras; you're bigger than you think you are, you know, and I read the other day that something like 80% of women are walking round in ill-fitting bras.'

Erica looked down at herself and had to admit that her boobs did have a tendency to leak out sideways. 'Please, Mummy, can I have a red one with lace and stuff?'

'Of course sweetheart; whatever you desire.'

'I was joking, you know.'

'Well, I wasn't. Come on; think of it as a birthday present.'

'My birthday isn't until October.'

'OK, look at it as an *early* birthday present.'

'Absolutely not; especially if it's the shop that I think you mean, it'll cost a bomb!'

'Please,' Maggie wheedled. 'I want to buy you something nice.'

'You don't need to buy me anything, Maggie.'

'I know I don't *need* to; I *want* to,' she pleaded. 'Go on, you know you want to see what you'd look like in a decent bra.'

Erica sighed. 'Whatever I say you will ignore and simply go on and on until I cave in, so lead on, but I swear to you if you *dare* buy me another present in October I will, I will…'

'You will, you will?'

'I will, I will, oh, come on!'

They made their way back towards the Hammersmith road. On the way they passed a second hand book shop called Black Moon Books. Erica ground to a halt; her penchant for stationary was as nothing compared to her addiction to books, especially those that might be hidden in the bowels of a decent second hand bookshop.

Maggie groaned.

'Oh, come on, just a quick peek,' pleaded Erica as she dragged Maggie past the fully laden trestle tables lined up along the pavement.

Inside, Erica took a deep breath. 'Oh, smell that, the unmistakable aroma of leather mixed with vanilla and dust.'

Maggie raised her eyebrows. 'Dust, I'll agree with,' she said, 'but leather and vanilla?' She took an exaggerated sniff. 'I'm just getting mould.'

'Charlatan,' said Erica

There were books everywhere: stacked on the floor, piled along the sides of the stairs leading up to further treasures, as well as neatly filed away on the many interlocking bookcases, which formed a maze to be negotiated at your own risk. The bookcases broke the sunlight streaming through the windows into wide shafts, hazy with motes of dust. The counter itself was also covered in piles of books, some teetering dangerously near the edge. Just visible behind these books was a thick crop of black wavy hair; impossible to determine whether this hair was attached to a female or a male head.

'Come on, let's explore.'

Maggie's squeal of protest caused the head of hair to speak.

'Do I detect a maiden in distress?'

'Not at all, not at all,' replied Erica. 'Just a squeal of excitement; isn't that right Maggie?'

Rubbing her arm in an exaggerated fashion, following the swipe that Erica had just given her, Maggie responded with a less than enthusiastic, 'Oh, absolutely; *nothing* I like better than an old, dusty…'

A further swipe from Erica prevented her from continuing.

The thick crop of hair rose up from behind the counter. The man wasn't handsome, but he pushed his John Lennon style glasses onto his head, revealing rich brown eyes, and the startling ebony black hair flowed around his face. His nose, although large, had an interesting tilt towards the left.

Maggie visibly cheered. 'Yes, as I was saying,' she affirmed with great enthusiasm, 'there is nothing I like better than a well stocked second hand bookshop.'

The man hesitated; he stared intently at Erica and brushed away a strand of hair that had fallen across his eyes. 'Well, you are most welcome. Please feel free to wander. I shall be here to offer assistance if you require it at any point,' he said as he slumped back down again, disappearing from view.

Maggie turned to Erica and gave her a wide eyed look as she mouthed the word, '*Wow*.'

'Thanks very much,' said Erica, dragging Maggie towards the bookcases. There they separated. Maggie made her way to the back of the shop, following a sign indicating where books on History were to be found, while Erica remained near the front amongst the Poetry and Drama books.

After forty-five minutes of aimless wandering, Maggie located Erica sitting on the floor, engrossed in *The Cantos*. Maggie collapsed onto the floor beside her. 'What have you found?'

Erica flipped the title page back. 'I studied this at University and found it incredibly difficult,' she replied.

'And now?'

'Sadly, I have to confess that I still find it formidable. What about you? Find anything interesting?'

'As it happens, I did,' replied Maggie. 'A couple of books, diaries really, written by women who were nursing in Jamaica.'

The tinkling sound of the shop door bell rang out into the silence.

'Gran, how lovely to see you! Have you brought me a treat?'

'I have, Dave. I hope you've had a good day.'

Erica gasped as she clutched the book tightly to her chest. 'That sounds like the lovely lady from the café who took the hit for me,' she whispered. '*And* she called the 'hair man' Dave!'

Maggie stood up quietly and peered around the end of the bookcase. 'It's definitely her,' she whispered back.

Dave came out from behind the counter. 'Whatever happened to your dress? I'm sure it never used to have that delicate brown stain resembling the continent of Africa.'

'No, dear, it didn't. It is courtesy of two charming young girls at the café a little while ago. Gertrude was most put out on my behalf. She really can be a bit of a grump.'

'Well, that's one way of describing her; personally I would have gone for something like…'

'Now, now, dear; she means well.'

'So, how did it happen?'

Maggie, realising how childish the story was going to make her sound, panicked. She dashed out from behind the bookcase. '*Mea culpa,* I'm afraid!'

'Gracious me; hello, dear.' She looked around the shop. 'Have you frightened off your friend with more missiles?'

'Missiles? What missiles?' Dave asked, eyes darting.

Maggie hastily explained. 'Obviously I wasn't aiming at your grandmother.'

Dave nodded sagely.

'It was just a bit of fun, and Erica, well, she was teasing me and so I, for reasons that elude me now, thought it would be funny to throw a rolled up cupcake case at her, the thing is, she ducked and well…'

'Gran didn't.'

'Quite.'

Erica appeared from behind the bookcase, head bowed. 'We are really sorry about your dress.'

Dave's grandmother exclaimed, 'Gracious, child, you look just like Melissa.' She grabbed hold of Dave's arm. 'Doesn't she, Dave. She could be her twin.'

Dave cleared his throat, looked at Erica and remarked casually, 'I suppose there's a *slight* similarity,' he said.

'Melissa?' said Erica.

'Just a woman I knew, years ago,' said Dave dismissively.

His grandmother threw him a confused look. 'Just a …?'

'Anyway,' continued Dave, 'it seems that you two have rather ruined my gran's dress.'

'Nonsense, as I said before, I never really liked this dress and now, well now, I've got the perfect excuse to turn it into rags.'

Maggie muttered an aside to Erica, 'Ask him.'

'Ask him what?' Erica replied through the corner of her mouth.

Maggie's eyebrows shot skywards. 'If he's the king of Siberia, what do you think?'

'What?'

'Is everything alright ladies?' asked Dave.

'Perfectly alright, thank you,' replied Erica. 'My friend obviously hasn't taken her medication.'

Maggie gave her a playful thump.

'No, definitely hasn't taken it; hence the tendency towards violence and missile throwing,' Erica confirmed.

Maggie strode over to the counter, causing Dave and his grandmother to back away, just a little. 'Don't listen to

44

Erica, she's quite mad. Now listen to me, I shall get straight to the point,' she gave Dave a hard stare. 'Dave, isn't it?'

'Yes,' he muttered.

'I have a question for you, Dave.'

'Fire away.'

Erica let out a squeal. 'Maggie, no, don't.'

Dave and his grandmother exchanged an amused look. 'I must say,' said Dave, 'this is turning out to be a most interesting encounter. Please, I am intrigued; what is your question?'

Maggie took the plunge. 'Is your name Dave Mardle, currently living at The Retreat, Aynhoe Road, or...?'

Dave's grandmother exclaimed, 'Gracious, that's where I live, dear, with Dave's mother, Deborah, my daughter you understand, and her husband...'

'That would be the other Dave Mardle then,' said Maggie. 'So, you must be Phyllis.'

'Goodness, yes I am,' said Phyllis, her eyes sparkling.

'Actually, I live at number 64, Flat 4...' interjected Dave.

'On the Auriol Road, yes,' said Maggie. 'And, to your knowledge, have several of your friends been having difficulty sending you text messages?' she asked bluntly.

A smile spread across Dave's face. 'Yes, several of my friends have been experiencing a little complication when it comes to contacting me via my mobile.' He paused and gave Maggie a hard stare of his own. 'Am I to assume that you are the ghost in the machine?'

Maggie made a theatrical deep bow and swept her arms and body in one smooth motion towards Erica. 'May I introduce you to Erica Woods, the ghost in your machine.'

Erica stood frozen to the spot. She opened her mouth to speak, but all she could manage was a rather feeble squeak.

Dave strode over and held out his arm. 'An absolute pleasure to meet you,' he said.

Erica shook his hand.

'Tell me,' he asked, 'how did you find me?'

Before Erica had a chance to open her mouth, Maggie replied, 'Surprisingly easily actually.' She quickly went on to explain in detail how they had researched his name, cross referencing it with various details like the pubs he visited and the doctors he attended.

Dave's mouth dropped open. 'You know which doctor I see?'

'I did text the surgery back explaining that I wasn't who they thought I was and that they should check their records,' explained Erica. 'But I have received several texts from them reminding me, or rather, you, that I, I mean you, have an appointment.'

'I see.'

'Actually,' said Maggie. 'She's been rather worried about you.'

'Maggie!'

'Well you have.'

Dave gave Erica a warm smile. 'As you can see,' he said, 'nothing to worry about.'

'I'll say,' muttered Maggie under her breath.

'Pardon?'

'She said, 'I see',' Erica blurted.

'Yes, I see,' repeated Maggie.

There followed a pregnant pause that was broken by Phyllis. 'Well, I'm glad that's all been sorted out; it's been driving my grandson mad,' she said. 'Now I really must be getting back, if for no other reason than to change my clothes.' She gave Erica and Maggie a smile and a nod. 'I do hope we shall meet again.'

'I hope so too,' said Erica.

'See you later, Gran, and watch out for any stray missiles.'

'Oh, I think I'm perfectly safe, as long as you manage to detain these two girls for a little longer, to give me a chance to make my escape.'

Silence again fell. Erica stared off into the distance and Maggie stared at the cupcakes that Phyllis had left for Dave.

Dave said, 'Would you care to partake of a cupcake with me? I can even offer you a tea or coffee.'

'If you knew Maggie like I know Maggie,' giggled Erica, 'you wouldn't need to ask.'

Maggie had the grace to blush.

'About the offer of cupcakes or the beverage?'

'Both,' exclaimed Erica.

'So, do I take that as a yes?'

'You do,' they concurred.

Dave led them to a small sitting area that was situated to the right of the entrance door, partially obscured by a particularly fine specimen of a *Ficus carica* that Erica had noticed when she first entered.

'You're so lucky to own such a wonderful bookshop, and this,' she said, pointing towards the seating area, 'this is fantastic. I've always felt that a bookshop should have a relaxing area. You should think about installing a coffee machine or something and maybe even getting wifi, it'd certainly boost your trade.'

'Boost my trade?'

'Um, gosh, I mean well, it's not exactly heaving with customers is it?'

'That's it, Erica. Jump in with both feet why don't you,' exclaimed Maggie.

'I didn't mean to imply…'

'Don't give it another thought. Let's face it, I'm hardly rushed off my feet, but the thing is I feel I ought to tell you…'

'You've got her hooked now,' said Maggie. 'She could never resist a decent bookshop and now I can see her cogs working overtime thinking about the possibilities for the place. She'll have you redesigning this entire ground floor…'

'Maggie!' Erica gave Dave a pleading look. 'She's being ridiculous. I would never presume…'

The bookshop door was thrown open. 'Ah,' said Dave. 'Do I spot that rarest of creatures just yonder, through the undergrowth?' He crouched down and pretended to raise binoculars to his eyes. 'Yes, yes by jolly, I'm right. It's a lesser spotted *vermis liber*. I'll be back in a moment, and don't worry, I haven't forgotten about the coffee.'

'What was he burbling on about? A lesser spotted what?'

'A lesser spotted *vermis liber*.'

'That's the one.'

Laughing, Erica explained. 'Loosely translated, it means bookworm.'

'Oh, I see; very good. Well, well, reasonably good looking, in a quirky sort of way, owns a bookshop, speaks Latin, *and* has a sense of humour. This could be your lucky day.'

Erica thumped her again. 'Oh, do shut up.'

'Ow; watch it,' exclaimed Maggie.

'Think of it as payback for the missile throwing.'

'Here we are; two coffees as promised.' Placing them on the table, Dave glanced at Maggie. 'Fear not, I haven't forgotten the cupcakes.'

'I never said a word.'

'You didn't need to,' said Erica. 'Your hang-dog expression said it all.'

They chatted casually until Maggie blurted, 'Tell me, Dave, given all the texts that Erica has sent to your friends explaining that she is not you, why didn't *you* text her at some point, you know, to explain or whatever?'

'Honestly, Maggie!'

'No it's fine. A perfectly reasonable question actually,' said Dave. 'And I hope that my answer to that question will also be considered perfectly reasonable.'

Erica and Maggie waited but Dave said no more. He simply stared out of the window, seemingly deep in thought.

Maggie, not known for her patience, implored, 'So, what is your answer?'

Dragging his attention back to the matter in hand, he went on, 'I actually thought it might seem a bit creepy.'

'In what way?' Maggie asked.

'I think I understand,' said Erica. 'I mean, I assume you know that I've had quite long conversations with a couple of your friends—obviously I don't know their names, just their numbers—and they assured me that they would let you know, so, that being the case, there would be no real need for you to contact me unless…'

Dave nodded with such vigour that his thick wavy hair flopped over his eyes in a most appealing manner. 'Quite; unless I was some sort of weirdo or stalker.' He grinned broadly. 'I'm not, by the way, in case you were wondering.'

'That's good to know,' remarked Erica.

'I certainly know that you had an amusing exchange with Julia,' continued Dave.

'Julia?'

'Yes, she's the wife of Steve, an old friend of mine. Didn't she inform you that I was completely disorganised and hopeless at staying in touch? Going as far as suggesting that I needed a PA; a job, I believe, that she felt you would be more than capable of fulfilling, given all your helpful feedback to her about various texts and voicemails that you'd received in error.'

'Oh, yes, I remember,' Erica chortled. 'Interesting; I didn't know what sex the person was but I felt that it was a 'her'. I must admit we did have a bit of a giggle. She seemed very pleasant.'

'She is,' said Dave. 'You and she would get on very well.'

Maggie threw Erica a knowing glance.

'You'd probably get on really well with my uncle actually,' said Erica. 'Not only is he called Dave, but he loves golf as well.'

'As well as what?'

'As well as you.'

'Oh, right, yes, I see. Sorry,' said Dave. 'I must confess I do enjoy a game of golf, even though many people believe, like Mark Twain, that 'golf is a good walk spoiled.' Dave cocked his head to one side. 'Do you make a habit of this sort of thing, by the way, tracking down mysterious men called Dave?'

'Of course not, it's just that...'

'It's alright, Erica I was joking.'

'Oh, right, yes, of course.'

'It's a thought though,' said Maggie. 'We could set up a 'Dave Club'.'

'What a terrifying prospect,' said Dave. 'There are vast numbers of men out there called Dave, and who knows what they're all like.'

'Well, you seem nice enough,' said Erica, immediately blushing.

'Why thank you. You seem nice too.'

'Ooer!' exclaimed Maggie.

'Will you give over,' Erica cried. Thankfully, she was spared any further embarrassment by the arrival of another customer.

Dave stood up and nodded at the gentlemen. 'I'll be with you in a moment, sir.' Turning back to Erica, he added with a wry smile, 'You're obviously good for trade. I seem to be rushed off my feet. It really has been a pleasure to meet you. Now, if you'll excuse me, I need to attend to this gentleman.'

Erica stood. 'Of course; it's been lovely to meet you too,' she said. 'A mystery solved. But we should be going so you can get back to normal, as it were.'

'Actually, I'm not sure I want to do that,' said Dave. 'Look; how about joining me for a drink in the pub one evening; The Bird in the Hand is very civilized, it's not far…'

'We know where it is,' said Maggie.

'Of course you do; your extensive research and cross referencing that you told me about. Anyway, what do you say?'

'We'd love to,' said Maggie, adding mischievously, 'Give Erica a call; you've got her number. Come on you, we have bras to hunt down.'

Chapter 4

Maggie would often buy a couple of coffees and some tempting morsels to share with Winton at his stall. He had been intrigued by Maggie's tale of finding Dave and, when she mentioned that he owned a bookshop, had asked if she could remember the name of the shop.

'It was something like Black Star; no, can't remember, I'm sure it was Black something though,' she replied.

'Was it Black Moon Books?'

'That's it,' Maggie cried. 'Why the interest?'

'My brother, Jay-Jay, is a book-runner and I...'

'A what?'

'Well, that's what I call him; he does what the term implies.'

'What? Runs after books? Strange; I had no idea that books had such capabilities.'

Winton flashed a smile towards Maggie. 'No, I think you'll find that the books remain quite stationary; it's Jay-Jay who does the running. He travels all over the country, searching for particular books that various bookshop owners have requested, you know, for some of their discerning customers.'

'And he makes a living doing that? It must cost him a fortune in travel alone.'

'You'd be surprised. He certainly isn't destitute.'

'I wonder if he knows Dave,' mused Maggie.

'I could ask him if you like; are you worried about him or something?'

'No, he seemed perfectly fine. Still, it would be interesting to know if your brother has come across him.'

'He's at a book convention at the moment, but I'll ask him when he gets back.'

*

Maggie was getting quite adventurous with her cooking, a task that she'd completely taken over. Two weeks after their encounter with Dave, Erica returned exhausted from her busy shift to find Maggie up to her eyes in vegetables of various shapes and sizes, as well as an assortment of herbs and spices and a jug of coconut milk. She was squinting at a very old, stained cookbook that Erica had no recollection of owning.

'Whatever are you looking at?'

Waving the book above her head, Maggie replied, 'Isn't it fantastic? Winton lent it to me; it belonged to his grandmother, or maybe it was his great-grandmother, I can't remember; it's certainly very old.'

'And well used from what I can see,' exclaimed Erica.

'I know! Anyway, Winton said this was one of his favourite dishes and so I thought I'd give it a try. He was so impressed when I said I was going to cook it that he actually gave me all this stuff free.' She surveyed the pile in front of her. 'Mind you, I think I know why now; it's a very complicated recipe.'

'So, what is this delectable dish going to be, and do you need any help?'

'Hopefully, Jamaican Veggie Patties and nope, I'm fine. You have your shower; I'm sure I can sort it out.' She consulted the cook book again, frowned and added, 'Failing that I'll simply phone out for a pizza.'

Half an hour later, rubbing her hair dry with a towel, Erica remarked, 'Well, it smells good.'

'I just hope it tastes as good as it smells; the problem is I've tasted it so often during the preparation that I think my taste buds have shut down.' She dipped a small spoon into the pot and held it out towards Erica. 'What do you think?'

'Oh, wow!'

'Good?'

'Yes, really good,' Erica assured her. 'Have you made the pastry too?'

'I could say that I have but…'

'You haven't.'

'Correct, I've never been very good with pastry for some reason. I read somewhere that you need cold hands or something, or is that just an old wives tale?'

'I've heard that too, but that doesn't mean it's true. Anyway, no matter, you've done the creative bit.'

'You are too kind; it should be ready in about 15 minutes,' said Maggie. 'The wine's cooling in the fridge.'

'Do you want a glass now?'

Maggie fluttered her eyelashes. 'That's like asking me if I like cake; which reminds me, have you heard from Dave?'

'Funnily enough I was thinking about that on the way back from work. It was all a bit of a let down really.'

'What was?'

Opening the wine, Erica replied. 'Well, once I got accustomed to the idea that we were going to become some sort of investigative team, I was looking forward to the challenge of hunting the man down, and then it was all over in a flash.'

'We're obviously bloody good; perhaps we should both reconsider our career options. Anyway, you didn't answer my question.'

'Sorry?'

Speaking slowly and emphasising each word, Maggie repeated her question.

'Have you heard from Dave?'

Erica concentrated on pouring the wine. 'Oh, no, nothing. I expect he's been busy.'

'Of course, rushed off his feet again I expect,' said Maggie with more than a hint of sarcasm. 'Still, I'm surprised. I felt sure that he would contact you, I mean it was as plain as a pikestaff that he fancied you.'

'Will you give over,' said Erica handing Maggie her drink. 'Is it ready yet?'

'I told you, 15 minutes.'

Pushing her plate away Erica collapsed onto the settee and announced that the meal had been a triumph. 'I'm stuffed.'

'It wasn't bad, was it,' agreed Maggie. 'Pudding?'

'You *are* joking; I couldn't manage…' The sound of church bells filled the room. 'Where the hell did I put my phone?'

Taking a swig of wine, Maggie replied, 'Sounds like it's coming from your bedroom.'

A few moments later, phone in hand, Erica said, 'You'll never guess who's just sent me a text.'

'Dave?'

'How did you know that?' demanded Erica.

'Educated guess; so, what does it say?'

'It says, 'Sorry for delay in getting back to you, it's all been a bit frantic. Anyway are you free on the 25th August, 8 o'clock? I thought maybe a drink in the Bird in the Hand, short notice I know. Look forward to hearing from you."

'That's this Saturday. Excellent,' said Maggie.

'I don't know.'

'Oh, for goodness sake, Erica, of course we should go. Text him back and say yes. Anyway, correct me if I'm wrong, but, as I said, I got the distinct impression that he took a shine to you.'

'Nonsense.'

'Don't give me all that blushing Miss Innocence; you know perfectly well that he fancied you, and you certainly fancied him.'

'I did not.'

Maggie's eyebrows jumped upwards and with an exaggerated sigh she said, 'Fine, if you say so; either way, I'm going. I feel an urgent need for a new outfit; we could go to up to Kensington on Friday.'

Erica's eyes flitted towards Maggie's wardrobe that now occupied the entire wall space from the corner of the room to the window frame.

Maggie grinned. 'I know; I just like clothes.'

'I'd never have guessed.'

Maggie aimed a playful swipe towards Erica. 'Oh, by the way, I don't think I told you, I was chatting with Winton the other day…'

'Again? You and Winton seem to be *chatting* together a lot these days; is there something you want to tell me?'

'Don't be ridiculous; we're just…'

'Good friends?'

'Precisely. Anyway, did you know his brother works in the book trade?'

'I didn't even know Winton had a brother; my, my, you *are* getting to know him well.'

'Very funny.'

'So, explain; what's the significance of his brother working in the book trade?'

'Probably nothing; I just thought he may have come across Dave and, you know, he could tell us whether the man's got any skeletons in his cupboard. I mean, he won't, obviously, but you never know.'

'This investigation bug seems to have gone to your head,'

'Guilty as charged.'

'Right, so as long as we understand each other here,' said Erica. 'I do *not* fancy the man but, as you say, he seemed nice so, OK, let's go.'

That Friday afternoon Erica arrived home, tired but looking forward to their shopping trip. The flat was empty. She checked the time, slung her jacket onto the settee, sighed and made her way over to the kitchen. She flicked the kettle on, snatched a mug from the cupboard, set it down onto the counter and heaped a teaspoon of instant coffee into it.

As soon as the kettle boiled she sloshed the water into the mug with such speed that half of the mug's contents ended up on the counter.

'Buggeration in hell,' she muttered.

Roughly snatching some kitchen towel from the roll, she mopped it up and flung the sopping mess into the sink. She checked the time again. Leaving the mug with what was left of the freshly made coffee on the counter to cool, she had a quick shower. Feeling more cheerful now that she no longer smelt of chips, she opened her wardrobe. Her heart sank as she surveyed the garments hanging forlornly on cheap metal hangers and decided that if Maggie wasn't back within the hour, she'd go to Kensington alone.

She hunted for her sandals and located them under the settee, then sat down to drink her coffee, which was by now horribly cold. She checked her mobile in case there was a message from Maggie. Nothing. It was then that she noticed the note on the table.

Erica,
Sorry to be a bore and let you down at the last minute but something's come up and I'm afraid I won't be able to go on our shopping spree today. If you don't fancy going on your own then feel free to borrow anything you want from my stuff. And yes, I can imagine what you're thinking, I know I'm taller than you but the tops and stuff will fit.
Have fun in the 'Bird in the hand' and give my apologies to Dave. All being well I should be back in a few days. I'll try and ring you on Sunday.
Yours, Maggie xxx

Erica leaned back and looked at the note again. It struck her as odd that Maggie had avoided saying *what* it was that had come up. She considered the possibility that it might be a family illness but dismissed that idea immediately, reasoning that Maggie would have said. The thought then flashed through her head that Maggie had changed her mind and decided to locate Jared. Again, she dismissed the idea immediately; Maggie had been adamant that she wasn't interested in the man's whereabouts. She refolded the note. There was nothing she could do; she'd have to wait until Maggie rang.

She took a final gulp of cold coffee, slipped her sandals on and decided that they too could do with replacing.

The following evening Erica arrived at the Bird in the Hand a fashionable ten minutes late. She was wearing a long multi-coloured skirt, a purple t-shirt, and a pair of brightly coloured leather gladiator sandals, all bought in a funky little shop near Camden market the previous day. She was also wearing the new bra that Maggie had treated her to. As she made her way to the bar where Dave was waiting, she noticed that he had a huge grin on his face.

'I'm surprised you made it safely through that lot,' remarked Dave. 'I must say, it's lovely to see you. Sorry it took so long to get in touch.'

Erica frowned and looked around, 'What lot?'

Dave's grin became even broader. 'The moment you walked through that door, heads turned. The men, and some of the women too actually, couldn't take their eyes off you. Surely you noticed?'

'Nope; but my mother is always telling me that I walk around with my eyes closed, and that I live in a world of my own; a world that she doesn't understand apparently.' She paused and added, 'The story of most mother-daughter relationships, I suppose.'

'And most father-son relationships. Now, what would you like to drink?' He looked back towards the door. 'Is your friend around?'

'Maggie? Oh, no, sorry, I meant to say, you see my mother is right, world of my own, dippy missy as my dad calls me, too much information, stop yakking Erica. Maggie, right, yes, no she isn't coming, she was called away;

no idea why, she didn't say, which is odd when you think about it.' She paused to take breath. 'Sorry, what did you ask me?'

'Two questions; one about your friend, which you have answered fully, and one about what you'd like to drink; I don't think I got the answer to that one.'

Erica felt the blush rise up her neck to her face. 'Warm in here, isn't it? Um, I'll have a glass of chilled white wine please.'

'Excellent.' He waved his arm above his head. 'Monica,' he shouted.

'With you in a tick, Dave.'

'There's a table just become free over there,' said Dave. 'If you go and bag it, I'll get the drinks. OK?'

'OK.'

'You'll have to be quick, otherwise we'll lose it.'

Erica hitched up her skirt and weaved her way skilfully through the throng. 'Excuse me, sorry, if you'd just, fine, thanks.' Reaching the table, she plonked herself down on one of the stools and placed her handbag on the other. Moments later she was joined by Dave bearing the drinks.

'Oh, well done.'

'One of the advantages of being short,' remarked Erica. 'And, if I do say so myself, I'm a mean little weaver.'

'So your friend was called away, you say. May I ask to where?'

'Well that's just it, I don't know; she didn't say. She's supposed to be ringing me tomorrow.'

Dave stared down at his beer. 'I see. Actually, I have to confess that I'm glad it's just you. Not that I didn't like Maggie, but I'm glad it wasn't you that was called away.' He raised his glass. 'Cheers.'

Erica's insides did a backwards flip. She held onto the edge of the table. 'Cheers.'

Erica took a sip of wine and stared around at the pub. She couldn't see much; it was heaving with people. She did notice the floor though: attractive Italian tiles coloured blue, green and red, and the lighting: stunning chandeliers that flickered through different colours in what appeared to be a random sequence; totally mesmerising.

'Great, aren't they? I think the owners got them made specially,' said Dave.

'They must have cost a fortune.'

Lowering his voice and leaning in towards Erica, he said, 'I think they have connections, if you get my drift.'

She didn't, but nodded in what she hoped was a wise and knowing manner.

They both sipped their drinks and peered at each other across the rims.

'Have you always...' they both began.

'You go first,' said Dave.

'I was just wondering, have you always lived in London?'

He nodded. 'And you?'

'No; I moved here when I graduated from York University; that's where I met Maggie actually.'

'What did you study?'

'English.'

'Me too,' said Dave. 'Not at York though; I went to Bristol.'

'When did you...' they both began again.

They started giggling. 'Honestly, what are we, sixteen again,' said Dave.

'I know. It's just a bit strange.'

Dave's face clouded over. 'Strange; strange in what way?'

'Not strange in a weird way,' Erica assured him. 'No, strange in a, in a, well, in an extraordinary way. You know, given how we met and everything.'

'Yes, true, and on that subject, it seems to me you know an awful lot more about me than I know about you,' said Dave, looking at her with wide puppy dog eyes.

'What?' Erica asked, feigning innocence.

'You know perfectly well. Come on, dish up, tell me about the essence that is you, and let's start with the basics. You know how old I am, so, indelicate though this question may seem, how old are *you*?'

'A perfectly reasonable request under the circumstances; I'm 24, as is Maggie. We were at York 2006-9.'

'And me?'

Erica scratched her head in an exaggerated theatrical manner. 'Now, let me think; you have recently turned 30 so you must have been at Bristol from 2000-03; correct?'

'Spot on.'

Within moments they were laughing and chatting, relaxed in each other's company. 'Another drink?'

Erica nodded.

'Same again?'

She downed the last few drops of her wine. 'Lovely, thank you.'

'There is just one thing,' said Dave when he returned from the bar. 'I don't want to frighten you off, but I feel I ought to be honest with you.'

He looked so worried that Erica felt apprehensive. Trying to cover up her concern, she was appalled to hear herself say, 'Oh, I know, don't tell me, you've been in prison or, worse maybe, you've done something awful but you were never caught and now you're going to confess.'

'Well, actually…'

Erica's blood drained from her face.

'No, panic not; no prison and um, no awful crime committed that confounded the law. It's just that, well, I feel you should know, and it should come from me, it always sounds much worse if it comes from a third party and…'

'Dave,' exclaimed Erica, 'just tell me.'

Dave hesitated, and Erica began to dread what he was about to say. *He's probably bloody married,* she thought. *With six kids and no doubt another on the way. No, that can't be it; if he*

61

was married with kids he wouldn't be living in a two bed flat, unless he was divorced of course. Maybe it's worse than that, maybe he's just come out. That would be just my luck. First decent man I've come across in over three years, and he's gay.

'Yes, right, well, the thing is; it's about the bookshop,' Dave was saying.

There was no reaction from Erica.

Raising his voice, Dave repeated, 'It's about the bookshop.'

Startled out of her thoughts, Erica said, 'What? Sorry, you were saying?'

'I was saying, it's about the bookshop.'

'What is?'

'Well, I think you got the wrong impression.'

'The wrong impression about what?'

'Well, the thing is you see, I don't actually own it. My mother owns it.' He bowed his head. 'I'm essentially just a shop keeper, working for my mother; pathetic really.'

'Nothing wrong with that. So, is that it? That's what you were worried about—me finding out that you didn't own the bookshop…?'

'Plus the fact that my flat is only just round the corner from my parents; hardly indicative of an adventurous chap.'

Erica could feel the smile creeping onto her face and quickly tried to mould her face into a more serious, compassionate expression.

'Are you alright?'

'Yes, absolutely fine,' she croaked. 'It's just, well, all sorts of scenarios were running through my head. And none of them touched on ownership of the bookshop.'

'So, the fact that I am not, as you first assumed, the respectable owner of a book shop, and the fact that, at the ripe old age of 30, I still live within spitting distance of my parents…'

'And your grandmother,' added Erica, still with an inane grin on her face.

'Quite; anyway, that doesn't bother you?'

'Why on earth should it?'

'So, I haven't totally wrecked my chances then?'

'Your chances of what?'

'Oh, God, Erica. With you; tell me I haven't wrecked my chances with you.'

'Gosh…'

'Oh, shit,' he exclaimed. 'If I hadn't already ruined my chances then I have now by asking you that stupid question; I'm an idiot. Listen, just forget…'

Erica held up her hand. '*If* you'd just give me a chance, I'll answer your question.'

'Sorry,' he muttered. 'Go ahead, but be gentle with me.'

Erica took a deep breath. 'As it happens, Dave Mardle, as far as I'm concerned you have in no way wrecked anything. What precisely your chances are, well, I'm afraid I'm not willing to divulge that at the moment.'

A broad grin spread across Dave's face. 'Fair enough.'

'Now don't take this the wrong way, but I've just noticed the time. I really should get going. I don't like to travel on the tubes late at night.'

Dave downed the remainder of his beer. 'I wouldn't hear of you travelling back on the tube. Please, let me get you a taxi…'

'Oh, I…'

Dave held up his hands. 'No protests.'

'Well, that's very kind of you.'

Phone in hand, he asked, 'So, where to?'

'Peckham.'

'Bloody hell, Peckham?'

'You sound like Maggie. That's exactly what she said when she found out that I lived in Peckham. I will say to you what I said to her, it's fine. The people are great and I haven't had a single problem since I moved into my flat. Peckham simply gets a poor press.'

'I apologise,' said Dave as he flicked his glasses from his head to his eyes. He scrolled down his contact list. 'Ah, hello; could you pick up Erica um, hold on,' he placed his hand over the phone, 'I don't know your surname.'

'There is a privacy button, you know.'

'Yeah, I know but I'm old, I'm still into old technology. Anyway, surname?'

'Woods.'

Removing his hand with a flourish, he resumed the call. 'Yes, sorry about that; so, could you pick up Erica Woods from the Bird in the Hand and take her to Peckham?' He listened for a moment. 'Yes, that's the one. And could you let me know the estimated cost so that I can pay up front? Thanks. Sorry, I missed that, when will you be here? 10 minutes? Fine, thanks, bye.'

'They'll be here in...'

'10 minutes, yes I heard. It really is very good of you.'

'Nonsense, it was good of you to come.'

An awkward silence fell. They smiled at each other and Dave blurted, 'I hope we can do this again.'

Erica had hoped he was going say something like that, and had planned to give the impression that she was torn between replying with a yes, or a no. Instead she, like him, blurted, 'I'd like that; when?'

'How about next Wednesday; we could go for a meal?'

'Lovely.'

'I'll pick you up, if you like; I know an excellent restaurant not far from you called Hanabi. They make exceptionally good sushi. Do you like Japanese?'

'I do,' Erica replied. 'Although I'm not sure about sushi; I tried some once and it was horrid.'

'You wait till you try it at Hanabi.'

Dave's phone suddenly began vibrating across the table. 'That'll be your taxi.'

'My God,' exclaimed Erica. 'Now that's what I call a smart phone.'

'They text you when they arrive, silly; saves them having to venture into busy places to locate their fare.'

Outside they were faced with the awkward protocol of saying goodbye. After a comical dance that led to an aborted attempt at a handshake, a continental kiss and a hug, they settled for a smile and a nod and, as the taxi drew away, he held his hand up to his ear, thumb pointing up and little finger pointing down; he would be ringing her soon. And he did; he rang that night. He also rang on Sunday, Monday, and Tuesday night.

Chapter 5

As promised, Maggie rang on Sunday. She rattled on, barely taking breath between sentences, saying she was fine and there was no need to worry. It was virtually impossible for Erica to interject, and the longer the call went on the more worried Erica became. Maggie did not *sound* alright; she sounded manic. When Erica did manage to ask Maggie where she was ringing from, all she said was that she was staying with some friends up north. She gave no indication of when she would be back. The entire phone call left Erica feeling uneasy.

Maggie knew she'd sounded agitated on the phone; she also knew that there was nothing she could do about it. She switched off her phone and went back into the hospital. Her breathing was erratic, each breath coming in short, sharp bursts. Standing outside the ward, she took a moment to compose herself before rejoining Helen and Patrick at Emily's bedside. No one spoke. They just had to wait and hope.

It was a couple of days later, on Tuesday, when Doctor Harris entered looking confident.

'She's out of the woods,' he proclaimed. 'I know she still looks very poorly but I can assure you that the worst is now over. The antibiotics are doing their work and her streptococcal levels are way down. She's going to be fine.'

Maggie thought she was going to faint, so great was her relief. Patrick, with tears streaming down his face, strode over and shook the doctor's hand so vigorously that the poor man was forced to cling onto his stethoscope with his free hand as it began to shake free from his neck. 'Thank you, thank you, thank you.'

'Don't thank me,' he replied modestly. 'Thank your wife. If it hadn't been for her prompt response to Emily's symptoms then, well, as I say, it is Mrs Cunningham who deserves the thanks. Meningitis is so easy to miss, you see, and every second counts; the sooner we can start treatment the better the chances. And I have to say, your little girl is a fighter.'

Helen, laughing through her tears, said, 'Tell me about it! She's a very determined young lady, and now, thanks to you, she always will be.'

'When will we be able to take her home?' Patrick asked.

'Given how well she's responded to the treatment, I would say that you'll be able to take her home on Friday. We will obviously be keeping a close eye on her progress, but I'm very confident that all will be well.'

Maggie was back outside; she'd left Helen and Patrick with Emily. They needed privacy. Desperate to share the news, she rang Erica.

'Hi there,' exclaimed Erica. 'Give me a second, I'm at work and it's very noisy; I'm taking you outside.'

Maggie could hear a cacophony of noises, then a loud bang followed by a sort of rustling sound and Erica's voice, distant and faint, exclaiming, 'Shit, shit, shit!'

'Sorry, dropped the phone into the rubbish,' explained Erica a moment later. 'Is everything alright?'

Maggie blurted out, 'Emily's going to be fine. Mainly because of Helen's quick actions, you know, when she first noticed the symptoms and Patrick, well he was in pieces, he still is really, but he's in good pieces now, not like before. It was a close call, Erica. It really was and…'

'Maggie, slow down.'

'Right yes, sorry. Anyway she should be going home on Friday. Helen has said that I'm welcome to stay over and everything but I think it would be best for them to be alone now, now that we know that Emily is going to be fine. The doctor said she was a fighter, probably gets that from me.'

'Gets it from you?'

Kicking herself, Maggie brazened it out. 'That's what I said.'

'Am I missing something here? Who exactly are Helen and Patrick and, come to that, who is Emily?' Erica asked.

'All excellent questions, Erica.'

'Thank you. So, am I going to get some excellent answers?'

'Absolutely; it's about time that you knew the full story. I was going to tell you when I first moved in but there never seemed to be the right moment, and then the Dave thing rather took over. Oh, how is he, did he miss me on Saturday?'

'Nice try Maggie, but you're not getting away with changing the subject that easily. *What* were you going to tell me when you first moved in?'

'Listen, I'm not trying to be mysterious or anything…'

'Well you're doing a pretty good job from where I'm standing.'

'Look, I'll be back on Saturday, sometime late afternoon. I'll tell you everything then. I don't want to tell you over the phone, is that alright?'

'Have I got a choice?'

'No, I suppose not; not really.'

'That'll be fine then. At least everything's alright now; I was very worried about you, especially after that phone call on Sunday. You sounded so stressed,' said Erica. 'Anyway, I'm looking forward to seeing you. I've missed you, *and* I'm now desperate to hear what the bloody hell is going on with you.'

It was four o'clock on Saturday and there was no sign of Maggie. Erica had tidied and rearranged every cupboard in the kitchen and had now moved on to the living room to tackle the bookcase. She was attempting to arrange the books alphabetically, but Erica had always struggled with her alphabet; she had to recite the whole thing in her head with each new author to determine their correct position. She kept looking at the clock.

'Where the hell is she?' she asked the room.

Clutching her copy of Jose Saramago's *All the Names*, and again reciting the alphabet in her head, Erica exclaimed, 'Oh, this is hopeless.'

She shoved the book back into the only free space available, the place she'd just removed it from. She turned and scanned the room, her eyes lighting on the beautiful roses that Dave had sent her after their meal at the Japanese restaurant. Erica grinned. It had hit her when they'd been at the Hanabi on Wednesday evening. They'd both reached for the same piece of sushi and, when his hand had touched hers, she knew. Nothing was said. And then today, when she got back from work, there was an enormous bouquet of red roses waiting for her. Erica again checked the clock. It didn't seem to have moved. She started to rearrange her roses, pricking herself as Maggie walked through the door. 'Hello, I'm home!'

Struggling to stem the drip of blood while trying to extract a plaster from its protective cover, Erica called out, 'Brilliant. Give us a hand; I'm at risk of bleeding to death here.'

Maggie dropped her bag and dashed over. 'A *slight* exaggeration, I would say. Hand me the plaster.' Gently pressing the plaster into place, Maggie said, 'There you are, all better now. How did it happen?'

Erica pointed to the roses.

'Wow! Where did they come from? They're gorgeous.'

Trying desperately not to sound smug, Erica said smugly, 'From Dave.'

'Ah,' muttered Maggie. 'From Dave; now there's a surprise. What did I tell you? He's really into you.'

'Oh, Maggie, he really is lovely. Last Saturday, you know, at the Bird in the Hand, we talked and talked; it was like we'd known each other for years.' She dragged Maggie over to the settee, eager to hear Maggie's news but also keen to talk about Dave. 'Sit down. I'll make us both a coffee, or would you prefer a drink, drink?'

Maggie fluttered her eyelashes and tilted her head coquettishly.

'Right, understood, a drink, drink; red or white?'

'White please.'

'Coming up.'

Armed with their drinks, Maggie asked, 'So, who's going first, me or you?'

'I'm dying to tell you all about Dave but, equally, I'm dying to hear what you have to say about your mysterious trip. Oh, I don't know. You decide.'

'Me then; I've been psyching myself up all the way back on the train.'

'Sounds serious; look, you don't have to tell me, not if you don't want to.'

'Oh, I want to. I was going to tell you ages ago but the longer I left it, well, you know, the harder it got.'

'As long as you're sure.'

'I am.' Maggie took a huge gulp of wine, hiccupped, and dribbled wine down her chin.

'Just let me get it all out in one go.'

'What, the wine?'

'No, you idiot; the story. Let me just tell it, and try not to interrupt, OK?'

'OK.'

'I told you all about Jared and his escapades and the fact that I'd found him and the lovely Donatella in a rather compromising position, remember?'

'I do; the image remained in my head for some time.'

'Well, I chucked all his possessions into a black bin liner and threw him out. I had no idea where he was going to go and frankly, I didn't care. I scrubbed the villa, paying particular attention to the steps, and then I took to my bed.

I stayed there for three days, hardly ate a thing, and on the forth day I thought, 'sod this,' and got up.

'I remember eating breakfast on the terrace overlooking the sea, the sun beaming down on me, and I realised that I was fine. The man was a jerk. I went for loads of walks along the coast. Collected shells and driftwood and generally chilled. That was in July. In August my parents arrived. They were surprised to see me; the original plan had been for Jared and me to stay in the villa until the end of July. We were supposed to be going to Rome for August.'

Erica kept taking sips of wine to stop herself interrupting.

'Anyway, around about the middle of August it dawned on me that I was late, very late.'

Erica's eyes became very wide.

'Then Mummy came right out and asked me, 'Are you pregnant, dear?' All calm and collected. And, of course, I bloody was!'

'Oh, Maggie, how?'

'Um, the usual way, Erica.'

'Yes, but, oh, anyway sorry, I interrupted. Carry on.'

'My parents were fantastic. Mummy took me to see her rather dishy Italian doctor in the town to confirm one way or the other; the tests were positive. Then, back at the villa, we discussed options. Daddy was of the firm opinion that I wasn't ready to bring up a child, especially on my own, and I certainly couldn't face an abortion, so that left adoption. We came back home in September and I had the baby in April. When she was two weeks old I handed her over to her new parents; two lovely people that I'd already met.'

'Patrick and Helen?' exclaimed Erica. 'And Emily, Emily must be the baby?'

'She's two now.'

'Oh, shit. So, it was your Emily who was so sick, Christ! What, what was wrong with her?'

'It was meningitis; luckily Helen spotted it early, but it was touch and go at first; it was awful.'

'So, you keep in touch with Emily's new parents. Isn't that awkward at all?'

'Surprisingly not. In fact they asked me to be Emily's godmother,' said Maggie, adding quickly, when she saw the incredulous look on Erica's face, 'I know; fully paid up member of the atheist society that I am.' Maggie downed the last of her wine. 'Ready for more?'

'Absolutely.'

'Right then, that's me done. It's your turn now. Tell me all about our Dave.'

Erica couldn't help flinching at the use of the word 'our', as far as she was concerned he was *her* Dave.'

'I say; have I touched a nerve? Come on, what's been happening? You haven't done the deed with him already, have you?'

Erica shrieked, 'No. I've only known him for a week, for goodness sake; credit me with some decorum.'

'The lady protests so passionately. This can only mean that she wants it to happen soon.'

Grinning, Erica wailed, 'I hate you.'

'Oh dear, and why is that my sweet; because I'm right?'

'You know you are.'

'So come on. I'm burning up with curiosity now.'

Erica launched into events of the last week. 'I don't believe he has a mean bone in his body,' she said. 'And I know I sound like a besotted teenager, but honestly we just seem to, I don't know, gel.'

'Two dates and a bunch of roses, Erica, does not a relationship make.'

'I know that! But it's a start, and we talk on the phone every night, and we're spending the whole day together tomorrow,' said Erica, adding guiltily, 'I didn't know you would be back when he asked me and so...'

'Don't be silly. I'll be fine; I'll be able to catch up with Winton, unless of course you want me to join you.'

Erica's face fell. 'Um…'

'Hah! You should see your face. I was joking. I wouldn't dream of being the gooseberry.'

Erica stared into her glass and swirled the wine around. 'Maggie?'

'Uh-huh?'

'Does, um, does Jared know about the baby and everything?'

'Absolutely not; and that's the way it's going to stay. Apart from Mummy and Daddy, and Helen and Patrick obviously, you're the only person I've told.' Taking another sip of wine, she added, 'Mind you, it wouldn't surprise me if there were others in the village who might have simply put two and two together and come up with an educated guess; still, nothing I can do about that. But as for Jared, well, I do have some control over that. I haven't spoken to him since I chucked him out of the villa back in 2009 and I have no intention of talking to him now. Anyway, I haven't got a clue where he is.'

'But you tried to find him at first, didn't you.'

'That was then, this is now.'

'I bet, with our new found detective skills we could find him easily though.'

'That may be so,' muttered Maggie. 'But the fact of the matter is, I don't want to find him.'

Erica concentrated on the remaining wine in her glass as she asked, 'But, won't Emily want to know, eventually?'

'Oh, Erica; yes, you're probably right, but that's a long time off. She's only two, remember, and who knows, anything could happen between now and the time she reaches eighteen. Jared may even metamorphose into a decent human being.'

At precisely ten o'clock the next morning, Dave arrived. Maggie let him in.

'Well, hello there. Back safe and sound I see. Is um, is Erica…'

Erica appeared from the bedroom, grabbed her jacket from the hook by the door, slung it across her shoulder and announced, 'I'm here, Dave, and ready to go. See you later, Maggie. Have a good day.'

Before Maggie had a chance to respond, the pair of them, hand in hand, were halfway down the hallway, and as they disappeared down the stairs, Maggie called out, 'Bye, you two lovebirds. Be good.'

Maggie, unlike Erica who slept at the back of the flat, had heard the market setting up early that morning. Normally this annoyed her, but this morning was different. She realised that she was looking forward to seeing Winton again and wondered if he had been in touch with his brother. Erica and Dave were obviously becoming quite close, and Maggie hoped that whatever Winton had found out, if indeed he had found out anything, would be mundane and boring.

It was a glorious morning, pleasantly warm with a light breeze, and the market, with its multi-coloured awnings, looked especially cheerful. As did Winton; his face lit up when he spotted Maggie coming out of the flats. 'Well, hello to you. I haven't seen you around for ages. I was getting worried.'

'I've been up in Yorkshire with some friends of mine; their little girl was very sick but, I'm pleased to say, she made a full recovery and is now back with her parents and so, here I am.'

All of this was of course perfectly true; it simply wasn't quite the whole truth.

'Well, that is good news,' he beamed at her. 'It's good to see you.'

She smiled back. 'It's good to see you too.'

There was a moment of silence as they faced each other.

'My brother is back, by the way.'

'I was going to ask you that; and?'

'He does know this Dave guy.'

'Please tell me there's nothing bad to reveal. Erica seems to be besotted with him.'

Winton's warm smile disappeared. 'Seriously?'

'Yes, why? Is there a problem?'

'It depends, I suppose, on what Erica knows about him; I wouldn't like to see her hurt.'

'And is there a reason she might be, hurt, I mean?'

'Well, according to Jay-Jay, there was some woman that he was involved with about six years ago…'

'But not now?'

'He doesn't think so.'

'So, what's the problem?'

'Probably nothing,' said Winton. 'It's just that Jay-Jay said that the pair of them had been very close and then, in 2005 or 6, sometime after the London bombings, their relationship seemed to take a nasty turn. He remembers several occasions, when he arrived at the bookshop with a delivery, stumbling in on quite heated arguments between the two of them. They didn't try to hide it or anything; they were screaming and shouting at each other in the front of the shop. But there was one time when they were out back, in the store room, and didn't know that Jay-Jay was there. Now my brother is not a wimp, far from it, but he says that Dave's vitriolic language and violent threats certainly scared the shit out of him.'

'Are you saying he hit her?'

'I've no idea. Suffice it to say that Jay-Jay only saw the woman a few times after that incident and according to him she looked like a trapped rabbit. He tried to talk to her on one occasion, you know, to ask her if she was alright, but Dave was hovering nearby and it was hopeless; Dave answered for her, saying that of course she wasn't alright, she'd suffered a recent traumatic incident. When Jay-jay asked what had happened, Dave turned on him and told him it was none of his fucking business.'

'So, are you saying that Dave could turn violent against a woman if things don't go his way?'

Winton thought for a moment. 'Well, I have absolutely no evidence to support that theory…'

'There's a 'but' there,' said Maggie.

'But, my mother would say, 'Yu shake man han', yn noh shake 'im heart'.'

'Excuse me?'

Laughing, Winton replied, 'It's an old Jamaican proverb; it means, what you see on the outside doesn't mean it's the same on the inside.'

'Ah, good one, I must remember that,' said Maggie, adding, 'Is that where you were born then, Jamaica?'

'No, I was born in Lewisham hospital, same as my brother. My parents came over here in 1976, in search of a better life.'

'And did they find it?'

'Not exactly, no,' he stammered. 'My father was, well, he was murdered; mugged by a gang of white kids in 1987; Jay-Jay was five and I was nine.'

Maggie didn't know what to say. She instinctively reached out to Winton and took hold of his hand. They stood there, in the middle of the hustle and bustle of the market, while people manoeuvred around them. Neither of them spoke.

After several minutes, Maggie said, 'I, I, oh, shit Winton; I have no words.'

'It's alright, it was a long time ago; things are better now.'

'But how did your poor mum cope?'

'She worked three jobs; she comes from hardy stock, my mother. Another of her expressions is 'When water trow weh i' cyaa pick it up,' which, loosely translated, means, you can't turn back time; what's done is done.'

76

'Your mother sounds awesome; I'd love to meet her one day.'

Winton gave Maggie a huge grin. 'Would you now?' he asked. 'Well, how about next Sunday? Come for lunch.'

Taken aback by the invitation, Maggie was again lost for words. She was also taken aback by the little flip of pleasure that she felt in her stomach. The prospect of spending time with Winton, away from the market, was something she'd never considered, at least not until now.

Waving his massive hands in front of Maggie's face, he asked, 'Hello; is there anybody there?'

'Sorry, right, gosh, yes; yes, that would be lovely.'

'Excellent. Jay-Jay should be there too.'

'I'm looking forward to it.'

'So am I,' said Winton. 'So am I.'

Winton's mother lived in a three bed terrace house on the Maxted Road. At the front door, Winton said, 'Prepare to be transported back to the '70's.'

As Erica followed him through the hall into the living room, she took in the décor and the furniture, furniture that today would be classified as vintage. 'My parents had a settee like that,' she whispered. 'Habitat, isn't it?'

Winton nodded. 'It was one of the first pieces that my parents bought when they moved into this house.'

Hanging over the fireplace was a large framed print, similar to the famous Rolling Stones logo on the *Sticky Fingers* album cover; this depicted a huge pair of lips around a gold spoon with a clear golden substance dripping down the bottom lip and onto the canvas.

'This is beautiful,' she remarked.

'It's a Michael English print,' said Winton. 'Dad gave it to Mum when I was born.'

Winton's mother, a woman of generous proportions, appeared bearing a tray loaded with delicious looking appetisers. 'I'm glad you like it,' she said with the same flowing cadence as Winton. 'I think Jerome was trying to imply that our Winton, being born in the UK, had more than a silver spoon in his mouth.'

'Here, let me take that, Mum,' said Winton. Nodding his head in the general direction of Maggie, he went on. 'This is Maggie; Maggie, this is my mum, Isobel.'

Isobel looked Maggie up and down. 'A bit on the skinny side,' she said, 'but you've got kind eyes.'

'Mum,' exclaimed Winton. 'You can't say things like that.'

'What? That she's got kind eyes?'

'You know perfectly well I didn't mean that.'

'It's alright, Winton,' said Maggie. 'There's no denying it; I am on the skinny side.' She gave Isobel a stunning smile. 'I *do* eat...'

'I can certainly confirm that,' Winton quipped.

She gave Winton a playful swipe. 'It's just that it doesn't seem to have any affect.'

Isobel patted Maggie's arm. 'Gracious child, you're all skin and bone. A few decent meals with us and I'll soon have some flesh added to you. Now, help yourself to the nibbles; lunch will be ready soon.'

'Can I do anything to help?'

'Just eat, child,' said Isobel as she handed Maggie a bowl of salt fish fritters.

'The dips are on the tray.'

'Is Jay-Jay here?' asked Winton.

'Not yet, precious; he rang to say he'd be late.'

Isobel was explaining to Maggie how to make the 'sticky jerk wings with sugared orange' that they'd just finished eating when Jay-Jay, a carbon copy of Winton but considerably shorter, arrived, all bounce and smiles; smiles that vanished from his face the moment he noticed the empty plates and dishes covering the dining table. 'Please tell me you saved me *something*,' he cried piteously.

'It's in the bottom oven, you silly boy,' said Isobel. 'Wash your hands. I'll fetch it for you.'

Having done as he was told, he returned to the living room. 'So, you must be the delectable Maggie, the one that Winton has been going on and on about,' he said.

Maggie shot Winton a wide eyed look.

'Yes, *thank you*, Jay-Jay,' said Winton.

'Here you go, son, tuck into this,' said Isobel as she placed his plate down.

'Great, thanks,' he exclaimed. 'Weirdest thing,' he went on, 'I bumped into Philip White last week at that book convention.'

'Now, there's a lovely man,' said Isobel, patting her son's shoulder. 'He took my Jay-Jay under his wing, stopped him from going astray and I praise the Lord for that.'

Picking up a sticky jerk wing, Jay-Jay scowled at his mother before addressing Winton. 'He was the one that introduced me to that Dave dude you were asking about,' he said as he took a bite.

'And?' said Winton.

Jay-Jay quickly swallowed his mouthful. '*And* we started talking about old times, and for some reason he started talking about that bird I was telling you about, Dave's chick; Melissa her name was.'

'Melissa was Dave's girlfriend?' exclaimed Maggie.

'Yea, what's the big deal?'

'Well, according to Phyllis…'

'Phyllis?' asked Jay-Jay.

'Dave's grandmother.'

'Now she's a real sweet old lady; never knew her first name though. She often…'

'Jay-Jay!'

'Sorry, Maggie; you were saying?'

'According to Phyllis, Erica is the spit of this Melissa woman, and when we asked who she was, Dave said that she was just some woman he'd known and she only bore a slight similarity to Erica.'

'Well, I can tell you they were tight, real tight,' said Jay-Jay.

'Interesting,' mused Maggie.

'Anyway, Philip said that he'd always liked Melissa but not Dave. He did business with him and everything, his jobs paid well, but he never liked him as a person. He said he was a control freak; never let Melissa out of his sight,' he turned to Winton, 'I said the same to you didn't I?'

Winton nodded.

'Anyway, he told me that Melissa's parents had been killed in the 2005 London bombings and that soon afterwards she'd moved in with Dave and his parents.'

'Hang on,' exclaimed Maggie. 'Melissa *lived* with Dave?'

'That's what Philip said.'

'Hardly just some woman he vaguely knew then,' said Maggie.

'No, like I said, they were tight. Plus, according to Philip, Dave's father had a bit of a thing for her too,' said Jay-Jay.

Maggie's eyes widened.

'Yeah; it seems that Dave senior fell under the spell of the delightful Melissa. He told Philip that she was marvellous with his wife, very caring and understanding. Said she was a great comfort to him. He believed that looking after Deborah had helped Melissa deal with the loss of her parents.'

'What was wrong with Deborah?'

'Tragic stuff; she was diagnosed with multiple sclerosis early in 2002, had a relapse in 2005, didn't you know?'

'I didn't; Erica might know I suppose, but she hasn't said anything.'

'According to Philip, Dave, Dave senior I mean, was devastated when Melissa upped sticks and left.'

'Did Philip know where she upped sticks to?'

'Yes, it was Australia, of all places.'

'Australia, bloody hell, that's a long way to go; was she that keen to put a lot of distance between them then?'

'Hah! Good point; no, according to Philip, Melissa had a friend out there called Penny I think he said; anyway, Dave senior was all for driving up to Yorkshire with his son...'

'I'm sorry to interrupt, Jay-Jay, Yorkshire? I thought you said she went to Australia?'

'She did, but before that Dave had driven Melissa up to Yorkshire; his grandmother owns a property up there. They'd gone up there for a break but it seems that, for Melissa anyway, it was going to be a permanent break. It's where she announced that she was emigrating to Australia.'

'And did he? Dave senior, I mean, did he go there, to Yorkshire obviously, not Australia?'

'No, Dave was incensed by the suggestion that his father should interfere, so he drove down to London to collect Melissa's possessions and then back up to Yorkshire alone. Dave senior never saw Melissa again.'

'And you've never heard from or seen this Melissa woman again either?'

Mid chew, Jay-Jay mumbled, 'Nope,' adding, once he'd finished his mouthful, 'But then, why would I?'

'No reason I suppose, it's just, oh, I don't know. Perhaps Erica's right; this investigation bug has gone to my head. Do you think I should tell her?'

'Tell her what exactly?' Winton asked.

'That Dave lied about his relationship to this Melissa woman for one thing.'

'Well, he didn't exactly lie, he just didn't go into details, and why should he, Maggie, he'd only just met the pair of you.'

'True,' Maggie conceded.

'Erica seems happy at the moment,' said Winton. 'She's been sad for a very long time; she tries to hide it, but I see it in her eyes. Why do you want to see complications where there are probably none? OK, so this Dave was a bit economical with the truth, but we've all done that on occasion, haven't we?'

Recalling her own economy with the truth the previous week, about her trip to Yorkshire, Maggie mumbled. 'I suppose so.'

His warm smile spread to his eyes, causing them to crinkle at the corners. 'Right then, excellent. Now, can I tempt you to a slice of one of my mother's delicious cakes?' asked Winton.

Chapter 6

Over the next three months Dave rang, emailed, or texted Erica every day. Flowers arrived every week, and once he even turned up outside the Lord of the Fries with a quartet to serenade her. Maggie found it creepy.

Coffee in hand, she was idly flicking through last month's copy of *Vogue*, muttering to herself that it was mostly adverts, when she glanced across at the new wall clock, a hideous, fluorescent, back-lit monstrosity that Dave had given Erica last week, and noted that Erica would be home in about half an hour.

Dave had dropped Erica back yesterday evening after their regular Sunday jaunt and, as usual, had rung 45 minutes later.

'Doesn't that get on your pip?' Maggie had asked.

'No, I think it's lovely. He's only ringing to let me know that he's safely back home.'

'Jesus, Erica; what could possibly happen between here and his place?'

'Nothing probably, but I still think it's nice. Anyway, he was also ringing to check that I was alright.'

'Why, what did he do to you?'

'He didn't *do* anything to me; honestly Maggie, why would you even think that?' said Erica. 'No, it's just that today, for the first time, he talked about his past; the girlfriend who deserted him, his parents, well, everything really.'

'A girlfriend deserted him?'

'He told me all this in confidence, Maggie.'

Maggie mimed zipping her lips, curious to hear Dave's version of events.

'It's awful; Dave told me that his girlfriend's parents were killed in those dreadful London bombings. He said that when she moved in with him at The Retreat, she became fixated on his parents and their relationship fell apart. He was very honest with me, Maggie, he told me that he'd been in love with her, but that she'd hurt him terribly.'

'So, did Dave mention this girlfriend's name?'

Maggie held her breath and waited.

Erica thought for a moment. 'No, now you come to mention it, I don't think he did. Still, that's not important, is it?'

Maggie hesitated momentarily before replying, 'Probably not; carry on.'

'He told me that they argued a lot…'

'Did he say what about?'

'No, Maggie, he didn't; and I thought you weren't going to interrupt.'

'Sorry; carry on.'

'As I was saying, he said they'd started arguing a lot. Dave was desperate to rescue the relationship, and so took her away for a break in Yorkshire; his grandmother owns a cottage up there.'

'And did it work?'

'Not really, no.'

'Why? What happened?'

'They'd been there for about a week when she suddenly announced that she was leaving the country; she needed space to think or some such gobble gook crap. Anyway, she told him that it had all been arranged; her passage had been booked, she was off to Australia for a year.'

'And how did Dave react to that?'

'How do you think?'

Maggie shrugged. 'Who knows? We're talking about a man who doesn't like to be apart from you for more than a few bloody hours, so…'

'Oh, give it a rest, Maggie.'

'Sorry; so, come on then, how *did* he react?'

Erica fixed Maggie with an intense stare. 'Not well. I mean he was shocked; it was the first time he'd heard about it.'

'And did he hurt her?'

'Sorry?'

'I mean did he hit her or anything?'

'Hit her?' exclaimed Erica. 'What is with you at the moment? No, of course he didn't hit her; he loved her.'

'These things happen, Erica.'

'Jesus, Maggie, do you think I don't know that?'

'I'm just saying; people do uncharacteristic things when they're upset.'

'What, like attempting to top themselves when their loved one buggers off,' said Erica. 'I told Dave about that, and, and, he confessed that he'd also considered that option.'

'Who'd have thought,' said Maggie.

Erica gave Maggie another hard stare. Maggie returned her gaze with an angelic smile.

'Anyway,' continued Erica. 'She didn't want to face his parents and so Dave drove back down to London to collect her stuff, and then drove back up to Yorkshire where she sorted through it. The stuff she wanted, he arranged to be sent ahead to Australia, the stuff she didn't want she told him to do whatever he wanted with it. So even though he felt overwhelmed, he was considerate, Maggie and *very* supportive.'

What is he, some sort of bloody saint now? thought Maggie.

'So, when did all this happen?'

'About a year after her parents had been killed. He said it was the North Yorkshire cottage that saved him. He stayed there for about a month after she'd left so that he could get on with the redecorating. He said it helped to take his mind off everything, and it would be a lovely surprise for his mother because it had all been hard on her, too.'

'I know; awful isn't it? And of course there's no cure for MS.'

'What?'

'Um, well, Jay-Jay was telling me that Dave's mother was diagnosed with multiple sclerosis back in 2002; I assumed you'd know.'

Erica went very quiet.

'Um, I expect he finds it difficult to talk about,' suggested Maggie.

Biting her lip, Erica muttered, 'Yes, that'll be it. Anyway, there you have it; he's just like me really; no murky past, no skeletons, just a normal person who got hurt by someone he loved; someone, like Jared, who simply abandoned him.'

'So, he never heard from her again?'

'Dave said that she did keep in touch for a while; she sent emails to him and to his mother, all saying how brilliant life was in Australia, and then she sent one final email saying that she wasn't coming back.'

'So, why all the secrecy and subterfuge? I mean nothing you've told me is remotely unusual. Sad, but not unusual; woman losing her parents, relationship breaking down...'

'It's not that. I just don't think Dave is very proud about how he dealt with it all, you know the suicidal thoughts and everything.'

'Oh, right, yes; the suicidal thoughts.'

'Yes, Maggie! The suicidal thoughts; he's ashamed, and he doesn't want me to think he's unbalanced. He thought he would never meet another woman that he could love and he says he feels blessed to have met me. He reckons that I would never do anything to hurt him. He said it would kill him if I left.'

'That sounds like emotional blackmail.'

'Oh, don't be so melodramatic; it's just an expression. He didn't mean it literally.' She pushed herself up from the settee. 'Now, do you want a drink before we go to bed or what?'

'Yes, OK, thanks.'

'Red or white?'

'Whatever's easiest.'

Erica handed Maggie a glass of white and settled back onto the settee. Maggie was desperate to tell Erica everything that she knew, but instead she said, 'So, what's happening with you at Christmas? Are you going to your parents?'

With a defiant look, Erica replied, 'No, I'm not; Dave's invited me to spend Christmas with him and his family.'

Maggie took a gulp of wine. 'And your mum's alright with that, is she?'

'She doesn't know yet.'

The wall clock alerted Maggie to the fact that Erica would be back in about five minutes. They were off to the Portobello market in search of Christmas gifts, and Maggie was looking forward to spending some time with her friend. Until, that is, the thought entered her head that Dave was going to show up; after all, by now it would be a whole fourteen hours since he'd last seen her.

She swallowed the last mouthful of coffee and was jigging up and down on the spot, rinsing the mug, when the phone rang. She snatched it up. 'Yes?'

'Erica?'

'No, this is Maggie, Erica's at work.'

'Maggie, yes, of course, this is Audrey, Erica's mum.'

Shit, thought Maggie.

'How lovely,' she said. 'How are you?'

'I'm very worried about Erica actually.'

'Whatever for? She's fine.'

'Is she? Well I wouldn't know, would I? She hasn't rung in weeks.'

Shit, thought Maggie again.

'Well, I can assure you, she's absolutely fine,' she repeated.

'I suppose *you've* met this new man of hers, Dud...?'

'Dave? Yes, yes I have.'

'And what's he like? The last time we spoke she was very vague about him. Is he much older, or worse, is he married? I mean when you don't know anything you just think the worst, don't you?'

'He's a little older,' said Maggie. 'Not by much; he's 30. He runs a bookshop and he's um,' Maggie crossed her fingers tightly. 'He's um, very attentive towards Erica.'

'And have you any idea what my daughter's plans are for Christmas? Are we actually going to have the pleasure of this Dud...'

'Dave.'

'Are we going to have the pleasure of this Dave for Christmas?'

'I'm really not sure; look, I don't want to be rude but I was just about to go to the loo when you rang and...'

'I'm back, are you ready?' cried Erica as she entered the flat.

Maggie thrust the phone into Erica's hand. 'It's your mother,' she whispered. 'I'm desperate for the loo.'

'Mum; hi,' said Erica brightly.

'I'm sorry, who is that? I'm afraid I don't recognise the voice.'

'Very funny, Mum; I get the message, I should have rung you, but I've been very busy.'

'With the mysterious Dave, I assume.'

'*And* work. I told you, I still do three mornings at the café and I'm writing loads of stuff for newspapers and magazines.'

'Oh, darling that *is* good news. So, what papers and magazines have printed your work? Your father will be thrilled, and wait till I tell the women in the book club, they'll be...'

Erica yelled down the line, 'Mum, Mum.'

'Don't bellow, dear; what?'

'I didn't say the work had been printed. I've sent it off but, as yet, there haven't been any takers. It's a very competitive field.'

'I see; so, still just the café then, really?'

'Yes Mum, still just the café. Anyway, Maggie and I are about to go out Christmas shop…'

Maggie re-appeared by Erica's side mouthing, 'Sorry'.

Erica gave a silent growl.

'I'm glad you mentioned Christmas, dear. It's why I rang; I just wondered, are your father and I going to be told, at some point, what your plans are?'

'Actually, I was going to ring you tonight.'

'Of course you were, darling,' her mother replied.

Erica clenched her fists. 'I'll be spending Christmas with Dave and his family, Mum. It should be fun. Now I must dash; talk again soon. Bye.' She slammed the phone down and whirled around to face Maggie. 'Don't say a single bloody word,' she cried. 'Just give me 10 minutes for a quick shower.' She gave Maggie's arm a stroke. 'We haven't had a girly outing for ages.'

They'd been in the Portobello Road about half an hour when, as Maggie had feared, Erica received a phone call.

'It's Dave,' she announced in a subdued tone.

Well, there's a surprise, thought Maggie.

She listened for a moment. 'The thing is, Dave, I'm with Maggie and—'

'Uh huh.' Erica glanced at Maggie and raised her eyebrows.

'Uh huh,' she repeated.

'OK, yes—No, no that's fine. Yes—I'll ask her. See you in a bit.'

'So, what's up?' asked Maggie.

'He's in the Castle at the top of Portobello Road and he says the food is great.'

'And I suppose he wants you to join him.'

Erica glanced away.

'Are you alright?'

Turning back to face Maggie, Erica smiled; it was, however, a smile that did not reach her eyes. 'Yes, of course I'm alright, why the hell wouldn't I be alright?'

'OK, don't get your knickers in a twist; I was just asking.'

'Sorry. Anyway, he says he's missing me.'

'Oh, give me strength,' exclaimed Maggie. 'What's wrong with the man? He only saw you a few hours ago, and anyway, hasn't he got a bookshop to run?'

'Phyllis is looking after the place. So, are you coming, he said he was concerned about me being out in this cold, damp November air.'

'For God's sake. What does he imagine you've come out in, shorts and flip-flops?'

'No of course not. Look, are you coming or not?'

'Not. I'll see you back at the flat.'

'I'm sorry about this.'

'You could always decline the offer from the wonderful Dave, you know, and explain to him that you want to spend some time with me for a change; I'm sure he'd understand.'

Erica mumbled, 'I'm not so sure.'

'What?'

'I said, 'Are you keeping score?''

Maggie was certain that wasn't what Erica had said. 'Absolutely, and I'd say that Dave was winning hands down.'

'Yes, you're probably right,' agreed Erica. 'You don't mind though, do you?'

Maggie did mind, she minded very much. 'Of course not, and anyway, it's easier shopping on your own; you don't have to keep waiting for the other person or worry about losing them in the crowds. Have a nice meal and I'll see you later.'

Maggie watched Erica plod up the road.

Something's wrong, she thought. *Perhaps I should have gone with her. Is he stalking her? Is she a substitute for the absent Melissa? Am I being paranoid?*

Maggie wandered aimlessly down the Portobello Road and turned right. Finding herself outside Notting Hill Gate underground station, she entered the concourse, bought a ticket and boarded the train.

Half an hour later and armed with a selection of cupcakes, Maggie stood, deep in thought, outside Black Moon Books.

The door flew open, revealing a beaming Phyllis. 'Hello dear, I thought it was you. How lovely! Dave isn't here; he's dashed off to see the lovely Erica, but I expect you know that,' her eyes alighted on the white box. 'I see you've been to Betty's again; no more missile incidents I hope.'

'Hello Phyllis, no, no more missiles thrown, not today. I just thought you might like some company and,' she held the white box aloft, 'a cupcake.'

'Lovely; come in, come in. I'll put the kettle on.'

They were enjoying their coffee and cakes when Jay-Jay walked in. 'Maggie,' he exclaimed. 'Fancy seeing you here.'

'Hello, Jay-Jay,' said Maggie. 'If you've come to see Dave you're out of luck I'm afraid; he's with Erica.'

'No problem. I'll just leave these books here then,' he said as he plonked them on the counter.

'Have you time for a coffee? And look, Maggie's bought cakes.'

'That's very kind, but sadly I'm already running late; another time perhaps.' He glanced at Maggie as he was leaving. 'See you on Sunday as usual?'

'Absolutely, Jay-Jay, bye.'

'So, how do you know Jay-Jay? Is he your beau?'

Maggie suppressed a giggle. 'My beau? No, Phyllis, no he's not. Actually, I'm a good friend of his brother, Winton,' she said. 'And when I told Winton that Erica and I had *discovered* Dave in the Black Moon Bookshop he mentioned that Jay-Jay worked as a book runner for him; amazing coincidence, really.'

'Yes, that's right dear. He was Philip White's apprentice, and when Philip retired the charming Jay-Jay took up the reigns. Dave tells me that he's one of the best. There was a time, oh, years ago now, when, for reasons that I never understood, Dave stopped using him, which was a shame.'

'Oh, when was that?' Maggie asked innocently.

'About five or six years ago I think; soon after Melissa left.'

'Melissa? Wasn't that the girl you said Erica resembled?'

Phyllis bit her bottom lip and nodded.

'Jay-Jay was telling me that Melissa went off to Australia of all places.'

'Yes, she went out there to join her friend, Penny.' Phyllis stared off into the distance. 'It was all very sudden.'

'And a very long way to go; was she intending to come back, do you know?'

'She told Dave that she was going for a year, but she never came back. Dave was devastated. All very sad; still, now that he's met Erica he's back to his normal self.'

And what is that 'normal self'? Maggie wondered.

'He's certainly very keen on Erica,' she said aloud. 'Given the choice I think he'd have her manacled to him.'

Phyllis started brushing away imaginary dust from the table. She gave a little laugh. 'Yes, I suppose he doesn't want to lose her. I'm sure you understand.'

'Was he the same way with Melissa?' asked Maggie tentatively.

'How do you mean, dear?'

Controlling, possessive and overprotective was what she wanted to say. What she actually said was, 'Attentive and considerate and, I don't mean to be rude, but a tad clingy?'

The brushing motion became more frantic. 'Oh, dear, well, it's really not for me to say, but, who knows, maybe you're right.'

'Didn't she move in with you all after her parents were killed in those dreadful bombs?'

Phyllis's eyes twinkled. 'Still investigating, I see.'

'Sorry, I don't mean to be...'

Phyllis patted Maggie's arm. 'I'm just teasing you, dear,' she said. 'Actually I thought that when Melissa moved in with us Dave would relax and become less clingy.' She wrung her hands. 'But he got worse; he and Melissa just seemed to argue all the time.'

'But why did they argue?'

'I'm rather ashamed to say that the silly boy became jealous.'

'Jealous? Jealous of what?'

'Of the time that Melissa spent caring for his mother. Dave didn't deal well with his mother's MS diagnosis, you see,' Phyllis frowned. 'Did you know about my daughter's MS, dear?'

'I did; Jay-Jay mentioned it. It must be very difficult for you all.'

'Deborah is not one to indulge in self pity, and she's currently in remission, which is good. But, back in 2005, she had a relapse; Melissa was a blessing, she really was.'

'So, Dave was jealous of the time that Melissa spent with his mother?'

'Yes, silly I know, but that boy has always been insecure.' She reached for another cupcake and pushed the box towards Maggie. 'Still, everybody argues sometimes. don't they?'

'Absolutely,' agreed Maggie as she helped herself to a cake. 'And sometimes it can all get a bit heavy.'

'Heavy?'

Licking her fingers, Maggie added, 'Yes, you know: passionate, forceful, intense; and, I suppose, in the right circumstances arguments may even turn violent.'

Phyllis recoiled. 'Not my little Dave, absolutely not; he wouldn't harm a fly.'

'Of course not, no; I wasn't trying to suggest…'

'More coffee, dear?'

'I'd love another coffee, but can I ask you just one more question, and then I promise that's it?'

Phyllis straightened her back and sat upright in her chair. 'Fire away.'

'I just wondered, did Dave ever meet this Penny?'

'No, dear. I think she'd already emigrated to Australia when Dave met Melissa. Why?'

'Idle curiosity, really. Listen, are you sure you've got time for more coffee?'

'I've certainly got the time,' she glanced around the empty shop. 'As you can see, I'm rushed off my feet.' She inspected the white box. 'And, more importantly, we've got more cakes.'

Back at the flat that evening, Maggie told Erica about her trip to see Phyllis. 'And you'll never guess who turned up at the bookshop.'

'Julia Roberts?' suggested Erica.

'Ha! Good one. No, it was Jay-Jay.'

'Winton's brother?'

'The very same; he had some books, unsurprisingly I suppose, for Dave. And after he'd gone Phyllis and I got to talking about how I knew him and everything, and she told me all about Dave's previous girlfriend, you know, the one you were telling me about who left him.'

'Uh huh.'

Maggie went on. 'Well, according to Phyllis, when Melissa emigrated to Australia it was to join an old friend of hers called Penny.'

Erica started. 'Did you say Melissa? Wasn't that the name of the person that I'm supposed to look like?'

Breezily, Maggie replied, 'Gosh, yes, I think you're right. That's weird.'

'Weird,' agreed Erica.

Maggie said nothing as she watched Erica digest this information; information that clearly pointed to the fact that Dave had lied to her, or at the very least, been economical with the truth.

'Still, it was a long time ago I suppose,' said Erica.

'And it was also a long way to go.'

'I'm sorry, Maggie, am I missing something here? I know Australia's a long way away and everything but I don't think that's the point you're trying to make, is it?'

'I'm just saying, you know, given how she cared for Dave's mother, and given that she'd lost her own parents in such tragic circumstances, I'd have thought that she would have wanted to remain in the UK.'

Sighing, Erica replied, 'You don't like Dave, do you?'

'Nonsense, of course I like him, it's just, oh, I don't know Erica, he never leaves you alone; don't you find it suffocating?'

Erica went quiet. Maggie held her breath and waited.

'Actually, I am beginning to find it all a bit much. I did try to decline his offer, you know, to join his family at Christmas, but he wouldn't hear of it. He simply went on and on about it until, coward that I am, I caved in and agreed, even though I knew how it would upset Mum and Dad. Dad will be very understanding but Mum, well I pity Dad, she'll whinge about all her hard work bringing me up, as if Dad had nothing to do with it, and their Christmas will be a disaster. I feel awful about it.'

'Oh, Erica, I'm so sorry. Listen, you'll just have to tell him, surely he'll understand. Christmas, whether we like it or not, is supposed to be a time that we share with our family.'

'But that's just it,' she wailed. 'He said that as far as he's concerned I'm part of *his* family now. I mean, what does that mean exactly?'

'Shit, Erica, I don't know. How long are you staying there, just for Christmas?'

'No,' Erica moaned, 'New Year too.'

'OK, don't panic, let me think.'

'Shall I open a bottle?'

'What a splendid idea.'

Maggie was well into her second glass of Chablis when she suddenly announced, 'I've got it!'

'What?'

'A plan to extract you from the demanding clutches of Dave.'

'I don't think he realises, Maggie; he tells me that he simply can't bear being apart.'

'Lovely as that sentiment is, dear friend, there is a limit. Anyway, listen. How about I ring you and tell a little white lie.'

'What sort of white lie?'

'Something like, your mother or father has been taken ill and you need to come home, or your nana, or an aunt, I don't know, you decide.'

Erica thought for a moment. 'Do you think that would work? It would mean lying, wouldn't it, and I don't feel very comfortable with deception.'

Would that Dave felt the same, thought Maggie.

'Actually, it strikes me as highly likely that your father, under the constant tirade of your mother's wrath at this happy time, *will* be in urgent need of medical assistance. Go on, what do you think?'

Erica was about to reply when her phone rang. She glanced at Maggie. 'It's Dave.'

'Oh, there's a surprise.'

'Hi there; long time no see,' said Erica.

'I know, don't be cross,' said Dave, 'it's just that when I got back to the bookshop, Gran told me that Maggie had popped in to see her and they got chatting.'

'Yes, Maggie was just telling me.'

Maggie gesticulated wildly. 'What?' she whispered.

Erica put her finger to her mouth as she listened to Dave's next comment.

'So, um, has Maggie told you what they talked about?' he was saying.

'She has, Dave, and I have to say I'm a little curious.'

'Um, right yes, about what exactly?'

'Oh, now, let me think,' said Erica. 'How about the fact that your girlfriend, the love of your life at the time I believe you said, the one that went off to Australia, was called Melissa and, correct me if I'm wrong, but wasn't that the name of the person that Phyllis said I bore a striking resemblance to?'

There was no response.

'Are you still there?' asked Erica.

'Yes, yes, sorry, yes, I can see why that might make you feel a little curious.'

'And?'

'Oh, I don't know, Erica, I just didn't want you to think that was the only reason I started dating you. And yes, like I told you, she was the love of my life and I did everything I could to keep her, but it wasn't to be, and maybe that was for the best. I mean, let's face it, if Melissa and I were still together I would never have met you, and that just doesn't bear thinking about. And anyway, you only look a bit like Melissa.'

'More than a bit; according to Phyllis, I could be her twin.'

'Yes, well, that's a bit of an exaggeration. As I say there is a slight similarity, but honestly, that has nothing to do with anything. Really, it doesn't, and I'm sorry that I didn't tell you in the first place; it was stupid of me. I see that now. Please forgive me.'

'And what about your mum? I find that a little more difficult to understand, I mean, I'm joining you all at Christmas; didn't you think I'd notice or something?'

Again there was silence down the line.

'Dave?'

'I'm still here,' he croaked.

'I'm sorry, Dave; I didn't mean to upset you. It must be very hard.'

Maggie raised her eyebrows. Erica thumped her.

'I *was* going to tell you, of course I was. I just...I just find it difficult. I feel so helpless, Erica. Mum's amazing, she really is, she copes very well, but it's been ten years since the diagnosis and, well, her time is limited. Every year that passes brings the inevitable,' he trailed off.

They both knew what 'the inevitable' meant.

'Oh, Dave, I'm so sorry.'

'You *are* still joining us for Christmas, aren't you? My parents are really looking forward to meeting you. I am so, so sorry; I had no intention of trying to deceive you; you do know that, don't you?'

Erica nodded mutely.

'Erica, Erica! Are you still there?'

'Yes, Dave, I'm here.'

'So, are you still joining us for Christmas?'

'Of course I am, Dave. I'm looking forward to it.'

'And you'll still on for our date tomorrow?'

'Yes.'

'Brilliant; I'll pick you up at 7 pm then. Bye, my love.'

'Bye.'

'I take it from your responses that the man gave you satisfactory answers to your questions.'

'Oh, Maggie, he sounded so contrite. I'm certain that there was no intent to deceive me. He's a very troubled man. Think about it, his mother has MS; she's dying, Maggie, and there's nothing he can do. He's powerless, and that's one of the worst situations to be in.'

Maggie sighed. If she revealed what Jay-Jay and his mentor, Peter, had said about Dave to Erica now, she would just say that they didn't understand him. It was hopeless. 'So, I take it that my mercy phone call is no longer required.'

'I don't think so, no; but thank you for the offer.'

Maggie left Peckham to join her parents on Christmas Eve. At the door, she turned and said, 'Erica, if it all becomes too much my offer still stands, you know.'

'Honestly, Maggie, don't worry, it'll be fine. I'm looking forward to meeting Dave's parents, and, don't forget, the lovely Phyllis will be there too.'

'If you're sure.'

'I'm sure; now go,' said Erica. 'Have fun and I'll see you next year.'

'2013; I can't believe it. What exactly happened to 2012?'

'We spent some of it looking for Dave.'

'Oh, yes that's right, and unfortunately, we found him,' mumbled Maggie

'Sorry?'

'I said, yes and fortunately we found him.'

Chapter 7
January 2013

The moment Erica walked into the café on her first morning back after her disastrous Christmas, she was overrun with customers. She'd just cleared table six for the third time that morning when Joyce elbowed her. 'Isn't that your young man hovering about outside?'

Erica glanced up. 'I don't know how he's got the nerve; I don't want to talk to him,' she whispered, walking away with her arms full of dirty crockery.

Dave pushed open the door and took a few steps towards the counter.

Joyce positioned herself directly in front of him. 'And where do you think you're going?' she said.

'To speak to my girlfriend if that's alright with you,' he snapped.

'It's of no interest to me, luv, but Erica doesn't want to speak to you.'

'We'll see about that; now, if you don't mind.' He shoved Joyce out of the way and marched towards the kitchen.

'Bloody nerve,' exclaimed Joyce as she watched Dave kick open the kitchen door.

The café fell silent. All eyes were fixed on the swinging door.

'Go away,' yelled Erica.

'Just let me explain, I know…'

'There's nothing to explain, Dave; nothing could possibly excuse your appalling behaviour.'

'If you'd just…'

'If I'd just what? Wait for some pathetic excuse, another lie…'

'I've never lied to you, Erica; I've merely been economical with the truth and…'

'You just don't get it, do you, Dave? I'm not an idiot, you know.'

'Of course you're not an idiot. I'm so, so sorry, Erica; please give me another chance.'

'I've already given you chances, Dave; too many. You're just a spoilt little boy and I can't be bothered anymore. I've, I've just had enough. I'm sick of your overbearing, controlling, and frankly idiotic behaviour. I need space to breathe, to be myself and work on my career, so just back off, Dave; it's over.'

'Jesus, you sound just like bloody Melissa.'

'Do I, do I?' Erica retorted. 'Well perhaps that should be your bloody clue. I'll tell you this, Dave; if I had the money I'd be on a plane to Australia this bloody minute; your precious Melissa and I could compare notes!'

'I suppose you think that's funny,' snarled Dave. 'Fine; do what you fucking like; you're not worth the time or the effort and *I'll* tell you this: you're not a patch on Melissa. You can go to hell.'

Mac stormed over and grabbed Dave by his collar. 'Right, matey, that's enough,' he said shoving him back out into the café. 'Joyce,' he yelled. 'Open the door; I need to remove this vermin from the premises.'

'With pleasure.'

The entire café erupted with cheering and clapping as Dave was unceremoniously ejected. Stumbling out onto the pavement he stuck his middle finger up and shouted, 'Fuck the lot of you.'

The texts started a couple of months later; each one more remorseful than the last. Eventually, Erica agreed to meet Dave in the Bird in the Hand. Maggie told her she was mad. Erica thought that Maggie was most probably right but nevertheless she went.

As soon as she walked in, Dave rushed forward to greet her. 'I can't tell you how grateful I am that you came,' he gushed. He looked her up and down and gently touched her arm. 'I can't believe it; you're really here. I am so, so sorry. I behaved like an imbecile. You should have heard my gran; she may look like a sweet old lady but, get her riled up and well, it's a sight to behold I can tell you.'

'Shall we sit down?' asked Erica quietly.

'Yes, yes of course, sorry. I've bagged a table. Come on.' He guided her gently towards the back of the pub to a small table enclosed within an alcove.

'What would you like to drink? A white wine?'

'Yes, that would be lovely,' she said politely.

'I'll get straight to the point,' he said as he set their drinks down. 'I'd been thinking about taking you up to Yorkshire for a while, and then I had what I thought was an inspired idea to surprise you with that invitation,' he began, adding quickly, 'That wasn't going to be my only present to you by the way, but that's not the point. My reaction to the news that the cottage had been sold must have seemed somewhat extreme.'

'You could say that.'

'Yes, well, quite,' he stared down at his beer. 'And, if I'm honest, well, it was. Extreme, I mean. And I really can't explain it, not even to myself. Gran says that I'd reverted to childhood and had a tantrum because I couldn't get my own way. Sadly, she's right.' He glanced up at Erica and noticed that she was smiling to herself. 'What?'

'Oh, nothing really,' she said. 'It's just that Maggie said you probably had tantrums as a small child.'

'And she was dead on the money; and, on current evidence it would seem that this behaviour still persists, it's just that these days it doesn't involve throwing myself onto the floor, kicking and screaming until I get my own way.'

'No, these days you just do a dramatic disappearing act.'

'Normally I just sulk; in a manly way obviously,' he said with a crooked grin.

'Obviously,' agreed Erica. 'Where *did* you go, as a matter of interest?'

'I descended on Steve and Julia.'

'Steve and Julia?'

'Julia, wife of my good friend Steve, she who exchanged texts with you…'

'Oh, yes, I remember; she was the one that suggested you needed a PA?'

'Spot on. Mind you, when I explained what had happened and how I'd walked out on you and my family, she reckoned I needed more than a PA.'

'And what, pray, did she suggest?'

'Can't you guess?'

'Oh, I don't know. Let me think; a nut doctor, therapy, a smacked bottom, or possibly all three?'

'The first two; she didn't come up with the smacked bottom idea but, if you're offering, I accept and I'll take my punishment like a man.'

'Idiot!'

'Oh, Erica, please say you forgive me. I'll do anything to make it up to you, and all those things I said about you not being worth it and everything, it was all nonsense. I'm so ashamed, I behaved like a monster. Frankly I was lucky that your boss didn't punch me to the ground. And before you say anything, let me also add that I heard what *you* said and I've taken it all on board.'

He went down on his knees. Erica nearly fainted. 'And I hereby promise faithfully,' he said, 'to stop being so possessive and clingy.'

Erica burst out laughing, mostly out of relief that he hadn't proposed rather than amusement. 'Get up Dave, honestly.'

He sat back down and looked at her expectantly.

Erica took a sip of wine.

Dave continued to watch her intently but said nothing. Under the table his fingers were tightly crossed.

Erica took another sip. 'I'm probably mad,' she said. 'But I do forgive you.'

Dave started to speak. Erica reached across and put her finger to his lips. 'But let me be clear here,' she continued. 'You've got to stop ringing and texting me all the time; you've got to go easy on all the flowers—apart from anything else it must be costing you a fortune; and finally, you've got to stop turning up everywhere unexpectedly. Generally you've just got to stop, well, hounding me, for want of a better word. One step out of line and that's it.'

A few weeks later, on a pleasantly warm spring day in early May, Dave and Erica were enjoying a lunchtime sandwich in the Marcus Garvey Park, a regular habit that they had recently fallen into on the days when Erica wasn't working. Dave was very quiet and when Erica asked him if he was alright he smiled and said, 'Actually, I was thinking about Black Sheep Cottage.

Erica's brow furrowed and her eyes clouded over.

'Don't look like that. I'm not about to throw another wobbly; no, I was just thinking that, at this time of year, it's particularly beautiful up there and I wish you could have seen it,' he mused. 'Still, never mind. It was obviously not to be.'

Without thinking, Erica suggested, 'We could still go up there, you know.'

'What, and ask the new owners if they wouldn't mind if we bunked down in the spare room?' he exclaimed.

'No, silly; I mean we could go up to North Yorkshire, not specifically to the cottage but...'

Dave's face lit up. 'That's a brilliant idea. We could book into a small family hotel for a week or something and I could show you around the area. We could even drive over to the cottage, you know, just to have a look.'

Erica cautioned, 'Well, not necessarily a week; I was thinking more like a weekend.'

Oblivious to Erica's concern, Dave blundered on. 'Yes; and you never know, the new owners might even invite us in, especially once I explain that I'm the grandson of the woman who sold it to them.'

Dave grabbed hold of Erica's shoulders, pulled her towards him and gave her a quick kiss. 'Right, when shall we go? Can you get some time off? Oh, this is brilliant!'

'Steady on, Dave.'

'Sorry, but oh, I don't know, it would give me a chance to say goodbye to the place if nothing else.'

Erica gave him a sideways glance. 'Do you mean it would give you closure?'

'That's just psychobabble; no, I simply mean it would be nice, nothing more, nothing less.'

'I *could* do with a break,' agreed Erica reluctantly. 'I'll have a word with Mac at the café and I'll let you know. Have you got any dates in mind?'

'Oh, as soon as possible I think. Now you've put the idea into my head I'm eager to get going.'

'But what about the bookshop; you surely don't expect Phyllis to look after it for a whole week, I mean over the lunch hour is one thing but…'

'No, no, of course not, but that's no problem; Philip White is always up for looking after the place. I'll ask him.'

'Philip White?'

'He's a good friend of my dad; he used to do the job that Jay-Jay does now, in fact he was Jay-Jay's mentor. He's a bit stuck up his own arse but he's honest and reliable.'

Erica swallowed. 'Um, right, so that's it then. There's no reason why we can't go.'

Dave's eyes were sparkling as he held Erica's hand. 'I love you, Erica Woods, I really do.'

Erica couldn't speak.

Dave watched her face intently and waited. Erica still said nothing.

'Erica,' he said quietly, 'did you hear what I said?'

Erica nodded mutely.

'I meant it, Erica.'

Erica closed her eyes. She had no doubt that he did mean it, and there was no denying that she enjoyed being with him; she was happy in his company. They had, of course, 'done the deed', as Maggie had referred to it back when they'd first *discovered* Dave; in fact they'd done it several times, not in Peckham obviously, not with Maggie just outside in the living room, but in Dave's flat. Erica felt her face flush as she recalled that it'd been less than a week after Maggie had asked the question when she and Dave had fallen passionately into bed together.

'Erica, are you alright; Erica, for God's sake, say *something*, anything!'

'I, I…'

'I'm not expecting you to reply in kind, Erica. Sufficient that you know how I feel about you, and this time away in Yorkshire, well, who knows, maybe you'll come to see that you might even be able to love me back.'

Erica started to speak.

'But, even if you don't,' Dave continued, 'I'll still love you.'

'Dave, I…'

'Shit, I haven't gone and repeated the same bloody error that I made when we first met, have I?'

'Sorry?'

'When I confessed to you that I didn't own the bookshop and then blurted out something about ruining my chances with you or some such guff.'

Erica smiled. 'No, you haven't,' she said. 'But, if you remember correctly, I told you that I wasn't prepared to divulge what those chances may or may not be.'

'Ah, yes, I remember; so, am I still alright, with you I mean?'

'Yes Dave, you are,' she said, adding enticingly, 'and a week away together could be just what we need.'

Erica had no trouble getting time off work, and so their trip up to Yorkshire was to take place at the end of May.

Maggie thought she'd lost her mind. 'Bloody hell, Erica, you've only been back together for a couple of months and now you're planning to spend a whole week away, on your own, with *him*.'

'What do you mean, 'with *him*'? What do you think he is, a psychopath or something?'

'Well no, obviously not, it's just that, well, what if he has another stupid tantrum and storms off, abandoning you in some far out, isolated and desolate place?'

'It's North Yorkshire, Maggie, not the outback.'

'Fine, you've obviously made your mind up; but promise me one thing.'

'What?'

'Any trouble, ring me and I'll come and get you.'

'Oh, Maggie, that's a bit melodramatic, don't you think?'

'Actually, no I don't; I refer you to December the 25th 2012, M'Lady, the date of the mysterious disappearing act of the accused.'

'Fine,' Erica conceded. 'I'll ring you at the first sign of trouble.'

'Good.'

The day before the Yorkshire trip, Dave and Erica were enjoying lunch in the park in the sudden spring sunshine after a gloomy grey morning, and Phyllis was minding the bookshop. She'd just dealt with a phone call from an irate customer anxious to know when his books would arrive when a feisty-looking redhead entered, dressed in attire more suitable for a chilly autumn day.

'Good afternoon,' said Phyllis. 'Can I help you?'

'Good afternoon,' replied the woman. 'I don't wish to be rude, but I was expecting to see a gentleman working here, a Dave Mardle.'

'He's my grandson, dear. I'm minding the shop for him.'

The woman closed her eyes and sighed deeply. 'Oh, I see,' she said as she turned to leave.

'He'll be back in about an hour, dear; he's simply out for lunch with his girlfriend.'

'With Melissa?' she exclaimed.

'Melissa? No, no, she's called Erica. Did you know Melissa?'

'Years ago, yes; I'm afraid we rather lost touch. The last I heard she was hanging out with someone called Dave Mardle, your grandson it would appear, and that he owned a bookshop. I was rather hoping he may know where Melissa might be.'

'She's in Australia, dear.'

'She's where?'

'Australia dear.'

'When? Why?'

'The 'when' I can answer, it was in 2006,' replied Phyllis. 'But as to the 'why' I'm afraid I don't really know. She *was* in rather an emotional turmoil at the time of course.' Phyllis hesitated a moment and then went on. 'I assume you know about her parents?'

'That they were killed in those terrible bomb attacks, yes, yes, I did know. We were still in regular contact then, but she never mentioned that she was moving to Australia. I assumed she was still in the UK with Dave.'

'No, dear,' said Phyllis. 'As I said she went...'

'To Australia, yes; I don't understand.'

'You don't understand what, dear?'

'Why she never said anything to me about it.'

'I can't really answer that,' said Phyllis. 'She did tell my daughter that she was very happy; she loved everything about Australia and she was especially pleased to be reunited with an old friend, so that's the main thing, I suppose; she never came back anyway.'

The woman gave a slight frown. 'She was reunited with an old friend, you say? Do you happen to know this friend's name?'

'Yes dear; it was Penny.'

'She went to join her old friend, Penny,' the woman repeated.

'Yes dear; that's what my grandson told me. Why, do you know Penny as well?'

'In a way,' replied the woman.

The doorbell rang out wildly as Jay-Jay rushed into the shop.

'Excuse me a moment,' said Phyllis. 'Hello there, Jay-Jay, what can I do for you?'

The woman gasped as she glanced across at Jay-Jay.

Brandishing two books tied together with string high above his head as if they were a trophy, he asked, 'Hi there, Phyllis, is Dave about?'

'Not at present, no; I was just telling this young lady he's having lunch with Erica. He should be back soon though. Do you want to wait? I could make us all a coffee.'

'Tempting though that offer is,' said Jay-Jay, 'I really need to crack on.' He brought the books down from on high and clutched them to his chest. 'If I could just leave these precious books with you; they're the ones that old Mr Fraser-Brown's been waiting for.'

'Oh, that is good news. He was on the phone just now, most anxious about the whereabouts of his books.'

Jay-Jay deposited them on the counter. 'Well, here they are,' he said. 'Sorry to interrupt your conversation with this delightful lady,' he added with a dazzling smile.

'Not at all,' said the woman. 'I really should be going now too.'

'You're most welcome to wait here until Dave gets back,' said Phyllis.

'Ah, so you know the infamous Dave?' said Jay-Jay.

'Actually no, I've never met him.'

'She's an old friend of Melissa,' interjected Phyllis helpfully. 'She was hoping that Dave might have an address for her.'

'She went off to Australia,' said Jay-Jay.

'So I hear,' said the woman. 'Anyway, as I said, I really need to get going. Lovely to have met you both.'

'I must shoot off too, Phyllis. See you again,' said Jay-Jay as he rushed towards the door to hold it open for the fresh-faced redhead. 'Allow me,' he said as he gave a deep, gracious bow.

'Why thank you most kindly, dear sir,' replied the woman.

Outside the shop, Jay-Jay announced in a stage whisper, 'I'm not really in a hurry; I'm ashamed to admit that, lovely as dear Phyllis is, she can be somewhat repetitious in her conversational style, an affliction that we will all suffer, according to my mother, as we age.'

The woman gave Jay-Jay a warm smile.

A sudden breeze snatched at their clothes. He returned her smile and said, 'Um, I'm Jay-Jay by the way, and I'm sorry, I didn't catch your name.'

'Penny.'

'And do you live round here?'

'My parents do, well, near here,' she said. 'I'm visiting from Australia.'

There was a pregnant pause.

Penny watched and waited.

'From Australia you say?'

'That's right.'

There was another pause.

'So, hang on,' said Jay-jay. 'Are you saying that you're actually Penny, Melissa's friend Penny?'

110

'That's right,' she repeated with a smile.

'I'm confused,' said Jay-Jay. 'Why are you looking for Melissa in Britain? She's in Australia with a woman called Penny, well, with you it would seem.'

'Because she's not; well, not as far as I know. She certainly never came out to join me. This is the first I've heard about her leaving the UK to travel to Australia.'

'And join you.'

'Yes, but as I said, she didn't.'

'How peculiar. Dave definitely said that Melissa went out there to join you,' said Jay-Jay. 'Oh, hang on, there he is, why don't we ask him?'

Penny froze. 'Where?'

'Behind you,' he said as he waved and called out a greeting.

Penny, head bent, grabbed Jay-Jay's arm. 'Oh, God; I don't want to speak to him, not now; can we go somewhere?'

'We most certainly can.' He called out to Dave, 'I've left some books with your grandmother, sorry, can't stop, I'll catch up with you later. Hi, Erica, bye!'

Arm in arm Penny and Jay-Jay dashed off.

'Will you look at that,' said Erica. 'It looks like Jay-Jay's got himself a girlfriend. I wonder who she is.'

'Couldn't give a monkeys,' remarked Dave. 'I hope he's referring to Mr Fraser-Brown's books.'

Deep in thought, Dave pushed open the shop door.

'Dave,' exclaimed Phyllis, 'you've just missed a young lady who was looking for you. You must have seen her, she was talking to Jay-Jay just outside.'

'The redhead?' asked Erica.

'Yes, that's her; you did see her then?'

'Yes, but only fleetingly. She and Jay-Jay rushed off.'

'What did she want?' asked Erica.

Dave spotted the books that Jay-Jay had left on the counter. 'Oh, bloody brilliant, that man deserves an award,' he exclaimed. Scrabbling around in his hair he untangled his glasses and quickly checked the books over. 'I'd better get these round to Mr Fraser-Jones immediately before he has a coronary.'

'Yes,' Phyllis was saying to Erica, 'she said she was friends with Melissa years ago and had lost touch. She hoped that Dave might have an address for her.'

Dave whirled around. 'What? Did you say she was looking for Melissa?'

'Yes, dear I was just telling…'

'What was her name?'

Phyllis thought for a moment.

'Her name?' repeated Dave.

'Don't snap, dear, I'm thinking,' replied Phyllis. 'Do you know, I don't think she actually told me her name,' she paused again. 'No, sorry, I don't know.'

Dave reached for his phone and started to scroll through his menu.

'Who are you ringing?' asked Erica.

'Jay-Jay; he might know her name.'

'I thought you weren't interested.'

Dave held up his hand. 'Ah, Jay-Jay, hi; just ringing to thank you for getting those books. You're a star.'

'No problem man; it's what I do.'

'Sorry you had to rush off like that, mind you I can quite understand, given who you were with.'

'Who I was with?'

'Oh, come off it, Jay-Jay; the woman that Erica and I saw you with, outside the shop.'

'Oh, right, the redhead?'

'Yes, Jay-Jay, the redhead. Gran says that she was asking after Melissa.'

'She was, yeah, but your grandmother told her that she'd gone off to Australia and so that was that really.'

'So what were you two talking about?'

'Not a lot; why?'

'I just wondered, did you happen to get her name?'

'Her name…?'

Penny shook her head with such vigour that several strands of hair fell across her face.

Jay-Jay cleared his throat. 'No, wish I had though, she was hot; no, she just wanted directions to Harrods.'

'Right; I see.'

'Anyway must dash; bye.'

Jay-Jay thrust his phone away and Penny Fisher smiled at him gratefully.

Chapter 8

Dave and Erica set off from Moor-House, a small, family-run hotel in Nether Sitton, immediately after breakfast. 'The cottage isn't far,' said Dave, 'well, not if you're a crow. Unfortunately we'll have to stick to the roads and head off down the A19 for a bit before we hit the A170 across to the Moors.'

'So, how long will it take to get there?'

'Not long; about half an hour I reckon.'

As they drove towards the cottage, Dave babbled on about the redecorating that he'd done after Melissa's departure while Erica stared out of the window at the passing scenery.

'I stayed up at the cottage on my own,' he was saying. 'It must have been for, oh, I don't know, about a month I suppose. I installed a couple of ramps, one up to the front door and one up to the back door, I expect they're gone now, and a massive set of French windows that led from the living room onto the terrace so that Mum could wheel herself outside whenever she wanted to. My piece-de-la-résistance was a fishpond with a fountain, well a *pond* with a fountain: there were never any fish in it. Even Dad was impressed with my skill, and as you know, he's the pond expert.'

Erica muttered, 'Uh huh.'

'Are you listening?'

Erica tore her gaze away from the window. 'Sorry; carry on.'

'I positioned it, and when I say 'it' I mean the pond,' said Dave, 'just in case you weren't paying attention.'

'Ha, ha.'

'I positioned it below the terrace, down a gentle slope under a willow tree. Mum used to sit under that tree in the shade for hours; she said she found it very relaxing and...'

'It sounds beautiful,' said Erica. 'It must have been hard work. My dad dug a pond once, oh, it was years ago, when I was little, and he said never again. He reckons his back has never been right since.'

Dave laughed. 'I know exactly what he means, but I did have help.'

'Your dad?'

Dave sighed. 'I *knew* you weren't listening; I told you, I was on my own,' he said. 'The help was from a small JCB, marvellous machine it was, saved me hours of back breaking work.' He fell silent for a moment and then added, 'I just hope the new owners haven't drained it and filled it in. Still, they wouldn't do that, would they?'

Erica shrugged her shoulders; the question was impossible for her to answer, she hadn't even *seen* the pond; for all she knew it could be a ghastly monstrosity. 'Well, if it's as fantastic as you say then it seems unlikely.'

'Yes, that's what I was thinking; so, nothing to worry about.'

'Worry? Why would you worry? I mean, it's not as if it's anyone's business really; it's up to them.'

'Perhaps worry is the wrong word; it's just that, oh, never mind, we're nearly there now and then I'll know; worrying about it, I mean, thinking about it isn't going to change the situation I suppose.' He gripped the steering wheel and stared straight ahead.

As Dave and Erica made their way across the moors towards Black Sheep Cottage, Jason and Nicole Morgan, the new owners, were relaxing in the back garden discussing their plans. Jason was all for ripping out the horrific mock electric fire that was designed to look like an old fashioned wood burner. 'I mean, it's bloody ludicrous, Nicole. There's probably a perfectly decent, authentic, inglenook fireplace behind all that modern crap.'

'I quite like it; it *is* convenient and anyway, what if there's just a massive hole behind it? It'd be pretty stupid to rip out a perfectly decent...'

'Hah!'

'Alright, let me put it another way. It'd be pretty stupid to rip out a perfectly functional, efficient fire, only to find nothing of any use or beauty behind it.'

'But when we moved in I'm sure Mr Mardle said something about blocking in the old fireplace for his wife's benefit; don't you remember?'

'Vaguely, but...'

'Look, how about if I drill a little exploratory hole, you know, so that I can have a peek? If it looks unpromising I can make good and then grit my teeth and continue to put up with the current arrangement; after all, I've put up with it for over a year now.'

'Do you really hate it?'

'More than I can say,' said Jason. 'And you have to admit, an inglenook would be more in keeping with the character of the cottage.'

Nicole sighed. 'Fair enough.'

Jason cupped his wife's head in his hands and kissed her forehead. 'I knew you'd understand.'

Nicole smiled and reached for the lemonade jug. 'Oh, it's empty.'

Jason shot out of his chair. 'I'll make up some more; you just relax.'

He was about to replenish the lemonade when there was a knock at the door.

Placing the jug on the kitchen counter with a sigh, he strode to the front door. 'Hello there, can I help you? Are you lost?'

'Hello there; you must be Jason, Jason Morgan?' said Dave.

'I am, yes; and you are?'

116

'Oh, sorry, of course, yes. My name is Dave Mardle, and this is my friend, Erica Woods.'

'Dave Mardle? I don't believe it,' said Jason as he stared at Dave's face. 'Are you by chance related to the Dave Mardle who negotiated the sale of this place?'

'I am indeed; I'm his son,' explained Dave. 'I hope you don't mind, it's just that we were in the area and I was telling Erica about this cottage that we used to own and, well, she was keen to see it.'

Jason turned and called to his wife. 'You'll never guess, not in a million years, who's standing at the front door.'

'Well at least give me a clue,' she called back.

'The plan we were discussing.'

'The plan we were discussing?' she said.

'Yes, the plan, Nicole; it's Mr Mardle!'

Dashing inside, she stopped mid stride, looked at Dave and Erica, and frowned.

'Obviously this isn't *the* Mr Mardle; it's his son, Dave, accompanied by his good friend, Erica.'

'Well, don't leave them standing on the doorstep, Jason, invite them in.'

'Right, yes, sorry, silly of me,' said Jason. 'Do come in; we were just enjoying the beautiful weather outside on the terrace.'

'Would you both like a drink?' asked Nicole. 'We're drinking homemade lemonade, but if you prefer…'

'A glass of lemonade sounds lovely,' said Erica.

'Yes, absolutely,' agreed Dave, his eyes straining to see past Nicole into the garden. 'Sounds lovely.'

As they stepped through the French windows onto the terrace, Dave's eyes sought out the pond.

'Is that the pond,' asked Erica, 'the one you constructed all on your own?'

'Spot on.'

'*You* constructed the pond?' asked Nicole. 'Surely not; Jason and I assumed it had been a professional job.'

Placing the refilled lemonade jug on the table, Jason exclaimed, 'Nicole.'

'No, sorry, that didn't come out right; I wasn't meaning to imply that you couldn't do a professional job, what I meant was...' she threw a panicked look towards her husband.

'My wife is trying to say that we love it,' said Jason. 'When did you build it?'

Dave hesitated momentarily. 'It must have been, um, about seven or eight years ago, I suppose.'

'Well you did a bloody good job; as you can see, looking at it now, it looks like it could have been there for decades.'

Erica asked, 'Can I go and have a closer look?'

'Of course,' said Jason. 'In fact, why don't we all go down there and admire the handiwork.'

The pond extended half way across the garden from the willow tree that stood near the perimeter on the right of the property. As they got closer Dave began to frown.

'Is everything alright?' Jason asked.

'Yes, um, well, I'm not sure; it looks different somehow, smaller.' Dave strode on ahead and began to pace out from the willow tree, counting each stride.

'*Smaller?* Well I can assure you that we haven't done anything to it,' said Jason.

'And don't forget,' added Erica, 'everything will have grown and matured since then and that might make the pond itself look smaller.'

'Yes, you're probably right; as far as I can remember it was about eight strides long and five wide and that's what it seems to be now.'

'Well, there you are then.'

Dave gave everyone a beatific smile. 'I must say the water plants have done rather well.'

'And the willow tree,' said Erica. 'It looks very happy, if trees can look happy that is.'

'Oh, yes, I absolutely think that they can,' said Nicole. 'And that is one very happy tree.'

Erica asked, 'I wonder; can I be nosey?'

With a huge smirk on his face, Jason said, 'It depends; there are some things that I feel should remain between...'

Nicole gave him a swipe. 'Ignore him, Erica; nose away.'

'It's just that your husband...'

'Jason,' said Jason.

'Yes, Jason said something about a plan and I wondered...'

'And you wondered what he was blathering about,' said Nicole. 'Nothing sinister...'

Dave gave a nervous laugh. 'No, of course not; I mean, why would it be sinister?'

'Well, quite,' she said, 'No, it was simply that Jason and I were discussing the possibility of ripping out the...'

'The pond? No! I thought you loved it,' Dave cried.

'Steady on, old chap,' said Jason. 'Nicole wasn't talking about the pond...'

'No,' continued Nicole, 'although we did consider it; I'm pregnant you see and...'

Erica's eyes were drawn to Nicole's abdomen. 'Oh, congratulations; when's it due?'

'The 'it' is a she, and she's due late August, early September.' Nicole beamed as she stroked her abdomen.

'Your first?'

She nodded.

'You must be so excited.'

'Almost as excited as Nicole's mother,' said Jason.

'Don't be mean, darling.'

'Oh, I can imagine,' said Erica. 'God knows what my mother will be like if and when I get pregnant.' She glanced at Dave. 'Its lovely news isn't it?'

Dave tore his eyes away from the pond. 'What?'

'The fact that Nicole's pregnant.'

'Oh, right, yes; lovely,' muttered Dave. 'Congratulations.'

'No, as I was saying,' Nicole went on. 'We were thinking of ripping out the modern fireplace in the hope that hidden behind would be an original inglenook thingy. But we didn't want to go to all that fuss and expense only to find a boring old Victorian monstrosity there.'

'Or just a bloody big hole,' added Jason with a smile directed towards Nicole.

'The fireplace you say, right yes, great; good idea,' said Dave. 'And you're in luck; there is an inglenook fireplace behind there. Dad was reluctant to block it in it but it was a matter of convenience. The modern replacement was easier to maintain; simple as that.'

'Absolutely,' agreed Nicole. 'Again, I wasn't meaning to be disparaging about the workmanship...'

Avoiding eye contact with his wife, Jason added, 'And it's not that we don't like it or anything, it's just that we've always rather fancied a proper old fireplace.'

'Yes, we do like a bit of retro,' said Nicole. 'We've installed an Aga in the kitchen; it's brilliant.'

'Oh, I love those,' said Erica.

'Come on, you two, I'll give you a tour of the place,' said Jason

In Peckham, shortly after waving Dave and Erica off on their Yorkshire trip, Maggie received a phone call.

'Is everything alright, Winton?' she asked. 'You sound a bit discombobulated.'

'I've just spoken with Jay-Jay.'

'And?'

'Well, the thing is, I'm not sure really, it all seems a bit strange.'

'Winton, you're not making much sense, is there something wrong with Jay-Jay?'

'No, no, he's fine. No, it's just that he met a woman yesterday, in Dave's bookshop...'

'Good for him,' exclaimed Maggie. 'So, what's the problem; is this woman some sort of cougar?'

'No, Maggie, it's a bit more complicated than that,' he said. 'Look, would it be alright if I invite myself, Jay-Jay, and this woman round to the flat? I'll bring a takeout or something; I don't want to put you to any trouble, it's just that you really need to meet her, Maggie; it's important.'

'When?'

'Would tonight be alright?'

'Tonight; it must be really important.'

'It is, Maggie; it is.'

Pointing her fork towards Penny, Maggie said, 'So, basically you're saying that Dave lied; Melissa did not join you in Australia back in 2006.'

'That's what I'm saying, yes,' said Penny. 'Of course that's not to say that Melissa didn't go to Australia at *some* point, but certainly not in 2006.'

'How can you be so sure?' asked Maggie.

'Well, she can't have been in Australia in 2006 because I received emails from her right up to early 2009; when she was living in London with Dave and...'

'You what; living with Dave; where exactly?' exclaimed Maggie, dropping her fork with a clatter.

'In a flat, not far from his parents,' replied Penny.

The look on Maggie's face prompted her to add, 'Well, that's what she told me.'

'Do you happen to know the address of this flat where they lived together?'

'Yes, it was in Auriol Road.'

Maggie frowned. 'But that's not possible.'

'Why?' asked Penny.

'Because that flat has only ever been occupied by one person and that person is Dave Mardle,' said Maggie. 'Hang on, I'll show you.' She dragged her laptop out from under the table, called up the link and turned the screen towards

Penny. 'There, you see, under occupants: one name and one name only; Dave Mardle.'

'Yes, so I see. I don't understand; that's definitely the address she gave me.' She retrieved her old Blackberry from her bag. 'These are my contact details for Melissa, and look, here's the address, Auriol Road.'

Jay-Jay glanced at Penny, his fully loaded spoon hovering midway between plate and mouth. 'Well, that's bloody weird,' he said before shovelling the spoonful into his mouth.

'OK,' said Maggie, 'let's start at the beginning. You said that you lost touch with Melissa and that's why you were looking for Dave, is that right?'

Penny nodded.

'So, presumably up to the point that contact was lost, you and she were in regular communication.'

'We were, yes; she and I would exchange emails about once a week at first, and then, I suppose, about once every few months.'

'And she was happy?'

'Yes, she was fine, well, until her parents were killed in those awful bombs, of course. That's when she moved in with Dave and his parents, but, well, I don't know now; did she?'

Maggie nodded. 'Oh, yes, that bit's true.'

'Well that's something, I suppose,' said Penny.

Jay-Jay reached across and gave her arm a gentle stroke.

'And how did Melissa say everything was after moving in with Dave and his family?' asked Maggie.

'She coped really well. She said that Dave's parents were wonderful, especially Dave's mum, the way she coped with her MS and everything.' Penny shook her head as Jay-Jay offered more rice. 'But she did mention that Dave behaved like a spoilt child whenever she chose to stay in with his mother rather than go out with him to some pub or dance or wherever it was that *he* wanted to go.'

'Sounds familiar,' said Maggie.

'Then, of course, the rows started; incidentally, that's how I recognised Jay-Jay's name: Melissa told me that he'd overheard them arguing on several occasions.' She smiled at Jay-Jay. 'She said Jay-Jay was a very kind man who'd tried to help her but Dave, who watched her like a hawk, was having none of it and was quite rude, telling him to butt out and mind his own business; although I think his language was a little more profane.'

'Yes, so Jay-Jay was saying,' said Winton.

'The most worrying thing is that during some of these heated arguments he hit her…'

Maggie clutched at her chest. 'Shit!'

'Melissa rang me after one particular incident. She told me that her arms were covered in bruises, and I told her to just get out.'

'Absabloodylutely,' said Maggie.

'The thing is, he was always mortified afterwards, begging forgiveness, telling her that he loved her and all that guff.'

'But they *always* say that,' exclaimed Maggie.

'I know, and frankly I was amazed that Melissa stayed with him, but she kept giving him second chances. And then, when she told me that they were going to some remote cottage in Yorkshire, well, I thought she was bloody mad and I told her so. She told me not to worry; she knew what she was doing.

'I heard nothing for a while; it must have been a month or so, I think, and then she sent an email saying that everything was wonderful. Dave had apparently turned some sort of corner, been to see a therapist or councillor or some such, and it was not long after that she informed me that they were moving into that flat in the Auriol Road.'

'The one she never actually lived in you mean?'

'Well, yes, so it would seem; the thing is it was about a year after they moved in together…'

'Or, didn't,' Maggie said.

'Well quite; anyway, wherever it was that she was living, it was about a year later that the emails stopped,' continued Penny. 'Up to that point they'd been upbeat and positive and so I couldn't understand why they'd suddenly dried up. At first I thought fine, no news is good news but then, as the days turned to weeks and the weeks turned to months, I began to worry. I emailed, I sent texts, I even resorted to snail mail and, eventually, she sent me an email; hang on, I'll find it.' Penny pushed her plate away and began scrolling through her emails.

'As a matter of interest,' said Maggie as she, too, pushed her plate away, 'what address did you write to?'

'To the one that she told me she was living at.'

'The flat in Auriol Road?'

'Yes,' said Penny. 'But she wasn't living there, was she?'

'No,' said Maggie.

'So she would never have got the letters.'

'No,' said Maggie. 'But Dave would.'

Penny looked up from her Blackberry. 'Well, he certainly never wrote to me.'

'But he may well have sent you emails,' said Jay-Jay.

'No, no emails either.'

'I don't mean from him,' he said.

'You're thinking what I'm thinking, aren't you?' said Maggie. 'Oh, shit, shit, shit.'

'What?' Penny asked.

'Melissa didn't send you those later emails...' began Maggie.

'Dave did,' said Jay-Jay.

'But why?'

'Well, that's the question,' said Maggie.

'Here it is,' said Penny handing her Blackberry to Maggie. 'She, or whoever it was, sent it on the 24th July 2009.'

Maggie held the Blackberry in both hands as if it were a precious object. She took a deep breath and scanned the email. By the end of the second sentence she stopped and looked up. 'This is unbelievable,' she said. 'Listen to this.'

Oh, Penny I'm so sorry that I haven't been in touch but well, oh, this is so difficult. Dave and I are parents, Penny; isn't it marvellous? I can see you now; thinking that I've lost the plot, wondering why such happy news should be difficult. It's just that the twins came too early. Penny, they're so tiny. They're all I can think about. I know you'll understand. I'm sorry, I can't talk about it any more; it's all so unfair. When they're out of the woods, and please God let that be soon, I'll get back in touch.

Jay-Jay's mouth dropped open, but no sound came out. In fact no one spoke. The noise of the ticking clock filled the room.

'There are no children, are there?' said Penny in a small, quiet voice.

'No, Penny, there are no children,' said Maggie.

'I think I might have noticed,' said Jay-Jay. 'As I said, the last time I saw Melissa it was 2006 and I can assure you that there wasn't an infant to be seen; not then and certainly not in 2009 for goodness sake.'

Maggie ran her hands through her hair. 'This is seriously weird. I mean, think about it; Penny is receiving emails from Melissa saying that all is well in London and that she and Dave are now parents whereas, at the same time, Dave and his mother are receiving emails saying that all is well and life in *Australia*, with *Penny*, is great.' She leaned back against the settee and took a generous gulp of wine. 'Right, what we need to establish first is, did she or did she not go to Australia, and, if she did, when did she go.'

'And how would we do that?' asked Winton.

'I was thinking; there are records aren't there, passenger lists and the like. It would be easy if we were dealing with

125

someone who travelled over there in the nineteenth or twentieth century, we could just check the national archive records, but I'm not sure how to go about it for people travelling across in the twenty-first century; any ideas, anyone?'

Everyone exchanged blank looks.

'Oh, hang on,' said Jay-Jay suddenly. '*I* don't know, but I think I know a man who might.'

'Who?' demanded Maggie.

'Philip White; he knows some pretty important people; I bet he'll be able to get hold of that information.'

'Brilliant, Jay-Jay; we can't afford to hang about. Dave and Erica are only away for a week.'

Jay-Jay gave a short, smart salute. 'Message received and understood.'

'You're not too big for a smacked bottom, you know,' said Maggie.

'Promises, promises.'

Maggie's eyebrows shot upwards. She turned to Penny and grinned. 'I warn you,' she said, 'he's worse than a child.'

Penny smiled. 'But a very kind child.'

'True. Um, do you mind me asking how long are you in England for?'

Penny's face clouded over. 'I'm not sure really; it all depends on how my father fares.'

'Oh, I'm sorry,' said Maggie. 'I didn't realise; I wouldn't have asked, sorry.'

'No need to apologise. You couldn't be expected to know that my father had been taken ill,' she said, adding with a smile, 'unless your skills as an investigator are even more impressive than Jay-Jay has led me to believe.'

'Well, my investigative skills are pretty awesome,' said Maggie. 'I did find Dave, remember.'

'That you did,' said Winton. 'But perhaps it would have been better all round if your skills hadn't been quite so good.'

Maggie exclaimed, 'Oh, Winton, shit, you're right; this is all my fault. If I hadn't stuck my nose in, Erica would never have bothered looking for Dave in the first place, and then…'

'Hey, hey, remember; when water trow weh i' cyaa pick up.'

'Pardon?' exclaimed Penny.

Maggie smiled. 'It means, you can't turn back time. What's done is done. That's right isn't it, Winton?'

'Absolutely, woman, absolutely,' replied Winton in his beautiful Jamaican lilt.

It didn't take long for Philip's contact to establish that Melissa *did not* travel to Australia in 2006. His contact also checked the records for the years after 2006; again there was no record of a Melissa Davies. So, why did Dave lie and, more importantly, where *was* Melissa?

Chapter 9

Following the visit to Black Sheep Cottage, Dave's demeanour improved. They visited the local sites together, and in the evenings, over a bottle or two of wine, they shared their hopes and dreams.

'I'm not expecting fame and fortune,' said Erica on one occasion. 'I just want to write a story that *somebody* will print.'

'Gran always says that good things come to those who wait; I mean, look at me,' said Dave. 'I'd almost given up hope of ever finding anyone after, after, well you know; and then serendipity brought you into my sad and lonely life.'

Erica beamed. 'Actually, I think you'll find it was Maggie rather than serendipity who was responsible for our meeting.'

'Ah, yes; the indomitable Maggie Hunter-Lopez,' said Dave. 'She doesn't like me much, does she?'

'Nonsense, of course…'

'Erica Woods, don't you start with the fibs,' said Dave. 'After all, you of all people should know what trouble they can get a person into.'

'Well, OK, perhaps that was the case at the beginning; but not now, not now that you've um…'

'Come clean about the old girlfriend's name being Melissa and opening up about Mum's MS?'

Erica nodded.

Dave's face clouded over. He bent his head and examined his shoes.

Erica's eye's widened. 'What now?'

'Well, um, it's just; oh, hell.'

'Jesus, Dave, what? You're frightening me.'

He looked up slowly, gave her a weak smile, and said softly, 'It's nothing really, except, given that honesty is the best policy and all that, I feel I ought to point out an important fact; you do bear a striking similarity to Melissa,' he said, continuing with fervour, 'Just in looks, I hasten to add; in all other ways you are completely, and I mean *completely* different.'

'Different good or different bad?'

Dave grabbed hold of Erica's hand. 'Oh, Erica, different good; and please, please believe me that it's not just your looks that I've fallen in love with, although they are quite delicious; no, I love your nature, your spirit, the indefinable essence that is you, and I shall be eternally grateful to Maggie for bringing us together, no matter what she thinks of me.'

Erica swallowed hard. 'Maggie's a good friend, Dave, and she just wants me to be happy.'

'And are you?'

She squeezed his hand. 'Oh, Dave, yes, I'm very happy, and it's amazing really...'

'What, that you're happy?'

'No, silly; I was thinking about what you said, you know, about serendipity bringing us together, because I suppose it did in a way. I mean, it was just a stroke of luck that I became an amateur detective and started looking for you in the first place. Maggie's research had ground to a halt, you see; she was fed up and needed a diversion.'

'Research?'

'Yes, she's researching unknown women in the history of medicine, particularly women from Jamaica as it happens.'

Dave raised his hand. 'Um, excuse me, Miss,' he said, 'but if the women are unknown how can they be researched?'

'Surely I don't need to remind you how adept Maggie is at discovering hidden facts.'

'Ah, yes.' He looked around furtively. 'I'd better be more careful in future then.'

'You're an idiot; you do know that, don't you?' she said, thumping his arm.

He shrugged. 'Guilty as charged.'

At the end of their week in Yorkshire, Dave announced that rather than returning to Peckham, Erica should move in with him. He maintained that they'd got on so well it seemed madness for them to maintain a flat each. He told her again that he was in love, and that she was too, but hadn't realised it yet.

He'd been so earnest and intense that it had frightened Erica.

When she turned the offer down, she'd waited with baited breath to see how he reacted, and had been surprised when he accepted her decision graciously.

Maggie was pacing back and forth, constantly checking the time and so, when Erica returned, happy and exhausted, Maggie rushed forward and threw her arms around her.

'I can't tell you how pleased I am to see you, safe and sound; I've been so worried and the thing is I just don't know what to do or say for the best; I mean, as far as I'm concerned, you need to know but, I suppose I have to accept that I might be reading too much into it and there may be a perfectly good explanation for everything; although, if I'm honest, I fail to see what such an explanation could be, still, as I say…'

'Maggie; what *are* you burbling on about?'

Maggie took in a deep breath and then slowly released it. 'Right, sorry. I suppose I should at least let you take your coat off.' She reached for Erica's bag. 'Let me take this; you sit down. Do you want a coffee? Or wine? Personally I think wine would be the best choice but it's up to you. The bottle's open and ready in the fridge so…'

Erica held up her hands. 'A nice cool wine would be lovely; thanks.'

Erica settled down on the settee with her legs tucked beneath her. 'Right then, I await an explanation. And, by the way, I had a fantastic time; thanks for asking.'

'Good, right, yes, sorry,' said Maggie. She studied her glass of wine for a moment. 'The day before you left for Yorkshire, do you remember seeing Jay-Jay with a woman?'

'Oh, yes,' exclaimed Erica. 'Why, have you met her? Who is she? Was I right, is she his girlfriend, oh, that's fantastic, how exciting.'

'I have met her, Erica, and the thing is…'

'She isn't very nice?'

'Actually she seemed very nice; no, the thing is her name's Penny…'

'Uh huh'

'You know, Penny; as in Melissa's friend, Penny.'

Erica put down her wine glass. 'I see. And um, so, what are you saying? Has Melissa come back too? Shit, Maggie, has she come back to make it up with Dave?' Erica's eyes began to fill with tears.

'Oh, Erica, no, that's not the problem.' She picked up Erica's glass. 'Here, have another drink.'

'What? Why?'

Maggie took another deep breath. 'Penny came over to England in the first place because her father is seriously ill and…'

'So, Melissa didn't come? Um, so, well; sorry, I'm confused.'

'If you'd just let me finish.'

Erica downed her wine and poured herself more. 'Carry on; you have my undivided attention.'

'While she was here, Penny decided to look for Melissa.'

'Pardon?'

'Look, I'm really sorry but there's no easy way to say this,' Maggie took a gulp of wine and held her glass out.

Erica refilled it. 'Go on.'

'The thing is, Penny was under the impression that Dave and Melissa were living together, in London. Melissa never went to Australia, Erica.'

'Don't be ridiculous, Dave's explained…'

'I know what Dave explained, Erica, but the fact of the matter is Penny is seriously contemplating contacting the police to report Melissa as a missing person, which, frankly, she is. I mean we know where she *isn't*; she isn't in Australia and she certainly isn't living with Dave, never has done; what we *don't* know is where she is at this precise moment. Essentially the last known sighting of her was when she left with Dave back in 2006 to stay at that cottage in Yorkshire.'

Erica kept her eyes down and said nothing.

'Erica?'

Looking up, tears flowing, Erica said, 'Oh, Maggie, what the bloody hell is going on here?'

'I honestly don't know, Erica. But ever since finding out about these complex machinations that Dave seems to have weaved around this Melissa woman, I've been feeling more and more uneasy. Perhaps he's a Walter Mitty type, you know, a compulsive liar who actually believes his own lies.'

'So, *where is* Melissa, Maggie; where *is* she?'

'I don't know, Erica; we don't even know if she *did* go to that cottage in Yorkshire. After all we only have Dave's word, and, um…'

'And you're saying that his word doesn't stand up to much scrutiny.'

'Well, yes, that's what it looks like to me,' said Maggie.

Erica sat quietly, sipping her wine.

'Are you alright?'

'Yes, Maggie; I'm fine. I know you think I'm stupid and I know you don't like Dave, you never have done, not really.'

'That's not…'

'Yeah, right! Anyway, I know he's told lies and everything but there's always been a good reason, in his

132

mind anyway, for the lies, and he's always sorry and contrite…'

'Only when he's found out.'

'You don't know that, Maggie. He might have been waiting for the right time to open up to me about everything. We got on so well in Yorkshire. We had fun and we were happy; he even asked me to move in with him.'

'Jesus; you didn't say yes did you?'

'I didn't, Maggie, no; and not because I don't trust him, but because, well it's a big step. He loves me, Maggie. I'm not an idiot you know…'

'I never said…'

'You've implied it, though. Look, I realise you've got my best interests at heart, but for God's sake, Maggie, you're not my mother!'

'Perish the thought,' said Maggie. 'I'm just suggesting that you need to exercise a modicum of caution.'

'There'll be a perfectly logical reason for all this confusion,' said Erica, adding, after a pause, 'Probably.'

With uncanny timing, Erica's phone rang. Holding the device as if it was about to explode, Erica groaned, 'It's him; I'm not ready, what the hell do I say?'

'Play it by ear, *but* if he suggests a meeting or whatever I'm coming too; got it?'

Erica nodded. She put the phone on speaker and took a deep breath. 'Well, hi there Dave; everything alright?'

'Couldn't be better; how about you?'

'A bit worn out actually; Maggie and I are just having a drink and then we're going to bed.'

'Me too; I just wanted to check that you're still on for our usual lunch in the park tomorrow?'

Maggie nodded and pointed repeatedly at herself.

'Maggie's going to join us, OK?'

A deafening silence echoed down the line.

'Dave; did you hear me? I said…'

'I heard you,' said Dave.

'So, that's alright, is it?'

'I suppose so.'

'Excellent; see you tomorrow.'

Maggie was looking forward to seeing the expression on Dave's face when she revealed the identity of Jay-Jay's mystery woman to him. Erica wasn't.

At the park, Dave dashed up to Erica and gave her a lingering kiss.

'Dave! Maggie's here too, you know.'

Without a glance in Maggie's direction, he said. 'It was wonderful being with you in Yorkshire. I wish we were still there. Let's go away again soon.'

'Lovely to be joining you,' said Maggie brightly. 'It's ridiculous, but I never even knew this place existed, and when I told Winton this morning that we were all meeting here, in the Marcus Garvey Park, he told me that this Marcus Garvey chap was a civil rights leader back in the day, and that Rastafarians consider him to be a religious prophet. He lived at 53 Talgarth Road; there's a plaque there apparently.'

Dave faked a yawn. 'Gosh, how fascinating.'

Erica thumped his arm. 'Did you know all that stuff then?'

'Of course I knew; common knowledge, isn't it?'

'Right; anyway, do you want chicken or beef?' asked Erica.

'Beef please; thanks.'

Erica rummaged in the paper bag and gave Dave his sandwich; Maggie handed him his flat white. 'Oh, the weirdest thing, I was telling Erica last night; you'll never guess who that woman was with Jay-Jay.'

Dave stopped chewing. 'Woman?'

'Yes, don't you remember? I thought she might be Jay-Jay's new girlfriend,' said Erica. 'The redhead, she'd been in the shop asking after Melissa.'

'Vaguely,' said Dave. He gave Maggie an intense stare. 'So, Miss expert detective, who the bloody hell was she then?'

'Her name is Penny, Penny Fisher.' Maggie took a slurp of coffee to hide the smirk that she could feel creeping onto her face.

Dave cleared his throat, took a sip of coffee and cleared his throat again.

'Something stuck in your throat?' asked Maggie.

His eyes darkened. 'Penny, you say; interesting.'

Maggie pressed on. 'Yes, I thought so too, and the thing is, and this is *really* weird, it seems that your Melissa never went to Australia at all; that's why Penny was asking after her. She'd lost touch, you see, about three or four years ago I think she said. Strange, don't you think?'

Dave didn't speak.

Erica said quietly, 'That is odd, isn't it? I mean you sent her stuff out to Australia, didn't you?'

Dave nodded. 'I did, yes.' He gave Maggie another hard stare. 'I sent them there because that's what Melissa bloody asked me to do. She told me that she was going to Australia for God's sake, and I believed her! What a bitch!'

Erica flinched.

'Sorry, love, but well, I genuinely thought she'd gone to Australia.'

Oh, he's good, thought Maggie. *Very good.*

'Strange, because that isn't what she told Penny, you see,' said Maggie.

'Well, if she had no intention of going to Australia, as you say, then she's hardly going to fucking tell Penny that she is, is she now?'

Erica glanced at Maggie. 'That's a good point.'

'Of course it's a good bloody point! She obviously lied to me.'

'And to your mother, too, it would seem.'

'Well, that's the thing about liars, Maggie; they need to be consistent, don't they?'

'Quite,' agreed Maggie.

'So, where did Penny think that Melissa was then?'

'Living with you, in your flat,' said Erica. 'With the twins.'

'With the what?'

'The twins.'

'What bloody twins?'

'The twins that Melissa gave birth to,' said Maggie.

Emphasising each word, Dave said, 'Melissa did not give birth to any baby, let alone twins.'

'We know,' said Erica.

'We just wondered,' said Maggie, 'why Melissa would have told her best friend that she had.'

'Haven't a bloody clue.'

'I wonder where she is then?' asked Maggie.

'How would I fucking know!' shouted Dave.

'Steady on, Dave,' said Maggie. 'It is intriguing though; I could probably locate her, you know, using my investigative skills.'

'Do what you like,' said Dave. 'I'm not in the slightest bit interested; not anymore. I have Erica now.'

Oh, pass the sick bowl, thought Maggie.

'So, you wouldn't mind then?'

'Knock yourself out,' said Dave. 'Now, if you don't mind, can we...?' His phone rang. 'Now what?' he exclaimed as he hit the answer button. 'What is it, Dad?' Then he yelled, 'What! What did you say?'

Erica and Maggie looked on as the colour drained from his face. His hand started to tremble. Erica reached out to him; he pushed her away.

'OK, right, yes.'—'No; of course not.'—'It's ridiculous, yes, I agree.'—'Don't worry, I'll sort it out; talk to you later.'

Dave slipped the phone into his top jacket pocket and looked behind him, towards the park entrance.

'Is everything alright?' asked Erica.

'I don't know; shall we ask Maggie?'

'Me? Why me?'

'Oh, I don't know,' said Dave. 'It seems that my father has just had a visit from the police and they're on their way here, to speak to me; now why do you think that might be?'

'*I* don't know,' said Maggie.

'Oh, is that right? You don't know?'

'Unless, um…'

'Unless what, Maggie? Been chatting to some colleagues in the police force, have we?'

'Don't be ridiculous; I haven't got any colleagues in the police force.'

'What, an ace detective such as yourself. I find that *so* hard to believe.'

'Leave her alone. She hasn't been to the police. I expect it was…'

Maggie shook her head. 'Erica, don't…'

'You expect it was who?' said Dave. 'Oh, Jesus, don't tell me; it was fucking Penny, wasn't it. So, what; is she bloody living with the pair of you now or something? Is that it? Three witches together.'

The church clock struck one. Erica felt her eyes burn. She turned her face away from Dave, and through the blur of tears she saw a mass of pigeons scatter noisily as Inspector Joe Reed strode down the path towards them.

It had been 8.45 that morning when Joe wandered into the reception area to greet Jay-Jay and Penny. 'Hello there; I'm Inspector Joe Reed. The desk sergeant tells me that Erica Woods suggested that you should speak with me. Is there a problem?'

'Well, to be honest, I'm not really sure.'

'I am quite busy, you know.'

'Yes; yes, of course; um, sorry, my name is Jay-Jay Dacosta.' He turned to Penny. 'And this is Penny Fisher.'

Penny inclined her head.

'And she's looking for a friend of hers who she *thought* was living in London; she'd received emails from her and everything. The thing is, when she made a few enquiries, the people here were under the impression that the friend had gone to Australia, to join Penny; they'd had emails from her too, you see.'

'So, you're telling me that we have two sets of conflicting emails, supposedly sent by your friend, whose name is?'

'Melissa Davies,' said Penny.

'Those sent to you implying that she was living in London and those sent here to…?'

'To Dave, Dave Mardle and his parents, well, his mother mostly, I think,' said Jay-Jay.

'Implying that she was living in Australia with Miss Fisher; correct?'

Penny and Jay-Jay nodded.

'A missing person report then; right, shall we go through to an interview room.'

Penny perched on a mottled grey plastic chair and gazed at the murky rectangular window and the drab walls; she gave a small shudder. Jay-Jay pulled up another chair, plonked himself down beside her and gave her a reassuring smile. 'Alright?'

Penny nodded.

'Not one of our most inspiring rooms, I know,' remarked Joe. 'It is what it is; now, can I get either of you a drink?'

They both declined the offer, and Melissa launched straight into her story, with Jay-Jay chipping in at various points. When she'd finished her eyes filled with tears. She gave Joe an expectant look.

'So, first things first, Miss Fisher; could Melissa Davies have travelled to Australia without your knowledge?'

'Well, I suppose so, yes,' Penny sniffed, 'but it seems unlikely and anyway, Jay-Jay checked.'

'You checked, Mr Dacosta?'

'Not personally; a friend did,' he replied as he gently stroked Penny's arm.

'And has this friend got a name?'

'Peter White; he's got a mate who works for Lloyds,' said Jay-Jay. 'The thing is, we're not only concerned about where Melissa is, we're also worried about Erica.'

'Because?'

'She's Dave's current girlfriend.'

'I see,' said Joe. 'And, just to be clear here, when you say, Erica, I assume you're talking about Erica Woods, the young lady who works in the Lord of the Fries café; the young lady who recommended that you should speak with me?'

'Yes, sir.'

'And how long has this been the case?'

'Um, since the summer of last year; they broke up sometime after Christmas, but they're back together now.'

'So, why exactly are you worried?'

'Well, first off, I reckon he's a bully, and now it seems he's a bloody liar too. I mean, he's told Erica all the same guff; he's even told her that he organised the shipment of Melissa's possessions out to Australia, for God's sake,' said Jay-Jay.

Joe glanced down at his notes. 'Mr Dacosta, you say that the only thing you know for certain is that Melissa moved in with Dave and his family after her parents were killed in the 2005 London bombs.'

'That's right.'

'And how is it that you know that?'

'Because Phyllis, Dave's grandmother, confirmed it with Maggie.'

'And Maggie is?'

'Maggie Hunter-Lopez. She's Erica's friend and flatmate,' said Jay-Jay.

'Right, I see. So, Miss Fisher, you say that when you became concerned about your friend, you wrote to her at the Auriol Road address and she responded via email.'

Penny nodded. 'That's when she told me she'd had premature twins and she and Dave were struggling to care for them.'

'But *she* wasn't living there, *Dave* was,' said Jay-Jay. 'So, *he* must have read the letter, and then sent the email to Penny to, well, to shut her up, I suppose.'

Penny bit her lips and dragged her hand through her hair. 'If only I'd flown back to England at the time, I would have found out that she wasn't living at that flat and there were no babies, and I could have reported her missing *years* ago,' she wailed. 'I mean why would anyone say such things if they weren't true?'

'I'm afraid I can't answer that at the moment,' said Joe. He consulted his notes again. 'Now, Mr Dacosta, you overheard Dave Mardle and Melissa Davies arguing on several occasions, and you say that these arguments were often centred on her relationship with his parents.'

'That's right, yes.'

'You also say that you suspected Mr Mardle of violence.'

Jay-Jay took hold of Penny's hand. 'Yes.'

'Did you ever witness any violence?'

'Um, well, not as such, but…'

'He did hit her, officer,' said Penny. 'Melissa told me.'

'And she said this in writing?' asked Joe.

'Well, no, but she spoke to me on the phone about it on several occasions.'

'But she didn't talk about the violence in her emails?'

'Not in so many words,' said Penny. 'But she did write about her extensive bruising.'

'And can you remember when these emails were sent?'

'Not exactly, no, but I've still got them so I can easily check,' said Penny. 'I *do* know that they were sent before she and Dave went to Yorkshire.'

'I see,' said Joe. 'So, my understanding is that you both believe that any emails sent by Melissa Davies after 2006 were in fact sent by Dave Mardle; is that correct?'

'It just seems the most likely explanation,' said Jay-Jay. 'The thing is, *why* would he do that?'

'And where *is* Melissa?' added Penny.

'Exactly,' said Jay-Jay. 'I mean, Penny is hardly going to report her friend as missing if she was actually living with her in Australia, as Dave claims, now would she?'

'Well, there is obviously a conflict of information here, I agree, but there could be a perfectly reasonable explanation. you know; there usually is.'

'But you are going to look into it, aren't you?' asked Jay-Jay. 'Penny is very worried.'

'It's just so out of character, officer; it really is,' said Penny. 'Melissa and I have always been very close; it just doesn't make sense. What if something has happened to her? I can't bear it.'

'You've done all that you can; you've reported a possible missing person and we are duty bound to investigate. Now, are you alright to wait here for a moment while I get these notes typed up for you to check through and sign?'

'No worries,' said Penny.

Twenty minutes later they handed their signed statements to Joe. 'Thank you officer, thank you,' said Penny.

'Oh, before you go,' said Joe, 'do you happen to have a photograph of Melissa?'

'Not on me, no,' replied Penny. 'But I can print one out from my laptop and drop it in later this morning.'

'That would be most helpful; now, try not to worry.'

'Thank you again,' said Penny.

'Oh, sorry, one other thing; did Melissa Davies have a Face Book account?'

Penny laughed. 'Absolutely not,' she exclaimed. 'She hated any type of social networking; she maintained that she knew who she wanted to remain in contact with and so couldn't see the point of them.'

'And did she? Keep in touch with people, I mean?'

'Well, she certainly kept in touch with me, at least up until the point where she didn't. Oh, that sounded really stupid; you know what I mean.'

'I do,' said Joe. 'No, I wondered if you knew who else she kept in touch with.'

Penny thought for a moment. 'Actually I think it was just me; she'd been very shy at school, and at University she kept very much to herself.'

Back at his desk, Joe read through the statements. The circumstances were odd, he thought, definitely odd; and as with all reports of missing persons the start point was the same; a serious crime may have been committed. He opened his desk drawer and removed a crisp sheet of A4 paper. He constructed a rough timeline and repeatedly tapped the point where Dave Mardle and Melissa Davies visited Yorkshire, the point where the major discrepancy occurred.

So, he wondered, did Melissa Davies lie to the Mardle family *and* to Penny Fisher? If the woman wasn't in Australia or London, then where was she? She must be somewhere, everyone is somewhere, and if she *was* hiding, living incognito, then it would have to be somewhere a long way from London. After all, Joe reasoned, she wouldn't want to bump into any of the Mardle family, not if they were under the impression that she was in Australia. He leaned back in his chair and closed his eyes. There was, of course, always the possibility that she was dead, he thought. Either way, she couldn't have known about the flat in

Auriol Road, bought by Dave Mardle in 2007, a year after she disappeared.

'Driscoll, get in here,' he yelled.

Carter, a skinny beanpole of a man, dashed in and skidded to a halt at Joe's desk. 'Um, Sergeant Driscoll transferred to Northallerton a few weeks ago, sir. I'm your new Sergeant.'

'So she did. Right, get your coat; we're going to pay a visit to The Retreat and have a little chat with Mr and Mrs Mardle.'

Joe and his sergeant arrived at the house at noon and parked their police vehicle behind a silver Rolls. 'Obviously not short of a penny or two,' remarked Joe as they made their way to the front door.

Dave's father flung the door open. 'Yes?' he demanded.

'Good afternoon; Mr Dave Mardle?'

'Yes, yes that's right.'

'Lovely car, sir, is it yours?'

Dave beamed. 'Yes; she's a beauty isn't she? You can't go wrong with a Rolls Royce.'

Joe held up his badge. 'Inspector Joe Reed, and this is my sergeant, Harry Carter.'

Harry pushed his large black-rimmed glasses a little further up towards the bridge of his nose as he too, held up his badge.

'I'm entitled to park there you know; I've got a permit.'

'It's nothing to do with your car,' said Joe. 'We're here to ask you a few questions pertaining to a missing person's report.'

'Missing person? I'm afraid I don't understand; nobody that I know is missing; well, not the last time I looked, anyway,' he quipped.

Joe smiled to himself. Guilty or not, people became nervous around police officers who wanted to ask questions. 'May we come in?'

Dave stood to one side. 'Yes, sorry; of course.'

Dave indicated the settee. 'Please take a seat. My wife is resting in the garden; she's been feeling rather tired these last few days; she has MS you see. You don't need to speak to her too, do you?'

'We may do, sir; but let's start with you, shall we?'

'Right, yes; so, who exactly is it that's missing?'

'A Melissa Davies, she…'

Dave gave a short laugh. 'But she's not missing,' he said. 'She's in Australia; she went out there years ago.'

'Well, that's just the problem; it seems that she may not have gone to Australia, sir,' explained Harry.

'But that's ridiculous; my wife and son received emails from her telling them how great the place was and how happy she was to be with her friend, Penny I think her name was; not a clue what her surname is, but they were school friends. Melissa used to live in Kent, with her parents, before they were killed in those bloody bombs; anyway I'm sure, with all your resources, you could find out this Penny's surname and then contact her, and then, you'd see that Melissa isn't missing at all.'

'We've already been in touch with Penny Fisher and she is adamant that Melissa never went to Australia,' said Joe.

'But, but, I don't understand; have you checked the shipping records? She went over in 2006, July, August, or September, something like that; my son will remember.'

'The records are being checked as we speak, sir,' said Harry.

'I see; well, as I say, she left the UK in the summer of 2006. She never came back.'

'I understand that she moved in with you and your family following the unfortunate death of her parents. Is that correct?'

'Yes, Inspector; she came to us in June 2005.'

'She had no other family?'

'No. She's an only child and both sets of grandparents were dead.'

'No aunts or uncles either?'

'Again, no; her parents were only children; it was awful for the poor girl. I mean, we were, effectively, the only family she had.'

'It seems strange that she left then,' said Joe.

'What's that supposed to mean?'

'It just seems strange, sir, that's all; still, probably not important.'

'She was a lovely girl and I was, well, we were all very upset when she left; my son, naturally, but also my wife; she and Melissa got on very well you see; she was a great support, kind, loving and considerate; yes, a lovely, lovely girl.'

'I wonder, sir, can you remember the last time you saw Melissa?'

'I certainly can; it was just before she and my son set off for a short break in Yorkshire; July, 2006.'

'I also understand that your son and Melissa were having some difficulties with their relationship around that time, arguments and the like?'

'Um, well, yes, but nothing of any importance; all perfectly normal in any relationship,' he said. 'As a matter of interest, how the bloody hell did you know that?'

'We have a witness to several of the arguments, sir; apparently they were quite heated, and I believe you and your wife were mentioned in some of them; have you any idea why that would be?'

Dave examined his nails. 'A witness you say; right, I see.' He looked back up and met Joe's eyes. 'I'll be frank with you, Inspector; I'm afraid my son was jealous of the time that Melissa spent with my wife, Deborah, and, well, with me too, I suppose. As I said she was a lovely girl, full of life and energy, such a contrast to my poor wife at the time, and I did rather lean on the girl.' He held up his hands. 'And before you jump to any nasty conclusions, I mean emotionally.'

'I see, and do you know where they stayed in Yorkshire?'

'At our cottage, my mother-in-law's cottage to be exact. We don't own it anymore, sold it last year, actually, to a very nice couple. It was a bit of a wrench, but my wife, you know, travel is getting more difficult for her, and of course it is very remote.'

'And where would that be?'

'It's in the North Yorkshire moors, not far from Scawton; it's called Black Sheep Cottage.'

'And the names of the current owners are?'

'Why on earth do you need to know that?'

'For completeness, sir; I'm sure you understand.'

'Fine,' he sighed. 'The current owners are Mr and Mrs Morgan; so, is that it, only I am quite busy.'

'Yes, thank you for your time sir. We may need to speak with you again.'

'I fail to see why; there's nothing more I can add,' said Dave.

'Oh, there was one more thing that you might be able to help me with,' said Joe. 'I'm told that your son arranged for the girl's belongings to be sent out to Australia; is that correct?'

A high pitched squeaking sound filled the room as Deborah wheeled herself through the French windows. 'Darling, could you find the oil; oh, I do apologise; I didn't realise that you had visitors.'

'This is my wife, Deborah,' said Dave. 'These two police officers are making enquiries about Melissa; apparently she's been reported as missing.'

'Missing? No, you must be mistaken, she moved out to Australia.'

'Yes, that's what I've been telling them, but it seems that there is now some doubt.'

'But, sorry, I don't understand,' said Deborah. 'She sent us emails from Australia; she was happy, that's why she stayed out there.'

'I wouldn't worry, darling; I'm sure it's a simple misunderstanding,' said Dave.

'I was just asking your husband about Melissa Davies's belongings,' said Joe. 'I understand that your son arranged for them to be sent out to Australia.'

'Yes, that's right,' said Deborah. 'My son drove back down here to collect it all and then drove back up to Yorkshire for Melissa to sort through it.'

'I imagine there must have been quite a lot,' said Joe.

'No, not really,' said Dave. 'She kept nothing from the old family home. There *was* a small silver butterfly necklace that belonged to her mother; she wore it all the time, but apart from that there was nothing really, apart from her clothes and bits and bobs.'

'There was also that old oak chest, Dave, don't you remember?'

Dave hesitated momentarily. 'Was there?'

'Oh, for goodness sake,' exclaimed Deborah. 'You can't possibly have forgotten; it was a hateful monstrosity, deeply carved with hideous gargoyles.'

Dave stared off into the distance. 'Um, yes; I vaguely recall something of that ilk now that you come to mention it,' he said.

'And do you happen to recall the name of the courier firm?'

'I've no idea; you'll have to ask my son. Now, as I think I just mentioned, I *am* quite busy…'

'Is your son here?'

'No, he's at work at my wife's bookshop, Black Moon Books, just off the Hammersmith road, near Windsor Way.'

'Thank you again, sir; we'll be in touch.'

Joe and Harry made their way towards the door and Dave stood to show them out.

'Don't worry; we'll see ourselves out,' said Joe. He turned to leave and then tapped his forehead with the heel of his palm. 'Honestly, I worry about myself sometimes; there was another question.'

Dave sighed deeply. 'Yes?'

'Do you happen to know the name of Melissa's GP?'

Dave frowned. 'Her GP?'

'Yes.'

'Well, yes, as it happens, I do,' said Dave. 'She was under our family GP, Dr. Saunders; his surgery is just down the road. Brook Street Surgery, although I fail to see how...'

'I know the place,' said Harry.

'You've been most helpful, and this time we really are leaving,' added Joe.

Outside, Joe instructed Harry to go to the Brook Street Surgery. 'I'll pop along to the bookshop and have a little word with the son.' He glanced at his watch. 'What do you reckon; meet back here in 40 minutes?'

'40 minutes should be fine,' said Harry. 'I'll text if there's a problem.'

As soon as Dave heard the front door slam he picked up the phone.

'Black Moon Books; how may I help?' said Phyllis.

Shit; I'm an idiot, he thought as he glanced at his watch; 12.40. *Dave will be with Erica, in the park.*

'Um, Phyllis, now don't be alarmed, I've just had a visit from the police...'

'The police,' she exclaimed. 'Has something happened to Dave or...'

'No, no; nothing like that; no. They were asking about Melissa; they seem to think she's missing.'

'She's in Australia, dear.'

'Yes, I *know* that, Phyllis, and that's what I told them, but it seems that there is some doubt...'

'Doubt? What sort of doubt?'

'Well, *I* don't know do I? They just said that Melissa had been reported as missing; they've even been in touch with that friend, Penny, that Melissa went out to join and she's apparently told the police that Melissa *isn't* in Australia, well, not with her anyway. Anyway, I forgot that you would be minding the shop. They're on their way to speak with Dave, so be a dear and let them know where he is. I'll give him a quick call on his mobile to warn him.'

'Yes, alright dear; gracious me, the police, whatever next?'

'Will you be alright? Do you want me to come over?'

'No, no, I'll be fine. I'll see you later.'

The church clock struck one. Erica felt her eyes burn. She turned her face away from Dave and through the blur of her tears she saw a mass of pigeons scatter noisily as Inspector Joe Reed strode down the path towards them.

'Sorry to disturb your lunch,' said Joe, holding up his badge. 'Inspector Joe Reed. I'd just like a quick word with you about...'

Dave stood and faced Joe. 'Melissa Davies?' he said. 'Yes, my father just rang me.' He turned and took hold of Erica's arm, pulling her to her feet. He put his arm around her shoulder and held on tightly.

Erica gave a little squirm. Dave tightened his grip. 'Erica and her friend, Maggie here, were just telling me that Penny Fisher, of all people, has turned up and she's looking for Melissa. I simply don't understand, officer; I was under the distinct impression that Melissa was out in Australia *with* Penny Fisher and now, well it seems that she isn't. It's quite a worry and it's really rather upset poor Erica; obviously I will do all I can to help, but I don't know how; as I said, I thought she was in Australia.'

Joe's eyes rested on Erica. 'Is everything alright, Erica?'

Dave gave her shoulder a squeeze. She nodded. 'Um, yes, fine.'

He turned back to face Dave. 'Now then sir, just a few questions; we can chat here or, if you'd prefer somewhere more private…'

'Here's fine,' he said. 'I have nothing to hide. Erica knows everything there is to know about my past relationship with Melissa; so, Inspector, shoot.'

'I understand that there were several arguments between you and Melissa in the weeks leading up to her disappearance.'

'She didn't *disappear*, officer; she went to Australia,' said Dave. 'Well, that's what she told me.'

'I was asking about the arguments.'

Dave hung his head. 'The arguments, yes; it's a terrible thing to admit, but I was jealous; jealous, can you believe it?'

'And what was it that you were jealous of?'

'Oh, give me a break; you've already spoken to my father, so you know what I was jealous of.'

'Just answer the question, sir.'

'Fine; I was jealous of the time she spent with my parents, especially my bloody father; time that she should have spent with me,' he exclaimed. 'Satisfied?'

'Could you tell me what happened at the cottage in Yorkshire.'

Dave took a deep breath and looked up at Joe. 'I'll tell you what happened, Officer; she buggered off to Australia, that's what happened. The trip to the cottage was my attempt to seek forgiveness for my selfish behaviour, but it was hopeless; she continued to argue. And then she announced that she was going out to Australia to join Penny, and not just for a few weeks, oh, no; for a whole bloody year.' He clenched his fist. 'I tried to understand. I tried to be supportive, Jesus, I even told her that I'd wait.

150

What a bloody fool I was; I loved her back then you see. She hurt me a great deal, and my mother, come to that, by choosing to stay out in Australia.'

'Leaving aside whether she did, or did not go out to Australia,' said Joe, 'your father mentioned that you arranged for her possessions to be sent out to Australia in advance; is that correct?'

'Yes, and?'

'The name of the courier firm that you used would be most helpful.'

Dave closed his eyes and thought for a moment. 'Sorry, can't remember.'

'Try.'

'I've just told you; I can't remember. Jesus!'

'It's important,' said Joe. 'So, when you *do* manage to recall the name, give me a call.' He handed Dave his card and turned to Erica. 'I'll see you tomorrow at the café; we'll have a little chat then, alright?'

'Why do you need to talk to Erica? She's never even met Melissa,' said Dave.

'Just following protocol; I'm sure you understand,' said Joe. 'And I may need to speak with you too; Maggie is it?'

Maggie flashed him a dazzling smile. 'That's right; Maggie Hunter-Lopez at your disposal, any time, Officer.'

Harry had just finished a call when Joe returned to the car. 'That was the station, sir; Penny Fisher has dropped off that photograph of Melissa Davies.'

Joe nodded as he rubbed at his neck. 'Right, let's get back.'

Harry inserted the ignition key. 'Is everything alright, sir?'

'I didn't take to our Dave, an arrogant little toe-rag if you ask me. I'm bloody certain he's lying.'

*

151

As soon as Joe turned to walk away Erica wrenched herself free from Dave's embrace. With tears streaming down her face she croaked, 'Don't you dare use me like that; one moment you're calling me a bloody witch and the next you're all lovey-dovey, clinging onto me like I'm your bloody possession.'

'I'm sorry, Erica, really I am; it's just all been such a shock. Melissa not in Australia; it just doesn't make any sense. She *told* me that was where she was going; I mean why else would I have sent all her stuff out there, for God's sake?'

'Why indeed?' said Maggie.

'And what's that supposed to mean,' he bellowed.

'Nothing, Dave; I was agreeing with you.'

'Oh, right; sorry, sorry; it's just that this has all rather unbalanced me. I just can't believe it. I've been a bloody fool.' He took hold of Erica's hand. 'I don't know what came over me earlier, really I don't. It's just when Dad rang and said that the police had spoken to him, and that Melissa was missing, well, I mean, what the hell is happening? I believed everything she said to me, you know, everything, and now...'

'Oh, Dave, I know; it's awful.'

'Jesus, Erica, what if something terrible has happened to her?'

'I'm sure she's fine; I mean if something had happened it would have been in the news wouldn't it?'

Dave nodded. 'I suppose.'

'Listen, we can talk later but I think it's important for you to be with your family at the moment,' said Erica. 'It's all been such a shock and your mum must be feeling as confused as you are.'

Dave took a deep breath. 'You're absolutely right, Erica. Less thinking about poor old me, more thinking about others; you are wonderful, you know, and you are definitely *not* a witch; it was a terrible thing to say to you. I'm really,

152

really sorry.' He squeezed her hand. 'I'm sure the police will get to the bottom of all of this soon and then, well, then we can concentrate on more important matters, like our future lives together, rather than going over my past life with bloody Melissa, especially as it appears that she was lying all along; lying to me, to my parents and, it would seem, to her good friend Penny too. Who'd have thought? It just goes to show; you think you know someone and then something like this happens.'

'Oh, yes, absolutely; whatever you see on the outside, you can never be sure that it's a true reflection of what's on the inside; rather like a book and its cover, wouldn't you agree, Dave?' said Maggie.

Dave threw her an icy look. 'I'd better get going,' he said. 'Make sure Mum's alright.'

'What about Phyllis?' Erica asked.

'Oh, Christ! Gran; she'll be in a state too…'

'You go; we'll let Phyllis know that you've gone home,' said Erica. 'Do you want her to shut the shop?'

'Yes, yes; good idea,' said Dave. 'This is all such a mess; listen, I'll give you a ring later.'

Erica watched Dave as he dashed off. At the gate he turned and blew her a kiss. She smiled and turned to Maggie. 'You see; I was right.'

'About what exactly?'

'Didn't you listen? He's just explained; Melissa told him that she was going to Australia so he wasn't lying; she was.'

'So he says,' mumbled Maggie.

'What?'

'Yes, that's what he said.'

Erica gave her a piercing stare. 'Right, so, there we are,' she said. 'Come on, we need to speak to Phyllis.'

Back at the station Joe picked up the photograph of Melissa. 'Look at this,' he said.

Harry took the photograph. 'A stunning looking girl.'

'I agree,' said Joe, 'stunning. But that's not the point; the point is, this Melissa Davies looks remarkably like Erica Woods.'

'That's the current girlfriend of our young Dave Mardle, right?'

'Right.'

Harry adjusted his glasses. 'I don't know if you are aware, sir,' he began.

'Probably not,' said Joe. 'But I sense that I soon will be.'

'It's just that there is some evidence to suggest that certain people choose new partners that look similar to their previous partners.'

'Oh, give me a break, Harry, that's just a load of psychobabble shit. So, what did you find out at the surgery?'

'Um, well, I spoke to Dr. Saunders, and he remembers Melissa Davies.'

'I don't doubt that for one moment, now that I've seen what she looks like.'

Harry pushed his glasses firmly onto the bridge of his nose. 'Quite. Anyway, he first met Melissa Davies when she came into the surgery with Mrs Deborah Mardle. He informed me that Melissa Davies never gave birth to twins, not while she was under him, as it were. He can't say what happened after she left the surgery, of course,' said Harry as he checked his notes. 'And his records show that her last appointment was in May 2006.'

'And did he know where she went to?'

'Yes and no,' replied Harry.

'Pardon?'

'Yes, he knew where she went, but it was young Dave Mardle who told him.'

'So he thought she'd gone to…'

'Australia,' said Harry. 'Yes.'

'Right, well someone's lying, and my money's still on Dave Mardle.'

'There was something else,' added Harry. 'Dr. Saunders prescribed Melissa Davies antidepressants following the death of her parents in 2005 but he was concerned that she was still on them right up to May of 2006 when he saw her last.'

'Was she indeed,' remarked Joe. 'Well, I can think of at least *one* plausible reason why that may have been the case.'

'Sir?'

'Any association with Dave Mardle would be enough to drive a saint to reach for the drugs in my opinion, humble though it may be.'

Chapter 10

Joe arrived at the Lord of the Fries at 10.30 the following morning. 'I can't really talk to you at the moment, Joe,' Erica explained. 'As you can see, we're short staffed. But if you can wait a little while, Joyce should be back soon.' She glanced at her watch. 'And Terry should have been here half an hour ago.'

'No problem,' said Joe. 'Gives me an excuse to have a coffee and relax for a bit; never seems to be enough time these days, what with all the paper work and bureaucracy that's crept up on us all. Still, not your problem; when you're ready, just give me the nod. I'll sit over by the window and watch the world go by.'

Joe was startled from his reverie as Erica collapsed onto the seat opposite him a short while later. 'Here I am, Joe; all yours.' She plonked another cup of coffee in front of him. 'On the house, alright?'

'Smashing; thanks.' He took a sip. 'Would you mind just talking me through how you first met Dave Mardle?'

Erica smiled. 'Not at all; although, to be honest, the way that he and I met was a bit strange.'

'In what way?'

'We didn't do anything illegal or anything; it's just that Maggie was convinced we could find him and ...'

Joe held up his hand. 'You found him? Why, was he lost?'

'No,' Erica chuckled.

'Perhaps you could start from the beginning.'

'Yes, right, of course.' She took a deep breath and told Joe about the misdirected texts to her phone and how Maggie had persuaded her to locate the mysterious Dave. 'Once we got started it was fun and, incredible though it may seem, we found him within a few days.'

'And that's when you and he started dating?'

'Pretty much, yeah.'

'And would you say that you and he have a good relationship?'

Erica hesitated. 'He was very attentive when we first started dating and I found it endearing, but after a while it all got a bit creepy,' she said. 'Maggie had been telling me for ages to get out of the relationship; she said he was virtually stalking me; a bit of an exaggeration, but well, I did end it.'

'But you and he are back together now?'

'Yes, much to Maggie's consternation.'

'So, Maggie isn't keen on the man?'

'Um, not really, no,' said Erica. 'The thing is, oh I don't know. I got the impression that he was very cut up, you know, about Melissa leaving him. He told me that he'd loved her and that he was prepared to wait for her and then, when she didn't come back, he moved out of the family home to be on his own, I suppose.'

She took a sip of coffee. Her hands were shaking, causing coffee to spill onto the table. 'When you told him that Melissa never went to Australia he was angry; well, I suppose that's understandable, you would be, wouldn't you, if you found out that the person you loved had lied to you, but well, I just don't know anymore. Everyone is convinced that it's Dave that's been lying all along, and oh, I just don't know.'

'Penny has given us a photograph of Melissa; were you aware that you and she look very similar?'

'Apparently so…'

'Dave never mentioned the fact that you looked like Melissa?'

'Well, not at first, no; hardly surprising really. It'd be a bit odd, don't you think?' she said. 'He did tell me recently, though, but he's adamant that I'm not like her in any other way; I mean, I wouldn't lie to him like Melissa seems to have done. It's just too awful. It's really shocked him, you know.' She examined the coffee spill and slowly etched a pattern in it.

Joe pressed on. 'So you've never seen her photograph then; there are none at Dave's flat or at his parents' place?'

'No, not that I've seen, and frankly I wouldn't have been too thrilled to find his flat stuffed with photographs of his ex.'

'No, quite,' agreed Joe. 'But perhaps there might have been one at his parents' place. Still, there you go. Tell me,' he went on, 'When was it that you broke off the relationship?'

'It was on Christmas day, last year, at his parents' house. I nearly didn't go actually, but Dave kept pestering me, saying how his parents were keen to meet me and everything, and so in the end I agreed.' Erica gave Joe a resigned smile. 'Maggie even had a plan to rescue me by ringing me up to say that there was some sort of family crisis.'

'And did she?'

'No, I told her not to be so melodramatic but, as it happened, she did ring me, not with the fake call, but just to chat; and thank God she did because I did need rescuing.'

Joe asked her why and Erica told him about the cottage key fiasco. 'It was bloody awful; he just left me stranded in the bosom of his family. Nobody knew what to do or say. He behaved like a spoilt child who hadn't got his own way; it was ridiculous.'

'So, what persuaded you to get back together with him?'

Erica looked down at her feet. 'You'll think I'm stupid.'

'Why would I think that?'

'Well, Maggie thinks I am.'

'I'm not Maggie.'

'No. Oh, I don't know, it's just that he seemed so remorseful, cross with himself really, and he said that it was because he'd been planning the surprise for a while and then, when he found out that his grandmother had sold the cottage, well, he was just so angry.'

'The surprise?'

'Oh, right, yes; he'd planned to take me up to Yorkshire, to spend the New Year with him at Black Sheep Cottage.'

'You're telling me that he wanted to spend time with you in the same cottage where he claims that he and Melissa spent their last few days together before she left for Australia? A place that was presumably filled with memories of what could have been; a place where he lost the love of his life that place, do you mean?'

'Well yes, put like that it does sound a bit odd and now, what with Penny turning up and everything, I just don't know what's going on. I mean, did this Melissa go to Australia or not?' She stared at Joe, eyes wide and full of trust. 'We went in the end, you know.'

'To the cottage?'

'Yes; he wanted to show me the renovation work that he'd done at the cottage after Melissa left for, well, for wherever she left for.'

'I thought you said the cottage had been sold.'

'Oh, it has; hence the Christmas debacle; no, we stayed in a lovely little family run hotel, and then Dave took me along to see the place. The new owners were really lovely and invited us in for a drink, and showed us around. They were amazed to see us actually; they'd just been discussing the possibility of ripping out the fireplace that Dave's father had put in to see if there was an original inglenook thingy behind it, and Dave was able to tell them that there was, and that his father had only blocked it in to make it easier for his mum, you know, what with the MS and everything.' She took a quick breath. 'Mind you, Dave got very upset at first, when he thought they were talking about ripping out his pond; he was very proud of his pond and I could see why.' Erica suddenly stopped talking. 'Sorry, I'm rambling, what was it you asked me?'

Joe laughed. 'I asked if you went to the cottage and I gather that you did; you met the new owners and they were very nice; I also gather that they're planning some renovation work of their own that involves ripping out a fireplace, and that Dave built a pond.'

'Right, yes,' said Erica sheepishly. 'Anyway, we had a lovely time and I was full of optimism for the future, and then, when I got back, Maggie sprung all this on me about Penny and the possibility, which seems to be getting stronger and stronger as each moment passes, that Melissa never went to Australia at all. I mean, where the hell is she?'

By early Friday morning of that week, Inspector Reed's team had established two important facts; one, there was no record of any items transported to Australia in the name of Melissa Davies in 2006; and two, there was no record of a Melissa Davies travelling to Australia in 2006.

'So, one obvious question that springs to mind,' remarked Joe, 'is this: how is it possible for Melissa Davies to send emails from Australia when she never actually went to Australia?'

'The emails were obviously sent from somewhere else,' said Harry.

'You don't say,' said Joe. 'Thankfully our techies will be more specific. And I bet you £100 that the 'somewhere else' will be London, and the person who sent them will be Dave Mardle junior.'

'We'll need everyone's computers then.'

'My God you're on fire today, lad,' said Joe. 'So, I suggest you get round to Penny Fisher and ask if we can have access to her laptop. I'll pay another visit to Mr and Mrs Mardle, and then I'll also pop along and have another little chat with their son.'

'Actually, sir,' said Harry as he scribbled the instruction in his notebook. 'I think those emails from Melissa Davies are stored on Penny Fisher's old Blackberry rather than her laptop.'

'Laptop, blackberry, hewn in bloody stone, I don't care; just get them.'

'Right you are, sir.'

'Well, go on lad; what are you waiting for?'

'There's just one other thing sir.'

'Spit it out.'

'Well, we all agree that Melissa Davies isn't in Australia, right?'

'Right, and?'

'But she's obviously *somewhere*…'

'How did I ever manage before you joined the team?'

Harry gave his glasses an unnecessary tweak. 'Um, well, I was just thinking that wherever she is, she'll need money won't she; and so I thought we could look into her banking activity to see…'

'Oh, good lad; get onto that ASAP.' He thumped Harry on his back. 'Don't get too clever though. I've only just lost Driscoll, a bloody good Sergeant, to the dizzy heights of Inspector. I don't want to lose another one so soon.'

Harry adjusted his perfectly straight tie and gave his glasses another push towards the bridge of his nose.

'So; what are you waiting for this time?'

'Right, yes, I see, you want me to get onto it right now; no problem.' He rose and attempted to leave with an air of authority, spoilt by the collapse of the coat stand as he relieved it of his coat. He scrabbled to right the thing and nearly decapitated Superintendent Marshall as he entered.

'Steady on man,' he cried.

'Sorry sir, I, I…'

Marshall grabbed hold of the stand and righted it in one swift movement. Harry stood stock still, clutching his coat tightly to his chest.

'Off you go, Harry,' said Joe. 'We need that information.'

'Right away sir,' said Harry and, with an apologetic glance towards the Superintendent, he left.

'Missing person's case, I understand,' remarked Marshall as he hauled his large bulk across the room to stand unnecessarily close to Joe.

'Yes sir,' replied Joe.

'Well don't waste too much time on it. You and I both know that the most likely explanation is that the woman left of her own accord.'

'Actually, I'm not so sure, sir,' said Joe. 'There are a few inconsistencies, and there's just something about the Mardle's son that doesn't sit right.'

Marshall poked Joe in the chest as he uttered each one of his next three words. 'Evidence, man; evidence.'

'Absolutely sir, it's being collected as we speak.'

'When did this woman allegedly go missing?'

'Seven years ago, sir.'

'Seven years, good grief. And why, pray, has it taken so long for someone to notice that she was missing?' he said, adding with a grin, 'Very tiny, is she?'

Gritting his teeth, Joe replied, 'Not especially, sir, no; it is simply that the people here were under the impression that she was in Australia, whereas the people in Australia were under the impression that she was here in London.'

'Well, there you are then,' exclaimed Marshall. 'The girl obviously wanted to disappear; it's a common enough story.'

'You may be right, sir,' said Joe. 'We just need to check the email records to ascertain where the woman actually is.'

'Well, what are you waiting for? Get on with it, man; there are other cases, slightly more current than seven bloody years ago, piling up on your desk. I'll expect your final report first thing Monday morning.'

Joe gave a curt nod as he stomped out through the double doors; doors that continued to swing violently for some time after he'd left.

Joe was admiring the ponds as he sat on the terrace waiting for Deborah. 'Do you take sugar?' she called from the kitchen door.

Joe held up three fingers.

'It's not good for you, you know,' she said as she removed the two mugs from a nifty little cup holder attached to her chair and plonked them on the table.

'Nothing we enjoy is good for us.'

'Oh, how true,' she agreed. 'Now what was it that you wanted to ask me?'

'Would you mind if I took your computer away so that our techies can have a look at those emails that Melissa Davies sent?'

'I don't see why not; hold on, I'll get it.' She wheeled herself away at some speed. 'Won't be a tic.'

Moments later she reappeared with her laptop. 'It's fully charged,' she announced. 'I keep it plugged in all the time.' She handed it over to Joe. 'There's no password or anything; I simply can't be doing with them. I think of a password that, at the time, seems inspirational and then, when I'm asked to enter the damn thing, I simply cannot recall it.'

Joe laughed. 'Oh, I know the feeling.' He opened the laptop and searched through the email file. 'Can you remember when you received her most recent email?'

'Funnily enough, I can; it was in 2009, Friday the 24th July, exactly three years to the day that she and my son set off for their holiday at my mother's cottage.'

'Ah, this is it, I think.' He passed the laptop back to Deborah.

Her eyes misted over a little as she reread the email. She cleared her throat. 'Yes, this is the one. She apologises for not being in touch and then goes on to tell me that she's married, to a sheep farmer of all things! Anyway, as you can see, she explains that the Internet is non-existent where they are, and not to be surprised if we never hear from her again; she adds a little smiley face but, as it happens, we never did hear from her after that. Still, there you go, she has her own life to live now and so I say good luck to her.'

Interesting, thought Joe. *In London, she's giving birth to twins, in Australia she's married to a sheep farmer. What a fascinating life this woman has.*

'I still can't believe she's not in Australia,' said Deborah. 'And you've spoken with her friend, Penny, Penny um...'

'Penny Fisher,' said Joe.

'And you've spoken with Penny Fisher and she's certain that Melissa isn't there.'

'Actually, I don't wish to be rude, but convention dictates that it should be me asking the questions.'

'Oh, I'm so sorry, do forgive me; it's just, well, it's just so hard to take in,' said Deborah. 'Ask away.'

'Perhaps you could tell me a little about the time that Melissa Davies was living here with you and your family.'

'Right, well, as you probably know, she came to us after the death of her parents, terrible thing, and I think, to a certain extent, my illness saved her from sinking into a dark pit of depression; every cloud has a silver lining I suppose. She was just what I needed; she didn't fuss, that was the main thing. My husband was still working full time back then; he's retired now of course.' Deborah's face clouded over. 'He still does a bit of private consultancy work, but essentially he's my full time carer; not the life we had envisioned for ourselves when we first married of course, but there you go.'

'Your husband seemed very fond of the girl.'

Deborah shot him a wry look. 'You could say that,' she said. 'Oh, I don't blame him, really I don't; he was under terrible pressure and Melissa had that sparkle of youth and vitality; she was whole.'

Joe nodded. 'I'm sorry to have to ask you this but, in your opinion, was your husband's relationship with Melissa

Davies a contributing factor to the arguments that took place between her and your son?'

Deborah hesitated. 'I don't want you to get the wrong idea, Inspector. I'm certain that there was no sexual relationship between my husband and Melissa, absolutely none; no, in many ways it was more serious than that, it was a strong emotional attachment between the pair of them. My illness, my dependency bought them together you see.' Her voice caught. 'He was very fond of the girl, very fond indeed.'

'And the arguments?'

'Oh, yes, sorry; yes, absolutely; well, I'm afraid to say that my son has always been the jealous type, likes to be the centre of attention and hates it if he doesn't get his own way; he used to tell terrible lies as a child and have the most spectacular tantrums, still does actually, have tantrums I mean, I'm sure he doesn't lie, not now, well not major lies you understand, I mean we all tell little white lies every now and then; I know I do, mostly to try and stop my husband from worrying about me. Anyway, sorry, what was it that you asked me?'

'I asked you about the arguments.'

Deborah rubbed her forehead and closed her eyes. 'He argued with both of us. He simply couldn't understand how I could be so relaxed about what he saw as an unhealthy relationship developing between his father and Melissa, and no amount of me trying to explain to him about adult feelings of trust and love would divert him from his anger. As far as he was concerned, Melissa was *his*, not to be shared with *anyone*, especially not his father.'

'You've getting tired,' said Joe. 'Look, you've been most helpful, but I'll leave you in peace now.'

Deborah gave a small shrug. 'Happens more frequently these days I'm afraid; the energy just seems to leak away, very frustrating.' She handed Joe her laptop. 'Don't forget this; I hope it will help you find out where Melissa is and, if

165

there's anything else you need, just ask; it's been lovely to meet you.'

'That's not what most people say,' quipped Joe. 'Oh, there is something else; I don't suppose you know whether your son kept hold of his old laptop, do you?'

'It must be your lucky day, Inspector; my mother has Dave's old one.'

'Is she in?'

Deborah glanced at her watch. 'She goes every Friday morning for coffee at Betty Blythe's; she leaves at 10.45 on the dot, in about five minutes as it happens; I'll give her a shout.'

Phyllis appeared at the kitchen door. 'Is there a problem, dear, only I'm just about to leave; oh, gracious, Inspector Reed isn't it?'

Joe gave a brief nod. 'It is. I'm sorry to bother you again, I know that you have an appointment, but your daughter has just informed me that you now own your grandson's old laptop.'

'That's correct, Inspector, I do, but why is that of any interest to you?'

Joe explained that he was looking into the email records of Melissa Davies, and Phyllis, after pointedly checking her watch, went to fetch the laptop.

Joe and Deborah exchanged a smile. 'While I'm on the topic,' he said. 'Did your husband also receive emails from Melissa?'

'Not to my knowledge, Inspector; you'll have to ask him.'

'Is he in?'

'No, sorry, he's at his club in town.'

'His club?'

'The City of London Club; he meets up with his old friend, Philip White, once a month; has done for years.'

'Here we are, Inspector,' said Phyllis. 'Now I really must be on my way, I do so hate to be late.'

With the two laptops safely tucked under his arm, Joe accompanied Phyllis to Betty Blythe's café where, as Phyllis put it, she was meeting her curmudgeonly friend Gertrude Flack. 'Miserable woman really, can't think why I remain friends with her; she was with me when I first met the lovely Erica and her friend Maggie, you know. Maggie threw a paper missile at me, well no, that's not technically true; she threw the missile at Erica, but she ducked and it hit me.'

'Erica Woods bears a striking similarity to Melissa Davies,' remarked Joe casually.

Phyllis gushed, 'Yes she does, doesn't she? Lovely girl, Melissa, I mean; oh, well, so is Erica, I didn't mean to imply…'

'I'm sure you didn't,' said Joe. 'Your daughter tells me that her husband was very fond of Melissa.'

Phyllis fiddled with her coat buttons and stared straight ahead. 'He was.'

'And that upset your grandson?'

'It did.'

'And do you know why?'

'Inspector, Melissa was a lovely young girl and Dave, Deborah's husband, is a normal red blooded male. I may be old but I'm not stupid. Quite frankly I would have been surprised if he hadn't taken a shine to the girl; always had an eye for a pretty young girl, that one.' She stopped and turned to face Joe. 'Deborah always sees the best in people, Inspector. She's a very trusting person, but in my opinion Dave was more than *fond* of the girl.'

'I wonder, can you remember when you last saw Melissa?'

'Oh yes, it was years ago, dear; when she and my grandson went off on their little trip to the Yorkshire cottage back in July 2006. My grandson, for once, had listened to my advice; I told him to stop behaving like a spoilt child and 'man up' as the younger people say. I told him to stop being so selfish. He's a good boy, Inspector, really he is, it's just that sometimes, well sometimes he seems to revert to childhood and I can't be doing with that. I told him that Melissa was being a great support to *both* his parents and for that he should be grateful.'

'But the trip away didn't end as it was supposed to.'

'No, quite,' remarked Phyllis. 'Probably explains why my grandson has never taken my advice again.'

'What do you think happened?'

'I'm sure I've no idea; up until a few days ago I was under the impression that Melissa had gone to Australia. Frankly, I still find it hard to believe that she didn't; she never struck me as a liar.'

'Whereas your grandson?'

'Whereas my grandson what?'

'Does he still tell lies?'

'That's a very loaded question, Inspector; a bit like that old chestnut, 'do you still beat your wife?''

Phyllis was saved from having to make any further comment by the bellowing voice of Gertrude Flack. 'You're late; do come along, Phyllis. I've been standing here for ages.'

'Gertrude, I'm so sorry.'

'Entirely my fault, Madame,' said Joe, extending his free hand. 'Inspector Joe Reed, at your service.'

Gertrude ignored Joe's proffered hand, 'Pleased to meet you I'm sure; now, goodbye.' She grabbed hold of Phyllis's arm and dragged her off through the doors of the café.

''Bye, Inspector,' cried Phyllis as she disappeared from view behind the bulk that was Gertrude Flack.

Joe returned to the station, handed the laptops over to the tech department, and sat slumped at his desk, watching the hands of the clock drag slowly from 12.30 to 12.35. He bit into his soggy sandwich and took a small sip of tepid coffee. He flicked through his notes, glanced at the clock again, and chewed unenthusiastically, examining the remaining portion of the sandwich as if it were an important piece of evidence before chucking it into the bin. Marshall blundered in, without knocking. 'Found your missing woman then?'

'Not as such, sir.'

'So; no, then.'

'I still think something's not right; the son is hiding something, of that I'm certain, hence all the lies.'

'Hiding what exactly?'

'The clue is in the word *hidden*, sir, so I'm not sure.'

'Oh, very droll.'

'Thank you.'

'It wasn't a bloody compliment, Inspector.'

'Right, well, I'm waiting on a couple of reports and once I get them, I'll have a clearer picture, you know, of what happened to Melissa Davies.'

'I shouldn't think anything's *happened* to the woman,' said Marshall. 'I expect she just decided to bugger off. I don't want you wasting any more time on this ancient case; you've got till Monday morning and that's it.'

Joe was mouthing Marshall's words to his retreating back when Harry entered with a huge grin on his face. 'Good afternoon, sir.'

Joe's mood instantly lightened; here was a man who, unlike Marshall, knew what he was doing. 'Tell me you have something interesting for me,' said Joe.

'I certainly do, sir; it's about Melissa Davies's bank account, and I think you'll find it most interesting, most interesting indeed.'

Joe beamed back at Harry. 'Something to wipe the smug expression off Dave Mardle's face I hope?'

'Oh, I think so, sir, yes.'

'Let's have a butchers then.'

And there it was, on the second page, the information that pointed to the fact that Melissa Davies had simply disappeared, seemingly without trace.

'Penny Fisher has forwarded all the relevant emails to the station, the techies are working on them as we speak and, just to let you know, sir, she has returned to Kent to be with her parents; I've got her mobile number and an address. She said she'd keep in touch but didn't know when she would be back, you know, what with her father being ill; apparently the prognosis is not good.'

'Right, excellent; well, not excellent about the poor girl's father, obviously,' said Joe. 'Now then; I've spoken to Mrs Mardle and she's not certain whether her husband received emails from Melissa Davies or not, so, I want you to go uptown to the um...' he consulted his notebook. 'I want you to go uptown to the City of London Club and have a chat with her husband; we need his laptop too.'

'Right you are, sir. Do you want me to accompany him home to collect it?'

'No, no; just ask him to drop it into the station at his earliest convenience. If he did receive emails then they're likely to be the same ones that his wife received anyway.'

Harry adjusted his glasses and pursed his lips.

'Fine; that's an assumption,' said Joe. 'Perhaps you should accompany him home and collect it yourself.'

Harry smiled. 'Right you are, sir.'

Erica still hadn't heard from Dave. She'd been convinced that he would ring her on the Wednesday night, if for no other reason than to ask how her chat with Joe had gone, but he hadn't. She didn't know if this made her more suspicious or less. There were logical reasons for his lack of contact. He was innocent, looking after his mother and feeling hurt that Melissa had lied to him and his family for all those years. Or he was guilty, hiding something and frantically trying to come up with some sort of plausible explanation for the fact that Melissa was not where he'd said she was.

'Oh, Maggie, please tell me that he hasn't been lying all along.'

Maggie quietly reminded her about the email that Penny had received from Melissa telling her that she and Dave had moved into the flat in Auriol Road.

'So?'

'Think about it, Erica; we all know that's not true…'

'Yes, I know *that*. Even Dave agrees it was rubbish for goodness sake! Surely that's evidence enough that it's Melissa doing the lying and *not* Dave.'

Maggie took hold of Erica's hand. 'When did Dave move into Auriol Road?'

'What difference does that make?'

'Think about it.'

'Oh, I don't know; 2007 I think.'

'Exactly.'

'*Exactly*; what do you mean, *exactly*?'

'Let's assume that, as Dave claims…'

Erica started to protest.

Maggie held up her hand. 'Hold on, let me finish. Let's assume that Melissa went to Australia.'

'Right…'

'But she didn't go to Australia, did she?'

'No…'

'But she must have gone *somewhere*.'

'Yes; but, look Maggie, where's this going?'

'Well, she's hardly going to go to London, or anywhere nearby, is she? She'd need to be as far away as possible to limit the likelihood of her ever bumping into Dave or his family again, you know, given that she'd told them that she was in Australia and everything.'

'Yes, *and*?'

'So how could she have possibly known about the flat in Auriol Road; a flat that Dave didn't move into until nearly a year after Melissa um, well, disappeared?'

Erica's chest tightened and an awful stillness came over her. Maggie was right. Wherever Melissa was, how could she have known? It was Dave; Dave was the liar; it had always been Dave; it was still Dave; he was, as Maggie had suspected for some time, a pathological liar.

Chapter 11

Harry marched into Joe's office at 6pm on Friday clutching a laptop.

'Is everything alright, lad?'

'Mr Mardle was a bit put out, sir; he didn't appreciate being disturbed at his club.'

'Is that so? Still, I see you have his laptop. Be a good chap and review the emails before handing it to the techies; we don't want to clog up the system if there's nothing new there.'

'Is there any news about the other laptops?'

'Not as yet,' said Joe as he picked up his phone. 'I'll check.'

'Ah, Mark, what progress on those laptops?'—'I see, and?'—'You're absolutely sure?'—'And when can I expect your report to appear on my desk?'—'That's great, thanks.' Joe grinned at Harry. 'Their report will be with me first thing tomorrow morning.'

Joe looked up from his desk as Harry entered the office the following morning. 'This is bloody gold dust, Harry,' he said, his eyes ablaze. 'Take officer Jenkins with you and bring Dave Mardle junior in for questioning; if he chooses not to come willingly then explain to him that you will be forced to arrest him on suspicion of perverting the course of justice; that should stir him up.' Joe chuckled as he looked down at the report again.

Harry cleared his throat.

Joe looked up again. 'Still here?'

'Yes sir,' he replied. 'It's just that I've got a bit of a problem.'

'Nothing catching I hope,' Joe quipped. Harry's hangdog expression prompted him to add, 'Sorry, what's the problem?'

'Well some of the emails on Mr Mardle senior's laptop seem to be password protected. I've rung him but he's unable to remember the password that he used back then.'

'How convenient.' said Joe. 'I wonder why he bothered doing that; so, what's happening now? Have you taken it down to the techies?'

'I have, sir.'

A couple of hours later, Dave was sitting in interview room A. The tape machine was running and Joe had started to question him.

'Thank you for coming in to speak to us, Mr Mardle.'

'No problem.'

Joe opened the file in front of him and studied it for a while.

Dave shuffled in his seat.

Joe looked up. 'I'm somewhat confused,' he said. 'I wonder; could you help me out?'

'Um, I'll try.'

Joe passed three printouts of emails across the table towards Dave. 'As you can see,' he said, 'these are copies of emails sent by Melissa Davies.'

'Uh-huh.'

'One to you, one to your mother, and one to Penny Fisher; they were sent on 24th July 2009. Do you notice anything strange about them?'

Dave retrieved his glasses from his head and examined the emails. 'Not really, no,' he said. 'Apart from the obvious fact that she's telling me and my mum a completely different story to the one she's telling Penny; is that what you mean?'

'No, that's not what I mean at all, no.'

'I'm sorry; what is it that you're expecting me to say?'

'I'm expecting you to be able to give me some explanation as to how it is that all these emails were sent from the same place.'

Dave went pale. 'The, the same place; I don't understand.'

'I'd have thought it was obvious; you see all these emails were sent from London, to be more precise, from Flat 4, Auriol Road, W14. That's where you live, isn't it, Mr Mardle?'

Dave swallowed and nodded.

'So, it seems to me,' said Joe. 'That you were the person who sent the emails to everyone, including to yourself it would seem, as if they were from Melissa Davies; now why would you do that, I wonder?' He glanced down at the file and slowly turned the pages, flattening each sheet by spreading the palm of his hand across it as he did so. He looked up again. 'Perhaps you could explain. And no more lies, there's a good lad; I can spot them a mile off.'

'It's, it's embarrassing,' muttered Dave.

'Don't worry about me and the Sergeant here; we've heard everything. You'd have to go some way to embarrass us, I can assure you.'

Dave took a deep breath. 'Everything up to the time that Melissa and I went up to the cottage in Yorkshire is true,' he began. 'The arguments and everything, you know, because I was jealous of her, of her, relationship with my bloody father! Anyway, we carried on arguing all the way up to Yorkshire, we slept in separate bedrooms that first night, bloody pathetic, right? Then, the following morning, the arguments continued until, that evening, she just upped sticks and walked out. She told me that she couldn't take anymore; she said her feelings for my father were complicated, or some such slush; she told me that ever since her parents had been killed her eyes had been opened, and, and she saw me for what I was; she was a bitch.'

'And what did she see you as, exactly?'

'You enjoy your job, don't you? I don't suppose that it's entered your head how *I* might have been feeling back then; I was totally humiliated when she walked out on me, totally;

I didn't have a clue that she was intending to leave, not a bloody clue.'

'I'm sure,' said Joe. 'If you could just answer the question.'

'Fine; have it your way! She saw me as a shallow, weak and selfish man; she said I needed to grow up. She was very forthright with her opinions, and the thing that hurt the most was that she was right. I *was* being selfish and I *did* need to grow up; Gran had told me that very same thing, several times. It was her idea that I should take Melissa up to the cottage actually; she said I needed to face reality.' Dave's voice cracked and he roughly wiped at his eyes. 'Sorry.'

Joe noted the lack of moisture around Dave's eyes. 'In your own time.'

Dave cleared his throat and went on. 'She saw me as a bully. I ask you, me? A bully; I *loved* her, with all my heart I loved her. I would have done anything for her, I wanted to protect and care for her, I wanted to be her family, and I wanted us to have children for God's sake! All perfectly normal stuff, and she just threw it all in my face.'

'So, you were angry with her?'

'Of course I was bloody angry, wouldn't you be?'

'And did the argument get out of control?'

'What are you saying? Are you suggesting I hurt her? That I hit her or something?' He leaned across the table and spoke very slowly, emphasising each word. 'I told you; I loved her. I would never hurt her.'

'Well, that's not quite true, is it?' said Joe.

'What do you mean?'

'Melissa Davies sent some emails in 2005, before she 'left', to her friend Penny Fisher stating that she was black and blue from bruising following arguments with you; so you *had* hit her. That, in my book, constitutes hurting her.'

'Yes, well; I bet they don't mention that *she* hit and scratched me first, though, do they?'

176

'You're saying that Melissa Davies used to hit a big strong man like you,' exclaimed Joe.

'Yes,' he screamed. 'Why is it that people find it so easy to accept a man hitting a woman but never a woman hitting a man? She could be quite spiteful and she was confident that I would never fight back; I used to grab her wrists and hold her away from me until she calmed down. I had to hold her quite firmly; and I admit she did bruise; but I never hit her; never.'

'If you say so,' said Joe. 'Right, going back to that evening at the cottage. She just left?'

Dave slammed his fists on the table. 'That's what I've just told you. Yes. She just bloody left.'

'Calm down, lad,' said Joe. 'It won't help your case if you lose your temper.'

'My case?' he yelled. 'What bloody case? I'm the victim here. I'm the one she abandoned.'

'And the emails?'

Dave took a deep slow breath. 'I admit that was stupid. I was, well, I was embarrassed. I had no bloody idea where she'd buggered off to; how could I admit that to my family? So I invented the story about her needing to get away from everything and Australia was the first place I thought of. I knew that her friend, Penny, lived out there and everything, but then everyone started getting concerned that they hadn't heard from her and so, to put their minds at rest, I started sending emails to Mum and to me as if they were from Melissa in Australia.'

'And the reason for the emails to Australia?'

'Same reason; Penny was sending more and more emails, each one more frantic than the last, asking Melissa if she was alright and why hadn't she been in touch.'

'And, just to be clear, whose computer did you use to send these false emails?'

'Melissa's,' he mumbled.

'Could you speak up; for the tape you understand.'

'I used Melissa's laptop,' he bellowed.

'Interesting; so, when she left the cottage in Yorkshire, she didn't take it with her?'

'She *didn't have* her laptop with her in Yorkshire.'

Joe opened another file on his desk. 'Remind me, when did you tell your family that Melissa had gone off to Australia?'

'I rang them that same evening.'

'I see, quick thinking then.'

'What's that supposed to mean?'

'No more than it says; quick thinking means what it implies, thinking quickly.' Glancing back at the file, Joe went on, 'Now, looking back, I see you told us that you drove back to London, presumably on the same evening Melissa Davies walked out, to collect all her belongings?'

Dave nodded.

'Now why would you do that; given that, as you have just said, you had no idea where she was going?'

Dave gave Joe a smug, patronising look. 'Well, as you have just said, Inspector, quick thinking. I reasoned that my family would understand that Melissa didn't want to face them and so she'd asked me to collect her things and send them out to Australia for her.'

'So, given that you didn't send Melissa's possessions out to Australia—we've checked—where are they all?'

'I burnt them,' he yelled. 'Happy now?'

'But not her laptop it would seem,' remarked Joe.

'No; obviously not.'

'Wouldn't burn? Or did you already have the idea about using it to send emails, you know, given that we've established that you're a quick thinker?'

'For God's sake,' Dave yelled. 'What are you trying to imply now? That I planned it all or something?'

'It's a possibility that cannot be ignored; all lines of enquiry need to be followed in the case of a missing person. I'm sure you understand. So, what was your reason for hanging onto her laptop?'

'I've no idea; I just did.'

'I see; well we'll need to take a look at that laptop. Where is it at the moment?'

'In my flat,' replied Dave curtly.

'Right; well, Sergeant Carter here will accompany you back home later to collect it.' Joe glanced down at his notes. 'Where were we? Ah, yes the burning; where exactly did you hold this burning ceremony?' asked Joe.

'It wasn't a bloody ceremony,' exclaimed Dave.

'If you say so,' said Joe. 'So, where did this burning take place?'

'In the back garden of the cottage.'

'And you stayed on at the cottage to carry out some renovation work; you built a pond as well, or so I hear.'

'I did, yes; I also installed a couple of ramps and a set of French windows; all very therapeutic activities.'

Joe didn't say a word; he just opened up another file.

'So, is that it, officer?' asked Dave jauntily. 'Or is there anything else I can help you with? Although what that could be, I'm not sure. The only person who could explain all this is Melissa, but of course no one knows where she is and presumably that was her intention. She's probably living it up somewhere, completely unaware of the mess she left behind.'

'There's just one more thing,' said Joe. 'I've got her bank records here and, to be honest, it's a bit of a worry.'

Dave kept quiet, and Joe was rewarded to see the smug expression drain away from his face.

'Yes, the strange thing is, her funds haven't been touched since July 2006; Friday the 21st to be exact, when it seems she withdrew £500. That's the same month and year that Melissa um, *left* you, isn't it?' said Joe. 'The bank, having had all their communications returned marked 'not known at this address', declared the account dormant in 2008; the money is sitting in a central fund. The government can legally claim it once it hasn't been touched for 15 years; they don't miss a trick, do they?'

Dave rocked his head slowly to the right and then the left, extending his neck muscles on either side. He said nothing.

'So how is it, do you think, that these letters got returned to the bank?'

Dave moved his shoulders in a small circle and still said nothing.

Joe sat quietly and waited.

'OK, OK; you win; I sent the bloody things back,' he yelled.

'I see,' said Joe. 'The thing is, and I find this most intriguing, the bank tells me that all these letters, as well as being marked, 'not known at this address', were also marked with the statement that they'd been 'opened in error'.'

'So?'

'I simply wondered why you bothered to open them,' mused Joe.

'I'd have thought that was bloody obvious.'

'Enlighten me.'

'I opened them, Inspector, because I hoped that her banking activity would give me a clue as to where she'd buggered off to.'

'And the lack of activity didn't alarm you?'

'Alarm me? Why the hell should it have alarmed me?'

'It's just that, bear with me—I'm a little confused—you have just explained how much you loved the girl, and how much you wanted to protect her. I would have thought that the fact that she hadn't touched her account for, what was it, three years?'

'About that, yes, I suppose,' muttered Dave.

'Yes, well, as I was saying, I would have thought that might have given you *some* cause for concern, for her whereabouts and her safety, I mean.'

Dave pushed himself back from the table so that his chair only had two legs in contact with the floor; he rocked back and forth and looked towards the ceiling. Slowly, he allowed the chair to right itself. He placed his elbows onto the table and lowered his head onto his hands. He moaned quietly. After a minute had ticked by, Dave raised his head. 'It didn't enter my head that it was odd, Inspector,' he said. 'I just assumed that Melissa had access to other funds. I was *trying* to find out where the hell she'd buggered off to.'

'So it wasn't another example of your quick thinking then?'

'What the hell's that supposed to mean?'

'Oh, I don't know,' said Joe. 'Let's suppose that Melissa just 'buggered off' into the night.'

'You don't need to *suppose*; that's what she bloody did!'

'*If* that was the case, opening her mail would be perfectly understandable as a means to ascertain where she'd gone, whereas simply returning them, unopened, would be seen as callous and uncaring and…'

'And so, the fact that I opened them *before* returning them shows that I wasn't callous and uncaring,' exclaimed Dave. 'What's your point?'

'My *point* is simple,' explained Joe. 'You've told us that you argued with Melissa that night and you've told us that the argument was quite heated, so maybe it went too far; you hit her, she fell, she struck her head and died.'

'Oh, don't be fucking ridiculous; so now you're saying that I disposed of her body and then set up the story of her escape to Australia to cover up my heinous deed.'

'Precisely,' said Joe. 'Hence my suggestion of quick thinking; you needed to open the correspondence from the bank before you returned them in order to maintain the illusion that she'd just 'buggered off."

Dave leaned across the desk and screamed into Joe's face. 'For the last bloody time, Inspector; I *loved* Melissa; the last time I saw her she was very much alive; I *don't know* where she went, or why she went. Jesus, even you haven't got a clue where she is, have you?'

'Not as yet,' said Joe, 'but fear not, I'm confident that will change soon.'

He made this statement with absolute conviction, but knew that his chances were slim. He felt in his gut that Dave had something to do with Melissa's disappearance; she could even be dead. The problem was, Dave's story sounded entirely plausible. Joe was convinced that the woman was dead. Murdered by Dave, possibly unintentionally and, in a blind panic, he'd made up the story of her phantom trip to Australia to cover his tracks. The question was, what had he done with the body? Without a body Joe could see no way forward.

Immediately after handing over Melissa's laptop to Harry, Dave drove over to Peckham. Maggie answered the door. 'Well hello; the prodigal returns. If you're looking for Erica, and I assume you must be, she's been out of her mind with worry; she expected to hear from you days ago. Anyway she's still at the café.' She glanced at the clock. 'She won't be back for another half an hour.'

Pushing past Maggie, he entered the flat. 'I'll wait then.'

'Oh, *do* come in,' said Maggie as Dave slumped down onto the settee. 'Make yourself at home why don't you.'

'Thanks,' he replied. 'You don't mind, do you?'

What could she say? He was Erica's boyfriend; it was Erica's flat. 'No, not at all,' she said, as graciously as she could manage, which wasn't very graciously at all.

'Coffee?'

'Smashing; milk, no sugar.'

Maggie turned away, growling to herself. She filled the kettle, checked the level, decided it was too full and so emptied some away; she checked it again and decided it wasn't full enough; she selected a cup, changed her mind and chose a mug; she opened the cupboard above the kettle and removed a coffee jar, studied it for a moment and then put it back; she picked a different brand. By the time she'd finished and walked back into the living room, brandishing the mug as if it were a masterpiece to be admired, Erica had arrived.

'Dave, goodness, what a surprise.'

Dave jumped up and rushed over to her. 'Forgive me for not getting in touch earlier; it's just all been so shitty,' he said. 'But, well, the thing is, I think it's about time that I explained everything.'

Oh, this should be good, thought Maggie.

'And you're going to tell the truth this time, the whole truth?' said Erica.

Dave clicked his heels and gave her a boy scout's salute; the smile he gave her would have melted the heart of the devil himself. 'I've just come from the station actually. I had another little chat with your friend, Joe.'

'I bet; 'helping the police with their enquiries,' were you?' hooted Maggie, before clearing her throat and apologising as Erica glared at her.

'Let's sit down,' suggested Erica, and giving Maggie a weak smile she added, 'Is that coffee for Dave?'

Maggie glanced at the mug clutched in her hand. 'This? Yes, sorry, did you want one?'

'Do you mind?'

'Of course not.' She handed Dave's coffee to him and made two more cups in record time. She sat opposite Dave and Erica.

'Thanks, Maggie,' said Erica.

'Yes, thanks, Maggie,' parroted Dave.

'Now come on, Dave; we're all ears,' said Erica.

'I can't tell you what a relief this is. I just want to get it all off my chest for once and for all; I'm sick of lying, especially to you, Erica; I'm so, so sorry.'

Oh give me a bloody break, thought Maggie. *He's going for the Oscar now.*

'Melissa never sent those emails,' he blurted. 'It was me; she just left me, no real explanation, no other man, or so she said, she just said she didn't want to be with me anymore. Can you imagine how much that hurt?'

Maggie felt like punching the air in triumph; she'd been right: he was a liar.

'So, you've confessed all to Inspector Reed then?'

'Yes, Maggie, I have,' said Dave. 'He was wise to the fact that Melissa never sent any emails. I made up all that guff about Australia and I'm ashamed to confess that I burnt all of her processions. Pathetic I know.'

'But why?' asked Erica.

'Why did I send the emails or why did I burn all her stuff?'

'Well, both, really.'

'The emails were to sustain the lie that she was in Australia; the burning because I was bloody angry that she'd just walked out on me.'

'So, where did she go then?' asked Maggie.

'That's the fucking point, Maggie; I didn't know back then and I don't bloody know now,' he yelled.

Erica reached across and took his hand in hers. 'Oh, Dave.'

He stared down at their entwined hands. 'Sorry; anyway, Inspector Reed found out about her bank account; I'd opened her mail from the bank. You see, I was trying to find out where she'd gone to, but it was useless; there was no activity recorded.'

'And you weren't worried by that fact?' asked Maggie.

'Jesus, you sound like Inspector bloody Reed,' snapped Dave.

Maggie took a sip of coffee, hiding her grin.

'And to answer your question, no, I wasn't worried at the time; I was too wrapped up in trying to find out where the bloody hell she was. The fact that she hadn't touched her account just said to me that she knew I'd look at her mail, and so, I don't know, I assumed she must have had funds elsewhere.'

'That's a possibility, I suppose,' said Erica.

'Oh, Erica, it's all such a bloody mess. Inspector Reed thinks I've done something to Melissa, hurt her, or worse; I mean it's ridiculous but I see how it looks, you know, from his point of view: the arguments; her disappearing; me burning her possessions; the emails; the lies; everything. But I swear to you I didn't do anything; she walked out on me and I was, well, I was embarrassed. If only I'd been honest right at the beginning and just told everybody that she'd left me and I didn't know where she'd gone, then, then I wouldn't be in this bloody mess.'

'But Melissa would still be missing, wouldn't she?' said Maggie.

Dave narrowed his eyes. 'Yes, Maggie; Melissa would still be missing, but, from a purely selfish point of view, her disappearance would not be casting any suspicion on me. As it is, I'm on the top of Inspector Reed's suspect list; he even accused me of *hitting* Melissa. I ask you! I would never do that, never; I didn't do anything, honestly.'

'Well, you did tell quite a lot of lies,' said Maggie. 'And, when I spoke with Penny, she said that Melissa was often covered in bruises after arguing with you; so how did that come about, I wonder?'

'There you go again, Inspector bloody Hunter-Lopez,' snarled Dave. 'Yes, I admit she had bruises…'

Erica gasped.

'Oh, Erica, no; not because I hit her, no; they were due to me defending myself; she used to hit and scratch me, so I had to restrain her; I didn't mean to bruise her.'

'*She* tried to hit *you*?' exclaimed Maggie. 'Oh, give me a break.'

'She could turn on you like a bloody wildcat,' exclaimed Dave. 'And I've just explained why I lied; I'm not saying it was the right thing to do, I mean obviously it wasn't, but it's too late now.'

'And so now, Melissa is officially a missing person,' said Erica in a small voice.

'And has been since she, um, walked out on you it would seem,' remarked Maggie.

'Yes, I know, which is awful and everything, but nothing to do with me; *she* was the one who left.' He pulled his hands free, snatched his glasses from his head and started polishing them with the bottom of his t-shirt. 'It wasn't really a huge surprise that Melissa didn't contact me; it was Mum, she was so upset, Erica. I was just telling a little white lie to make her feel better,' he said as he shoved his glasses back into his hair.

'Hardly a little white lie,' exclaimed Maggie. 'More like a massive deceit.'

'That's not how I saw it at the time, but now, well, I suppose if Mum had known the truth from the beginning she would have reported Melissa as missing years ago; as it is, with it being so long ago…'

She could be anywhere,' said Erica.

'Exactly,' exclaimed Dave. 'And she obviously doesn't want anyone to know where she is; that's why she hasn't touched her bank account, you know, to avoid setting up a trail or whatever it's called.'

'I wonder how she's managed to survive all these years without any money?' said Maggie.

Erica looked at Dave. 'Dave?'

'Well, I don't know do I; how does anyone survive without money? She's a good looking woman; I'm sure she's fine. She probably found herself a rich sugar daddy or something. She could even have changed her name.' He stared into Erica's eyes. 'Erica, I swear to you I never hurt Melissa. Please tell me you believe me,' he pleaded.

Erica looked at him long and hard. He returned her gaze. With a furtive glance towards Maggie, she said, 'I believe you.'

Maggie sighed audibly.

He pulled Erica towards him and they hugged. 'Oh, thank God; we can move on now, can't we, Erica; put all this behind us.'

Erica gave a muffled reply. 'Yes.' She withdrew and asked, 'But what about Melissa?'

'The police are dealing with all that; they'll find her and if, when they do, she tells them that she doesn't want anyone else to know where she is then that's her right. I want to concentrate on us now; alright?'

Erica nodded.

'Can I see you tomorrow? We'll have lunch or something?'

'That would be lovely.'

'Excellent; I'll pick you up at noon, OK?'

'OK.'

Maggie followed him to the door, closed it slowly and stood with her hand clasped firmly onto the handle for a moment before turning back to face Erica. 'Tell me you didn't buy all that crap.'

'Crap?'

'Yes, Erica, crap! He's a nasty piece of work; a charming liar, and they're the worse.'

'But he's just explained…'

Maggie stared at her friend. 'No, Erica, he has simply made up another story.'

'You don't know that!'

'I know one thing for bloody certain,' said Maggie. 'He *did* hit Melissa…'

Eyes blazing, Erica screamed, 'How could you possibly know that?'

'Because Penny told me; she said Melissa rang her to say that Dave had hit her.'

Erica snorted. 'Well, she would say that wouldn't she? She's hardly likely to admit that she was the violent one.'

Maggie chewed her lip and sighed deeply. 'Think about it, Erica; how many variations of a theme has he told you about his relationship with Melissa? I mean he never even admitted to you that Melissa, the woman his grandmother said you bore a striking resemblance to, was his ex girlfriend did he?'

'No he didn't; but we've been over this before, and he's explained his reasons why.'

'Oh, yes; he's very good at explaining, I'll give him that.'

'Maggie, you're being unfair. At least it's all out in the open now and, as Dave said, he and I can move on.'

Maggie gave up.

Back at the station, Joe was working late. He was concentrating on the transcript of his interview with Dave. He was missing something, he was certain; something that Dave had said at the beginning of the interview. He played the tape through again and again, until at last, triumphantly, he hit the stop button.

'That's it,' he exclaimed. 'She just 'upped sticks and walked out'.' He thumped his desk and continued explaining to the wall. 'The cottage is bloody miles from anywhere; she didn't take the car—Dave drove it down to London that same evening. So, how did she leave and where did she go?'

He picked up the phone and rang Dave Mardle's number. There was no answer. He checked his watch; only just gone eight pm. He rang The Retreat.

'Hello,' said Deborah.

'Ah, Mrs Mardle, I'm so sorry to bother you on a Saturday evening, but I'm trying to get hold of your son and he doesn't seem to be answering his mobile.'

'That's because it's switched off, Inspector; strict rule in this house, no phones on while we're eating...'

'I've disturbed your evening meal. I can only apologise again.'

'No need; we've just finished,' said Deborah. 'Hang on; I'll fetch him.'

Moments later Dave picked up. 'What now?' he retorted.

'Good evening,' said Joe. 'Sorry to disturb you, but there was just one more thing I wanted to check.'

'What?'

'Saturday evening, when Melissa left Black Sheep Cottage, how exactly did she leave?'

'What do you mean, *how* did she leave? What are you suggesting now? That I had her manacled to the fireplace or something? How do you *think* she left? She walked out the bloody door!'

'The thought that you might have had her manacled to the fireplace is an interesting idea,' remarked Joe, 'but, I have to confess, not one that crossed my mind. No, it's simply that the cottage is very remote, as I understand it, and of course it would have been dark...'

'I don't bloody know; I expect she rang George.'

'George?' said Joe.

'The local taxi man,' bellowed Dave. 'He was the postman too, not sure if he still is, he was quite old; I wouldn't be surprised if the old codger isn't dead by now.'

'And does this George have a surname?'

'Of course he bloody does!'

'So, what is it?'

'Haven't a clue.'

'Be a good lad and ask your mother.'

Dave banged the phone down muttering expletives. Joe heard retreating footsteps. Moments later Dave snatched up the phone. 'Broddle,' he snapped. 'Happy now?'

'Yes, thank you so much for your help, and sorry again...'

The line went dead. 'Bloody nerve,' exclaimed Joe. 'The bastard hung up on me.' He slammed his own phone down and thought for a moment. A smile crossed his lips. *Richard,* he thought. *He moved back to Northallerton after a stint in the Met; I wonder....*

Richard Soames was an old colleague of Joe's, the classic tall policeman. He'd gone back to Yorkshire after his marriage, back in 1999. Joe unfolded his map as he dialled Richard's number and saw that, as he'd hoped, Black Sheep Cottage was on Richard's patch.

'Joe Reed. As I live and breathe,' exclaimed Richard. 'How the devil are you...?' He broke off as a coughing fit overtook him. 'Sorry about that; I'm down to 20 a day for all the good its doing.'

'Last time we spoke you said you were giving up.'

'What can I say?'

'How's Madeline settling in?'

'The Driscoll girl? Fine; you know she got her promotion to Inspector?'

'Yes, and about bloody time. Bonehead Marshall was never going to agree to it.'

'She's in the middle of a tricky child abduction case at the minute. Anyway, come on, you didn't ring me to chat about your old Sergeant, so to what do I owe the pleasure? I'm betting a hundred to one this isn't a social call.'

'You know me so well,' laughed Joe. 'I'm just tying up loose ends really.'

'Pull the other one, mate,' said Richard. 'You're working on a case and you suspect foul play. Am I right or am I right?'

'You're right.'

'Thought so; what's it all about?'

Joe briefly outlined the case and asked him if he knew George Broddle.

'Everyone knows George,' exclaimed Richard. 'Life and soul of our little village, and your man's right; he's the postman and local taxi service round here, vital given that there's no public transport available. Marvellous chap. Lived here in Cold Kirby all his life.'

'Still alive?'

'Without question; built of sturdy stuff, these Yorkshire folk.'

'Do you think he would remember if he picked up Melissa Davies from Black Sheep Cottage near Scawton back in July 2006?'

'Was she pretty?'

'Very.'

'Then he'll remember,' said Richard. 'Tell you what, email me the girl's photo and I'll ask George tonight, it's our Saturday night Dominoes match in the Bull and Feather.'

'I'm sending it as we speak,' said Joe.

'I see,' said Richard. 'So, you had it all set up and ready to go, did you?'

'Got me again,' confessed Joe. 'It should be with you now.'

Richard opened his email. 'What a stunner; if George picked this one up he'll certainly remember,' he said. 'Listen, you should come up for a visit some time. Sally would love to see you.'

'I might just do that, Richard, I just might. Talk to you tomorrow.'

Richard rang Joe at home at seven the following morning with the news that George did remember Melissa Davies, but said that he'd never picked her up from Black Sheep Cottage on her own; he'd only ever picked her up with the Mardle family when they used to go over to The Green Man in Scawton for an evening meal.

Joe dressed and drove over to Auriol Road. Dave answered the door, dishevelled and bleary eyed. 'It's Sunday bloody morning! Don't you ever sleep?' demanded Dave.

'Just one more question…'

'You said that last night, *Inspector*, so got that wrong then.'

'Do you want to chat on the landing or can I come in?'

Dave threw the door open wide. 'Oh, don't mind me. Come in, why don't you, make yourself at home. Shall I be civil…?'

'That would make a pleasant change,' said Joe.

Dave gritted his teeth. 'Coffee?'

'Milk, three sugars.'

While Dave made the coffee, Joe did a quick scan of the room; there were certainly no photographs of Melissa in the living room. He wandered over to the window next to the bedroom door and peered in; again, no photographs.

'Lost something?' asked Dave as he entered the living room, bearing a small tray that he dumped onto a modern glass monstrosity of a coffee table.

'No, no, it's just that I notice you have no photographs of Melissa, the love of your life; still, understandable I suppose,' he said as he picked up a framed photograph of Erica displayed on the windowsill. 'It would be a bit insensitive, even for you, to flaunt the ex in front of the current.'

Dave snatched the photograph from Joe's hand and replaced it.

'Is everything alright? You seem edgy.'

'As it happens,' announced Dave, 'your suggestion that something awful might have happened to Melissa has rather upset me.'

'Oh, dear me; I *am* sorry to hear that,' remarked Joe.

'Your concern is admirable, Inspector,' he said. Returning to the coffee table he picked up the mugs and thrust one at Joe. 'Now, can we get on; you wanted to ask me something?'

'It's a funny thing. I was sitting in my office last night going over the case, my notes, statements, reports and recordings, you get the picture.'

Dave nodded impatiently. 'That's part of your job isn't it; to review *the case*?'

'Indeed; anyway, it's a small old world, I was sitting there and I suddenly remembered about Richard, lovely chap, solid and reliable, salt of the earth.'

'And who, pray, is Richard?'

'A colleague of mine; works up in Yorkshire as it happens, and, wonder of wonders, Black Sheep Cottage is on his patch, so that's a stroke of luck isn't it?'

Some of the colour drained from Dave's face. 'On his patch, you say?'

'Yes, and not only that,' Joe went on, 'but he's a good friend of your taxi man, George Broddle; they play dominoes together.'

'Fascinating,' remarked Dave.

Joe noted a small tremor in Dave's voice. He pressed on. 'Yes, and it seems that George didn't pick up your Melissa Davies from Black Sheep Cottage back in July 2006. Odd that; you did say that she got a taxi, didn't you?'

Dave took several deep breaths, followed by a huge swig of coffee, and nearly choked.

'Steady on there, lad.'

Dave spluttered. 'Went down the wrong way; give me a moment.'

Joe pictured the cogs turning in Dave's head.

'He remembers who he picked up from over seven years ago? I find that very hard to believe.'

'Oh, trust me,' said Joe. 'I'm assured that George has an excellent memory, especially if it involves a pretty girl. So, given that we have now established that she did not, as you claimed yesterday, leave by taxi, it begs the question: how did Melissa leave the cottage that evening?'

'I didn't claim she'd left by taxi,' exploded Dave. 'I merely *suggested* that she might have rung George; after all, we had used him in the past.'

'So, you simply let her go out into the night all alone with no clear idea of how she was going to fare.'

'Yes,' shouted Dave. He took a breath. 'In fact, I encouraged her to leave.'

'Encouraged her?'

'Yes. I may even have given her a gentle shove.'

'How gentle?'

'Just enough to push her outside so that I could close the door on her; I didn't hurt her if that's what you're implying.'

'I wasn't implying anything; I was simply seeking clarification. So, you gave her a gentle shove out into the night and shut the door; hardly the action of a man in love.'

'I told you before,' barked Dave. 'I was bloody angry with her; you can be angry with someone and still love them, you know. She was going on and on about how she had nothing; no family; no friends; she kept fiddling with that bloody stupid butterfly necklace, saying it was the only connection she had to her mother. I mean, how ludicrous, a silly piece of sentimental, crappy jewellery.'

'And you told her that, did you?'

'Too right I did! *And* I told her she had me, and if that wasn't enough then she could bugger off.'

Arrogant fool, thought Joe. 'And you weren't worried at all about sending her out onto the desolate moors, alone and upset?'

'It's Yorkshire, not bloody Siberia,' retorted Dave. 'Anyway, I'm pretty certain she was lying; there must have been another man, why else would she leave? And if, as you say, George didn't pick her up, then I'm sure that as soon as she was out of sight of the cottage she rang him to come and get her.'

'And who might that have been?'

'Jesus,' exploded Dave. 'How the hell would I know?'

'I just wondered; you suggested it was a man; so, did she have any male friends in the area?'

Emphasising each word, he replied, 'I don't bloody know!' Dave shrugged and went on. 'Anyway, I set off back to London soon after she left and I didn't see her wandering the lanes, so, there you go.' He took another swig of coffee before slamming his mug down. The coffee sloshed and slowly spread across the thick glass table like blood oozing from a wound.

'Fuck, fuck, fuck,' he yelled as he watched the coffee inch towards the edge of the table.

Joe set his untouched coffee down onto the windowsill. 'I'll fetch a cloth.'

'Just leave it,' yelled Dave. 'Is that it, Inspector, or have you suddenly remembered something else you want to ask me?'

'No, that's it for the moment,' said Joe.

Chapter 12

Superintendent Marshall called Joe into his office at 2 pm the next day. 'I've read your report and it seems pretty clear to me that the suspicions, or *gut feelings* you have about this Dave Mardle are completely groundless. There is *no* evidence whatsoever of foul play; this woman,' he shuffled through the report, 'Melissa Davies, simply took it upon herself to walk away.'

With his fists clenched, Joe retorted, 'The man lied for years, sir, and if Penny Fisher hadn't turned up, he would have continued to lie.'

'The man accepted that; he explained his reasons; all perfectly reasonable as far as I'm concerned. You cannot continue to make accusations against the man without a shred of evidence; you need to let it go. I'm closing the case.'

'But…'

Marshall's face flushed. He stood, leaned over the desk and banged his fist down violently; so violently that Joe jumped. 'Enough!' exploded Marshall. 'The case is closed; you need to inform the relevant parties of that fact and move on.'

'If I could just follow up on the Yorkshire connection, sir,' pleaded Joe. 'There may well be something…'

'Did you not hear what I said?' demanded Marshall. 'The case is closed and that is my final word on the matter.'

Joe said nothing. He gave Marshall a curt nod, turned on his heal and left the office, making sure that he closed the door behind him with sufficient force to cause a satisfying slam of wood on wood. He marched down the corridor, muttering expletives, and crashed into his own office. He walked to the window and looked out, seeing nothing but a black mist. The thought of speaking to Dave Mardle to inform him that he'd effectively won stuck like sour vomit in his throat.

A gentle tap at his door caused him to whirl round.

'Sorry to disturb you, sir,' said Harry clutching several manila folders tightly to his chest like a protective shield. 'But these have just landed on my desk and um, Marshall…'

'Fuck bloody Marshall; fuck him to hell and back,' Joe said. 'No, amend that instruction; fuck him to hell and fucking leave him there.'

Harry placed the folders onto Joe's desk. He removed his notebook from his top pocket and, with pen poised, he said, 'So, that's fuck him to hell, and *don't* bring him back, correct?'

Joe could feel the smile creeping onto his face. He picked the folders up. He opened the first one, sighed and dropped it back onto his desk. He opened another, sighed again and chucked it aside. He glanced at his watch. 'Have you eaten yet?'

Harry had, but replied, 'No.'

Snatching his jacket from the back of the chair, Joe said, 'Right; come on.'

Harry's eyes slipped towards the manila folders.

'Nothing urgent; come on, get your coat.'

Erica greeted them warmly as they entered the café a short while later. 'Hello there Inspector; Dave tells me you paid him a visit yesterday. He was quite excited when you turned up so early on a Sunday morning; he thought you'd come with good news and that you'd found Melissa.'

Jesus, thought Joe, *the man's a professional liar.*

'No, sadly not,' he said. 'I was just seeking clarification on some details around the time that Melissa Davies left the cottage.'

'He'd assumed she'd rung for a taxi because there was no sign of her on the road when he left the cottage shortly

197

afterwards, you know, to drive back to London,' said Erica, her wide eyes full of concern.

'Yes,' said Joe. 'So he said.'

'Anyway; what can I get you both?'

'Two coffees and two All Day Breakfasts please.'

Harry's face paled. 'Um…'

'What?'

'Um, well, I'm not sure if I could manage an All Day Breakfast.'

'Nonsense, lad,' said Joe as he poked Harry's thin frame. 'You could do with a bit of building up.'

Erica bought their coffees to the table. 'So, what happens now, with the case, I mean?'

Harry gave Joe a sideways glance.

'Unfortunately,' said Joe, 'the case is now closed. We're going to speak with the family later.'

'So, what, you just stop looking?'

'For the moment,' said Joe. 'The case remains on file and, in the event of any new information turning up, it will be reopened.'

'I see,' said Erica. 'Poor Dave; it looks like he'll never know what happened.'

Joe tensed his jaw. 'Yes, poor Dave,' he mumbled.

'And then of course there's Penny; she'll be devastated too; what with her father being so ill and now, when she finds out the case has been closed, well it's all so, so…'

'Unsatisfactory,' offered Joe. 'Yes, I quite agree; all very unsatisfactory. But, fear not, I shall be keeping my ear to the ground.'

Back at the station Harry rang Penny with the news, and then he accompanied Joe to speak with Mr and Mrs Mardle at The Retreat. Deborah opened the door to them.

'Inspector, Sergeant, do come in,' she said. 'My son informs us that you called in to see him yesterday, something about George not remembering picking up

198

Melissa. He was quite taken aback; he'd been convinced that Melissa must have rung him. Still, I suppose she must have been collected by a friend, who knows?'

He's consistent; I'll give him that, thought Joe.

Mr Mardle and Phyllis joined them in the living room.

'It's all so sad,' said Phyllis. 'I wonder where she is. My grandson is full of remorse that he wasn't honest with us all from the beginning. Fancy making up that convoluted story about her going to Australia, I ask you. And the trouble with stories like that is that they rapidly escalate out of control, with one lie leading to another and so on. He got himself into a right old pickle; still, he's told us all the truth now and that's something at least.'

Joe felt the bile rise in his throat. 'Yes, as you say, that's something at least. We've just come to let you know that the case is closed, pending further information. You've all been most helpful,' he said. He turned to Mr Mardle. 'I don't want to disturb your son at work,' he said. 'Would you be good enough to let him know we called round and the case is now closed?'

Dave gave Joe a hearty thump on the back. 'Absolutely, Inspector, I'd be delighted. So, I assume I can expect my laptop back now?'

Joe blinked. 'Your laptop, yes, sorry. Carter, Mr Mardle's laptop?'

'It's with our technical team at the moment; I'll get onto them as soon as I get back to the station,' said Harry.

'Excellent; is there anything else?'

Plenty, thought Joe.

'No, that's it,' he replied. 'Come on, Sergeant; work to do.'

They drove back to the station in silence.

Inside, Marshall pounced.

'I assume you've just got back from informing the Mardle family that this missing person's case is now closed,' he said curtly and, without waiting for confirmation, he continued. 'I gave Carter here a set of files; all urgent cases. I need them sorted, and I need them sorted *now*. I want results, Reed, do you hear me, results; so get to it.'

Joe stomped back to his office with Harry trailing behind. All thoughts of Mr Mardle's laptop vanished from his head as he began to go through the tedious cases that Marshall had foisted on him.

In the park the following day, Dave and Erica were enjoying their lunch in the sunshine. 'Apparently we're in for something of a mini heat wave over the next few weeks,' said Dave. 'And I don't know about you, but now all this Melissa stuff is out of the way...'

'But she's still missing,' said Erica.

He reached across the bench and took Erica's hands into his. He turned them over and examined them closely. He didn't look up. 'I know, Erica; but I think we have to face the fact that she made a conscious decision all those years ago to escape out of our lives and we have to respect that; after all, she's a grown woman.'

'I know,' agreed Erica, 'but...'

Dave looked up, his deep brown eyes moist and wide. 'No more buts,' he crooned. 'Look at you; I'm so lucky. I was a bloody idiot back then. All those lies; I wove such a tangled web and then trapped myself in it. Mum has been brilliant; she, and Gran, both understand that I made all that stuff up about Melissa going to Australia to protect my own stupid pride. And Dad, well Dad, took me aside and had a quiet word with me.'

'About what?'

'About me and my lies; although he understood that the false emails were sent with the best of intentions, he said it was irresponsible of me; I should have told the truth.'

'Has he got any ideas about where Melissa might be?'

'Not really, no; he's certain that Melissa's fine, wherever she might be; he reckons, like you, that if anything *had* happened to her then we would have heard, it would have been in the news, you know, if she'd been killed or something, and he couldn't understand why Inspector Reed hadn't come to the same conclusion much sooner, especially after I admitted that Melissa hadn't gone to Australia. I've caused so much trouble and upset, especially to you. I'm so, so sorry.' There was a crack in his voice, he closed his eyes briefly, and again looked down at Erica's small hands still resting in his. 'I was an idiot.'

Erica squeezed Dave's hands. 'It's all over now,' she said. 'And, if nothing else, you've learnt a valuable lesson.'

Dave looked up again and gave Erica a dazzling smile. 'Oh, Erica, I have, I have; you are *the* most amazing person and I love you so much, really I do.'

'I know,' she whispered. 'And I, like your father, understand why you lied but, again, like your father, I think you were foolish.'

'In my defence; I was only 24.' He shuffled closer. 'I've had a word with Mum and Dad and they both agree that a couple of weeks away would do me the world of good; Dad's already spoken to Philip and he's agreed to look after the shop, and so I was hoping that we could go away together.'

'Um, right, and um, where were you thinking, because I…'

'It's alright; *not* Yorkshire, although I would like to meet your parents sometime soon. No, I was thinking we could go to Paris; we could go on the Orient Express, they do 12-day excursions, hotel included; what do you think?'

'The Orient Express,' exclaimed Erica. 'Wow; well, I don't need to think too long and hard about *that* suggestion; the answer is, yes please.'

'Brilliant; so, how about the beginning of August?'

'Um, no, sorry, I'm pretty sure that slot's taken.' Erica rummaged in her bag. 'It's written down in my diary, *if* I can find it; ah, here we are; yep, the earliest we can go is the 16th.'

'That's when we shall go then.'

Maggie, like Joe, was convinced that Dave had replaced one set of lies for another, but she knew that there was no point trying to convince Erica of that; after all, she didn't have a scrap of evidence. When she found out that the police had closed the case she made a decision; she'd do a bit of digging for herself, and the news that Erica and Dave were to go off on a jolly jaunt to Paris gave her the ideal opportunity; she'd go up to Yorkshire then.

On a scorching day towards the end of July, Maggie confessed her plan to Winton. 'What do you think?' she asked. 'Am I mad?'

'Probably,' said Winton, 'But I admire your motives; you and I both want Erica to be happy, and if there is *any* doubt about Dave, and personally I have to agree with you—I think there most definitely is doubt—then we ought to do all we can to ascertain the truth.'

'You said, 'we'; will you come with me?'

'If you'll have me,' replied Winton with a crooked smile.

'In a heart beat, Winton, in a heart beat.'

Winton busied himself with some unnecessary rearrangement of fruit at the front of his stall and, without looking at Maggie, he said, 'I shall look forward to it.'

'So will I,' said Maggie smiling to herself. 'Oh, by the way, has Jay-Jay heard anything from Penny about how her father is?'

With an apple in each hand, Winton turned towards Maggie. 'You must have some sort of sixth sense,' he said. 'Penny rang Jay-Jay this morning. Her father passed on a couple of weeks ago. She's staying with her mother for a few weeks more and then flying back to Australia.'

'Oh, that is sad news,' said Maggie. 'And I expect Jay-Jay is upset; I got the impression he was rather taken with Penny.'

'He's besotted with her,' said Winton. 'He's hoping he'll be able to accompany her back to Australia.'

Maggie's eyes widened. 'What, to stay?'

'No, no; just for a visit,' said Winton. 'Mum's thrilled, not that he's going to Australia of course, no; she's thrilled for Jay-Jay because she rather took to Penny herself. She's always believed that every hoe ha dem tick a bush.'

'Sorry, you've lost me.'

Winton carefully replaced the apples, took hold of Maggie's hands and stared deep into her eyes. 'It means there's a perfect someone for everyone.'

Saturday the 17th August, the day after Erica and Dave left for Paris, Maggie and Winton set off for Yorkshire. They'd booked into Moor-House, the same family hotel that Erica and Dave had stayed in. Mrs Fletcher, the receptionist, became quite flustered when she clapped eyes on the imposing figure of Winton, and her hand shook a little as she handed them their key. 'Welcome to Yorkshire,' she said. 'I hope your room is to your liking. It's at the front; it has a marvellous view across the moors.'

Sitting on the terrace the following day, Winton glanced at the darkening sky. 'Looks like a storm is brewing.'

'Who for, us or Dave?'

'Us,' said Winton. 'But, if you're right, then possibly there's an even bigger storm brewing for Dave.'

'I did make some notes,' said Maggie.

'Ever the professional investigator,' said Winton.

Maggie gave Winton a playful swipe. She delved into her handbag and removed one of Erica's spare notebooks. She opened it and pressed the spine flat with the palm of her hand.

'Taking it as read that Melissa didn't go to Australia, I've just noted down some of Dave's other lies,' she said.

'Like?'

'Like Dave saying that Melissa just walked out on him and called for a taxi.'

Winton held up his hand.

'What?'

'To be fair, he only *suggested* she might have rung for a taxi.'

Maggie gave a dismissive wave. 'Whatever; he certainly lied about hitting Melissa.'

'But, how do we know that's a lie?'

'How do we know,' said Maggie. 'We know, Winton, because Penny *told* us that Dave hit Melissa.'

'Yes, but Penny is only reporting what Melissa told her; we don't *know* if it's true.'

'Are you saying you believe Dave? I thought…'

'I'm just saying we need to keep an open mind.'

'Alright; well, what about the fact that he opened all her mail from the bank?'

'Like he said, he opened them in the hope of finding out where she'd disappeared to.'

'And yet didn't seem concerned when he saw no activity; not worried about how she was surviving or anything.'

'Because he believed she had access to other funds.'

'That's what he *said*, yes,' said Maggie.

'You have to admit it's plausible.'

'Oh, for goodness sake,' exclaimed Maggie. 'What are you now, Dave's bloody lawyer?'

Winton leaned back in his chair with his arms behind his head and closed his eyes. After a short while he allowed his chair to right itself, opened his eyes and asked, 'When Dave brought Melissa up to the cottage to, as he claimed, save their relationship, was that the first time they'd been up here?'

Maggie, arms folded across her chest, replied. 'I don't think so. Why, what are you suggesting now: she had some lover up here that Dave knew nothing about and he's done her in?'

'No, Maggie, I wasn't suggesting that. I was just thinking that they might have been out to a local pub and somebody may have witnessed Dave's behaviour towards Melissa.' He pursed his lips and screwed up his eyes. 'I'm trying to help, you know.'

'Sorry,' said Maggie. 'Let's ask the receptionist where the nearest pub or restaurant is to Black Sheep Cottage.'

'And we could also ask your friends,' suggested Winton.

'My friends?'

'Yes; the ones you stayed with in Yorkshire last year,' explained Winton.

Maggie shuffled about on her seat and started rearranging the condiments on the small table.

'It *was* Yorkshire, wasn't it?' he asked. 'I appreciate that it's a large county; I just wondered...'

Maggie leaned back and placed her palms flat on the table. 'Yes, Winton, it was Yorkshire; they live in Northallerton.'

'And is that far from here?'

'No, it's not far; but the thing is, oh, dear.'

Winton placed his hands over hers. 'What's the matter? Have I spoken out of turn? I didn't...'

'No, Winton; you haven't spoken out of turn, it's just that I wasn't entirely truthful about my reason for coming up to Yorkshire. I hadn't known you very long back then, you see. Helen and Patrick are not exactly friends; well, they *are* friends, it's just that, well, what I'm trying to say is that they're, um, they're, oh shit.'

'I *have* spoken out of turn,' said Winton.

'No,' exclaimed Maggie. 'You haven't.' She took a deep breath. 'They're the people who adopted my baby, Winton.'

'Your baby; right, fair enough.'

'She's three now,' said Maggie. 'And she's very beautiful.'

'I would expect no less, given who her mother is,' said Winton with a warm smile. 'And the father?'

'A shallow minded dick head,' said Maggie.

'I take it you are no longer enamoured with this man.'

'Correct,' said Maggie. 'So I'm afraid I was as guilty as Dave in telling you a lie.'

'Nonsense,' said Winton. 'An entirely different situation; and, as you said, not a lie as such, merely a part truth.'

Maggie smiled weakly.

'Anyway,' said Winton. 'Let's get that list of pubs and restaurants and then we can draw up a plan of action.'

Rather surprisingly, given the remoteness of the cottage, there was a huge number of pubs and restaurants in the near vicinity. They therefore decided to visit Black Sheep Cottage to ask the current owners if they knew of a place that the Mardle family used to frequent. Maggie didn't hold out much hope but, as Winton said, it was worth a try. And they were in luck; Jason and Nicole were very helpful and told them about a small family run restaurant called the 'Green Man' that Deborah had recommended. It was situated just a few miles away. Maggie and Winton managed to book a table for that Wednesday evening.

The drive to the Green Man, just outside Scawton, proved to be quite a challenge. The storm that Winton predicted had arrived, yet though rain lashed down and the wind howled, the air was thick with heat. The restaurant was set back from the road and surrounded by trees. There was a small raised terrace at the front with steps and wheelchair access. On the terrace were two oak tables, currently lashed to the railings. Several huge, multicoloured, Chinese paper lanterns lighted the inside; original oil paintings, depicting Yorkshire life, were displayed on the white painted walls, and the floor was slate-tiled.

Maggie and Winton were shown to a small bar area at the back of the restaurant. 'This is a beautiful place,' said Maggie to the man behind the bar.

'Thank you,' he said. 'Are you up here on holiday?'

'Sort of,' said Maggie.

'Sounds intriguing,' he said.

'Actually,' she said. 'We were wondering if you remember a couple that used to come here regularly, up to about 2009; specifically during 2005. A Dave and Deborah Mardle. Deborah would sometimes have been in a wheelchair as she suffered from MS.'

A female voice behind them exclaimed, 'Oh, absolutely; I remember them; a lovely couple.'

Maggie whirled around. 'And did a young lady ever accompany them? Small, with brown hair...'

'Melissa, do you mean?'

Maggie gripped Winton's hand. 'That's her; yes.'

'She was their son's girlfriend, he was called Dave too,' she said. 'A selfish brute of a man, he was.'

'Susan,' exclaimed the man behind the bar.

'Well, I'm sorry, John, but I speak as I see,' Susan declared. 'And as far as I'm concerned that boy was a nasty piece of work; I can't see what she saw in him. How is she these days? Not still with that boy, I bet.'

'No, she isn't,' said Winton. 'It seems she's disappeared.'

'Disappeared?' exclaimed John. 'When?'

'In 2006, shortly after she and Dave came up to stay at Black Sheep Cottage,' said Maggie.

'So, she did a runner. I'm not the least bit surprised,' Susan continued. 'I distinctly remember a very nasty event when they all came for a meal years ago; it must have been, oh, let me think, seven or eight years ago, I suppose. Melissa was going to sit next to Dave, the father I mean, and young Dave kicked up a hell of a fuss. You'd have thought she'd elected to sit at an entirely different table. Mr Mardle told his son to grow up and Dave told him to mind his own f'ing business. Deborah tried to calm everyone down, Melissa was in tears, and Dave, after trying to physically force Melissa to move, stormed out, telling them all to go to hell. All very awkward.' She turned to her husband. 'Do you remember, John?'

'Difficult to forget,' he said. 'Mr and Mrs Mardle and Melissa stayed and ate their meal, but it was a very strained affair.'

'And did you ever see Melissa again?'

Susan took a moment. 'No, I don't think we did. So, has no one got any idea where she is now?'

'It would seem not, no,' said Maggie.

'That is a worry,' said Susan. 'I hope she's alright.'

'Well, that's just it,' said Maggie. 'I'm quite concerned that she's not alright. It seems that she left the cottage after a row with Dave late one evening back in 2006 and was never seen again.'

'She might have been picked up by George, our local postman and one-man taxi service. Hold on, I'll get you his card.' She handed them the menus she'd been holding onto for the entire conversation. 'This is our menu for this week; limited, but all local and freshly prepared on site. Have a look and I'll fetch that card for you.'

'Thank you,' said Maggie as she took the proffered menus. 'But don't worry about that card; it's already been established that Melissa wasn't picked up by George.'

'I am surprised,' said Susan. 'The cottage is very remote.'

Maggie and Winton woke the next morning to find that the storm was still raging. The rain lashed down in sheets and lightning forked across the sky; several roads had been closed due to flash floods, and there had been reports of buildings being struck by lightning. The proprietor of the hotel said he'd never seen the like in all the years that they'd lived here, and suggested that whatever plans Maggie and Winton had for the day were likely to be unfulfilled.

Over breakfast Maggie peered morosely out of the large bay window at the rain-battered back garden.

'It's all been rather a waste of time, hasn't it,' she groaned.

'Not entirely,' said Winton.

'How do you mean?'

'Well, we've got further evidence that Dave was jealous of his father's relationship with Melissa, and that he could be a bit rough with her, which is contrary to his assertion that she was the feisty one, with him playing the role of the pacifier.'

'True,' said Maggie. 'But we're no closer to finding out where Melissa went that night; it's hopeless.'

Winton concentrated on his bacon and eggs. Maggie was right; they were no further forward, not really. He glanced up at her as she continued to stare out of the window and immediately looked down again when she turned towards him. Maggie stared at Winton as he slowly cut a piece of bacon ready to spear onto his fork. He glanced up again, fork held midway between the plate and his slightly open mouth. This time, he held her gaze. Neither spoke. Winton put down his fork. He reached across the table and took hold of Maggie's hand. He smiled warmly. She smiled back.

'I'm not really very hungry,' said Winton.

'Nor me,' said Maggie. She again peered out of the window. 'It looks like we're stuck here for the day.'

Winton pushed his chair back. 'So, come on, let's not waste it,' he said.

Maggie grinned. 'My, my, sir, what *do* you mean?'

The proprietor watched them as they scuttled back upstairs. 'Lucky sod,' he muttered.

Chapter 13

As Winton and Maggie were staring into each other's eyes over breakfast, Joe was staring out of his office window at the London rain continuing to pour down. The pile of folders on his desk didn't seem to be getting any smaller, and his thoughts dwelt on how many years he had left before he could retire gracefully. The insistent ringing of his phone dragged his attention back to the present.

'Morning, Joe; Richard here, and you'll never guess where I am.'

'Not a clue.'

'I'm standing in the garden, or rather, what's left of the garden, of Black Sheep Cottage.'

'Black Sheep Cottage you say; the cottage that Melissa Davies allegedly stormed out of back in 2006?'

'That's the one, mate.'

'Bloody hell; are you telling me you've actually found something?' asked Joe. 'And what do you mean you're standing in *what's left of the garden?*'

'To answer your second question first, I don't know if you are aware, but we are experiencing a bit of weather up here in the north.'

'Forget the bloody weather, Richard; what have you found?'

The relentless rain and lightning of the previous evening had battered the old willow and it now lay, branches akimbo, amidst the wreckage of the pond; the small beck, running down by the side of the cottage, had burst its banks, sending a rush of water through the garden to join the water of the pond as it too burst free, and the contents of the pond—rocks, plants, and garden ornaments—were currently scattered across the garden.

Wedged firmly in the muddy base of the pond was a wooden chest. Shreds of black plastic sheeting, still attached in places, flapped about in the wind whistling through the newly erected incident tent. Bryan Hopkins, forensic anthropologist, was inspecting the contents of this chest as Richard spoke with Joe.

Joe rested his forehead on the window and closed his eyes. He pressed the phone firmly against his ear. 'Skeletal remains you say?'

'Yes, initial examination indicates that they've been here for more than a year but less than a decade. According to Hopkins the bones belong to a female, early to mid 20's; she'd been wrapped in thick plastic, stuffed into an old oak chest…'

'An oak chest,' exclaimed Joe. 'What does it look like?'

'Difficult to say at the moment, mate; it's covered in mud and slime, wrapped in thick plastic and buried beneath what was the pond.'

'The pond constructed by Dave Mardle. Bloody hell, Richard, it's her, isn't it?'

'I thought you might be interested. Do you fancy having a look for yourself? You could have a chat with the Morgans, the current owners of the cottage; they've lived here since February 2012.'

'I'll be there sometime this evening; God knows what time.'

'And perhaps you could bring your file on the Melissa Davies case,' suggested Richard.

'I'm emailing a request to records as we speak,' said Joe.

'I say; multi-tasking: I'm impressed.'

Late that night, Joe booked into a bed and breakfast near the Northallerton police station, and the following morning he was shown up to Richard's office.

'Right; where's the description of that oak chest that Dave Mardle brought up from London?' said Richard.

Joe scanned through his notes. 'Um, here we are; Deborah Mardle described it as; 'hateful, deeply carved with hideous gargoyles'.'

'Interesting,' said Richard.

'So, come on; is it the same chest?'

'The oak chest currently residing down in our evidence room is hateful, deeply carved and with hideous gargoyles.'

'It *is* her,' exclaimed Joe.

'It seems highly likely,' agreed Richard.

'When will you get the autopsy report?'

'Hopkins assures me that it will be soon.'

'Soon?'

'He doesn't like to commit himself.'

'It'll be Melissa Davies, I'm positive,' said Joe. 'I knew I was right about that smarmy toe rag.'

Richard smiled. 'Not your favourite person, I take it.'

'Not in the slightest; I took against the creep from the first moment I set eyes on him.'

'Right; so, would you like to view the crime scene and have a chat with the Morgans?'

'Lead on.'

On their way out of the station, Joe almost bumped into a woman coming through the door.

'Joe? What are you doing here?'

'Madeline, or should I say *Inspector* Driscoll. Good to see. Settled in alright?'

'Fine, so come on, you're not thinking of transferring up here too, are you?'

'Hah, no it's a missing person case I was working on back in June. I had my suspicions that something wasn't right but Marshall…'

'Oh, don't tell me—couldn't see past his ever expanding ego and told you to close the case.'

'That's about it.'

'So, has this missing person turned up here?'

'Might have done.'

Madeline glanced at Richard. 'The remains at Black Sheep Cottage?'

'It's a possibility.'

'Look, great to see you, Madeline but…'

'No, that's fine. I understand. You need to get on. Good to see you again though.'

Nicole Morgan was still in a state of shock. 'The whole thing was terrifying enough,' she said. 'What with the sheet lighting, the thunder and everything, and then the crash as the poor willow tree was struck, and the volume of water that came gushing out from that tiny beck; I couldn't believe it—so much water from such an innocent looking thing. The garden's ruined.' She gasped. 'Jesus, listen to me; as if that matters.'

'Just tell us what happened in your own time,' said Richard.

'Well, when the storm subsided we, we both donned our wellies and ventured outside,' she said. 'The pond was all churned up and that chest was on its side, the lid smashed, and the skull, the skull was jutting out, oozing mud; it was like some awful horror movie.'

Jason put his arm around his wife. 'At least the remains have been taken away now, to do whatever it is that they do at the lab. And Inspector Soames here said we could start clearing up the mess in the garden…'

Richard's eyes widened.

'It's alright, Inspector, I know we mustn't touch anything within the taped-off area and under that tent thingy, but you did say we could tackle the rest of the garden, you know, so it doesn't look like a bomb site, so that will be better, I suppose…'

'It doesn't alter the fact that a murder may well have taken place in our cottage; it may even have been committed by the people we bought the place from; it just doesn't bear thinking about,' cried Nicole.

'I can't believe that it was Mr Mardle; he was such an avuncular chap, very upstanding and obviously well bred,' said Jason. 'But the *son*, well, I didn't take to him at all, there was just something about him. Nicole found him charming, but I'll tell you this: I wouldn't be the least bit surprised to find out that he was the murderer.'

'Jason,' exclaimed Nicole, 'you can't go around making accusations like that.'

'I'm just saying,' he muttered. 'Anyway, what happens now?'

'The coroner will carry out an autopsy to ascertain the cause of death,' explained Richard. 'Inspector Reed is here to ask you a few questions about the visit you had from Dave Mardle and his girlfriend, Erica Woods; I believe they were here earlier this year.'

'Yes, that's right; they turned up, completely out of the blue,' he squeezed Nicole's shoulder. 'When was it, love?'

'It was late May, early June, I think,' said Nicole.

Joe glanced at his notebook. 'According to my notes, they were here on Saturday, the 25th of May.'

'Yes, that sounds about right,' said Jason.

'Did Dave Mardle say why he called in?'

'He said it was because they happened to be in the area and his girlfriend was keen to see the place.'

'I see, and how did he seem?'

'How do you mean?'

'Was he relaxed, anxious; how did he behave?'

Jason thought for a moment. 'Hard to say really; I mean we'd never met the bloke before.'

'He did behave a bit oddly when he thought we were planning to rip out his pond,' said Nicole. 'Which seemed a bit odd at the time, but now, well…?'

'That's right,' exclaimed Jason. 'He became quite agitated. It was only when I explained that we meant the fireplace that he relaxed; he was all charm after that, telling us that there was a inglenook hidden behind the modern fireplace that his father had installed,' he waved his hand in the general direction of the front room. 'You passed it when we walked through to the kitchen.'

'Anything else?'

'Not really, no, sorry,' said Jason. 'We gave them a tour of the place and they left shortly after that; never saw or heard from them again.'

'But some other people came to see us,' said Nicole.

'Some other people?' inquired Joe.

'Yes, a couple of days ago actually,' said Jason. 'She said she was a friend of Dave's girlfriend; Maggie I think she said her name was. She turned up with a huge Jamaican guy who looked just like Reginald D. Hunter.'

'Is that so,' said Joe. 'And what did they want?'

'They wanted to know if we knew of a local pub or restaurant that the Mardle family used to frequent.'

'And did you?'

'As it happens, yes; we told them about 'The Green Man'; Deborah Mardle recommended it to us.'

'The one just outside Scawton?' asked Richard.

'Yes, that's the one.'

'Well, thank you, you've both been most helpful,' said Joe.

'They didn't have anything to do with that awful murder, surely,' said Nicole, stroking her abdomen. 'They both seemed so nice.'

Joe smiled. 'When is the happy event?'

'The sooner the better,' laughed Nicole.

'Early September,' added Jason.

'Not long then,' said Joe. 'I hope this unfortunate discovery hasn't turned you against the place.'

'A new life, Inspector,' said Nicole. 'That's what this place needs now.'

'Good for you,' he said as he stood to leave.

Nicole pushed her hands through her long hair and held it up on the top of her head. 'It's so humid,' she moaned. 'You'd have thought the storm would have cleared the air but, if anything, it's made it worse.'

'I'll run you a cool bath in a bit; that'll help,' said Jason. 'Do you need to have a look round or anything, Inspector?'

Joe was staring at Nicole's neck.

Jason cleared his throat loudly. 'Inspector.'

Joe tore his eyes away. 'I'm sorry. What did you say?'

Jason repeated his question.

'No, no that's fine; I'll liaise with Richard, Inspector Soames.' He returned his gaze to Nicole's neck. 'I've just noticed your necklace,' he said. 'Was it a gift?'

Nicole put her hand to her neck. 'This? No, Jason found it when he was doing the fireplace. It's lovely isn't it?'

'Would you mind if I took a closer look at it?'

'No, not at all,' said Nicole as she removed the necklace and handed it over to Joe.

It was a silver chain; attached to the chain was a small silver butterfly.

'The chain's new,' said Jason. 'The one it was originally attached to was broken; probably because it was too thin for the pendant.'

Joe reached into his inside pocket and removed a small plastic evidence bag. 'Would it be alright if I held on to this for a bit? It will be returned to you, don't worry.'

'I, I suppose so,' said Nicole. 'Do you think it's connected to the remains in the garden or something?' She rubbed at her neck. 'Have I been wearing a dead person's necklace? God, how awful.'

'It may be nothing,' said Joe. 'I just want to check, and to do that I need to show the necklace to some other people; alright?'

'Yes, yes; take it,' said Nicole waving her hands.

'Could you show us where you found it, Mr Morgan?'

'Well, yes, but why?'

'Just show us, if that's alright.'

'Fine,' said Jason. 'Follow me.'

Kneeling in front of the fireplace, Jason indicated a small crack behind one of the slate slabs making up the hearth. 'It was wedged in there,' he said. 'It was only because I started to loosen the slab to reposition it that I found it. I assumed it had been there for years; it was filthy.'

Joe and Richard peered at the slab. They both noticed that it was significantly paler than the others. Straightening up and rubbing the small of his back, Joe said, 'I don't suppose your team examined this area.'

'We had no reason to; the remains were discovered outside.'

'So, can you get SOCO back here?'

'I'll ring them now,' said Richard as he retrieved his phone from his top pocket.

'Excellent, we…' Joe began.

Richard held up his hand. 'Meredith. Hi. Listen I'm back at Black Sheep Cottage with a colleague of mine, Inspector Joe Reed, and we have just discovered something potentially important….'—'No, inside...'—'Yes, I know. Can you get over here?'—'Great; see you in about 20 minutes. We'll wait in the car.'

'You're most welcome to wait inside,' said Jason.

'That's very kind of you,' said Richard, 'but I think your wife would appreciate that cool bath, and she won't want two great hulks hovering about the place. We'll be fine.'

The rain had started again; the noise of the drops falling on the car roof sounded like heavy gunfire. Richard had to shout in order to be heard. 'Don't mind if I smoke, do you; I'm gasping,' and without waiting for a reply, he lit up. 'So, what's all the excitement about the necklace?'

'I think it's the one Melissa Davies inherited from her mother; it certainly fits the description that Dave Mardle (senior) gave me,' Joe shouted back.

'It must be her,' said Richard. 'What are the chances of some random dead female turning up in the garden of the very same cottage that Melissa Davies was last seen in?'

'Quite; I'll ring Harry; get him to track down Melissa's dentist and get her dental records sent up here to Hopkins.'

'So,' said Richard when Joe finished his call to Harry, 'how's life in jolly Peckham?'

'It would be great if it wasn't for the fact that Superintendent Marshall is the boss.'

'Yes, well, you have my sympathies. We, on the other hand, have the rather delightful Inspector Avery. Not only did she manage to get shot of the incompetent Curtis but she managed to snap up your old Sergeant Driscoll, promote her to Inspector, and improve the morale of the station all within a few months of her appointment. Plus she's easy on the eye, if you know what I mean.'

'Unlike Marshall.'

Richard coughed and spluttered. 'Well yes, quite. Still, give the man his due; he didn't object to you coming up here.'

'Actually, Richard, that's not entirely true.'

'Bloody hell, you mean he doesn't know you're here.'

'Come on, Richard, you know Marshall, the man's so full of his own importance that...'

The banging on the roof of the car suddenly intensified. 'Come on, you two,' yelled the hooded creature standing outside. 'It's bloody wet out here.'

'Ah, the dulcet tones of dear Meredith, head of SOCO,' muttered Richard as they exited the car followed by a cloud of smoke.

After a quick examination of the fireplace, Meredith was able to confirm what both Joe and Richard had suspected;

there had been repeated attempts to clean it. 'Fear not,' she said. 'Luminol works even after cleaning with bleach, and if, by some remote chance, that bleach contained hypochloride, then I simply add my magic ingredient, which will remove any remaining traces of the stuff, allowing the Luminol to react with blood that may be present.' She began to prepare the area. 'Plus, of course,' she continued, 'the effects of the bleach lessen as time passes. If one of you could just draw the curtains; we need darkness to view the reaction.'

Curtains drawn, Joe and Richard stood back. A short while later a blue glow emanated from the tested area. 'There you are; presence of blood confirmed,' said Meredith. She took several photographs before the glow faded, and sampled the area.

'How the hell does that work?' asked Joe.

'Oh, shit,' said Richard.

Joe frowned, but before he could ask Richard what he meant, Meredith was in full flood. 'Glad you asked; it's fascinating. The light is emitted when an oxidising agent, like blood, catalyzes the oxidation of Luminol by hydrogen peroxide in a basic solution,' she said. 'The iron in the blood, and there doesn't need to be much, acts as the catalyst…'

Richard raised his eyes to the ceiling; Joe's glazed over.

'That's the issue with bleach you see, it can catalyze the reaction as well. Anyway, the Luminol gains oxygen atoms and…'

'Meredith, Meredith,' exclaimed Richard.

'And, at the same time it loses nitrogen and hydrogen; this produces a compound called 3 aminophthalate…'

'Yes, that's *fascinating*, Meredith but time marches on…'

'The electrons in the 3 aminophthalate are in an excited state,' she continued, 'And because of that they release energy; the blue light. Beautifully neat, isn't it?'

219

'Um, yes, beautiful,' said Joe. 'I'm *so* glad I asked; I've always wondered.'

Richard had to avert his eyes. Clearing his throat and keeping his head down, he set about taping off the fireplace area.

Jason wandered into the living room. 'Nicole's having a lie down.' His eyes alighted on the newly erected tape barrier. 'Oh, I say; have you found something?'

'We're not at liberty to discuss any aspects of the enquiry, Mr Morgan; I'm sure you understand,' said Richard.

'Right, yes, sorry, of course.'

'Just one thing,' said Joe. 'You mentioned that it was Dave Mardle's father who installed the modern fireplace, is that right?'

'That's right, yes.'

'Do you happen to know when that was?'

'Nope, sorry; you'll have to ask him.'

'Right then, we'll leave you in peace for the moment,' continued Richard. 'Please don't disturb this area or the taped area in the garden.'

'Understood,' said Jason.

'And don't talk to anyone; do you understand?'

'Absolutely,' said Jason. 'Oh, um, well, oh dear,' he added as he threw his hand up towards his face.

'What?'

'It's just that Nicole's mum rang last night and you know what mothers are like, she detected immediately that something was wrong and well, the thing is, she didn't mean to or anything, but…'

'Your wife told her mother about the skeletal remains in the garden,' said Richard with a sigh.

'Well yes.'

'Is your mother-in-law local?'

'Yes; she lives in the big house on the hill in Nether Sitton; it's about 20 miles away.'

'I'll have a word with her, don't worry. We don't want the local press getting hold of this, not until we've got a bit more to go on.' He turned to Meredith. 'Joe and I will see you back at the station; we just need to pop along and have a little word with Mrs, um…'

'Fletcher,' said Jason. 'But she'll be at work at the moment; she's the receptionist at the Moor-House Hotel; it's in Nether Sitton too, not far from her house actually.'

Richard nodded. 'No problem; I know the place. Thanks for all your help, Mr Morgan.'

'Right, that's me done. I'll get these back to the lab,' said Meredith.

As Richard opened the front door a gaggle of reporters, cameras and notebooks poised, rushed forward. A particularly scruffy individual thrust a microphone under Richard's nose.

Richard leant forward and tapped it. 'Testing, testing; ah, excellent, it appears to be working.' He cleared his throat. The reporter skipped up and down and waited.

'No fucking comment.'

Meredith shoved Richard out of the way and addressed the mike. 'As soon as we have some more information there will be a press statement issued.'

'Until that time I suggest you all bugger off,' added Richard.

They continued to shout out their questions.

Richard fixed them with an icy stare and one by one the reporters fell silent.

'Right then,' he said. 'Off you pop; and if I hear that any of you have tried to question the owners of this cottage, I will be down on you like a ton of proverbial shit; do I make myself clear?'

The general mutterings as the reporters dispersed indicated that Richard's point was very clear; universally disliked, but nevertheless clear.

'Bloody vultures,' muttered Richard. 'Come on, Joe; we'll pay a quick visit to Mrs Fletcher.'

'Is there much point? It seems to me that the cat's already free and running wild.'

'That is indeed very true,' said Richard as he lit another cigarette. 'But we don't want her spreading the news to the hotel guests as well, do we?'

They arrived at the hotel reception desk at one o'clock. Maggie and Winton, having missed breakfast, were making their way across the small foyer towards the dining room for lunch.

'Inspector Reed,' exclaimed Maggie. 'Whatever are you doing here?' She blushed. 'Oh, God, sorry, none of my business, it's just, well, it's such a shock seeing you here, I mean, so far from Peckham and everything, I just wondered...'

'Good afternoon, Maggie, isn't it?'

Maggie nodded.

Maintaining a straight face, he added, 'And, Winton Dacosta; good afternoon to you, too.'

'Good afternoon, Inspector.'

'Now then,' continued Joe. 'This is a surprise; and what, may I ask, brings you two to these parts?'

Maggie swallowed and chewed her lower lip. 'Um, well, um...'

Mrs Fletcher popped up from behind the reception desk, waving sheets of blotting paper above her head triumphantly. 'I knew I had some here—gracious me; Inspector Soames. Have you managed to identify the remains already?'

'Remains,' asked Maggie. 'What remains?'

'It's awful; my daughter found...'

'Mrs Fletcher!' yelled Richard. 'Please!'

Eyes wide with innocence, she gasped, 'What?'

222

'The investigation is ongoing and it would be best if you kept what little you know to yourself, to avoid any spurious speculation, as I'm sure a woman of your intelligence will understand.'

Mrs Fletcher bowed her head briefly. 'Understood officer; mum's the word.' She turned to speak to Maggie and Winton. 'So sorry about this rather nasty turn in the weather; I do hope it hasn't spoilt your holiday. Are you heading to the dining room?'

'We are,' said Winton.

'Well I'm sure lunch will cheer you up; I hear that chef has prepared one of his specials today.'

'Lovely,' said Winton. 'Nice to see you, Inspector Reed,' he added as he tried to steer Maggie away.

'So, you're both up here on holiday,' said Joe.

Maggie nodded her head furiously.

'I see,' said Joe. 'And what made you decide to come to North Yorkshire? It obviously wasn't for the weather.'

Maggie found a sudden interest in the carpet pattern as her brain tried to conjure up a plausible reason for their visit to the area. *Fuck it,* she thought. *We haven't broken any laws.*

'Actually Inspector, we came up here to see if we could find out anything more about Melissa Davies; is that a problem?'

Mrs Fletcher began to tap down the sheets of blotting paper, slowly easing herself forward as she did so.

'Ah, Mrs Fletcher,' said Joe.

She straightened up immediately. 'Yes?'

'Is there somewhere Inspector Soames and I could speak privately with your guests?'

'Yes, yes, of course,' she said, pointing to a small room to their left. 'The lounge is free at the moment.'

'Excellent,' said Joe. 'If you could see that we are not disturbed.'

'Certainly, Inspector, of course.'

'Now then,' said Joe as they each took a seat in the lounge. 'Did you happen to discover anything about Melissa Davies at all?'

Maggie explained about their visit to the Green Man. 'We found out that Dave behaved aggressively towards Melissa, contrary to what he's always maintained.'

'Apparently Dave wasn't too pleased when she chose to sit next to his father; he tried to drag her out of the seat, and when she argued, Dave stormed out,' explained Winton.

'I see,' said Joe.

'Anyway, the owners said that Melissa was a lovely girl. They didn't like Dave though; so, no surprise there,' added Maggie.

'Well, that was all very enterprising of you,' he said. 'Erica did mention you were a bit of a detective.'

Maggie managed a weak smile. 'These remains, Inspector, are they…'

'You know I'm not at liberty to talk about…'

Maggie held up her hand. 'I know, I know, sorry, it's just, well; it's her isn't it? It's got to be, otherwise, well, why else would you be here?'

Joe's mobile rang. 'Excuse me, I need to take this; enjoy the rest of your, um, your holiday.'

'As we explained to Mrs Fletcher,' said Richard. 'Please don't discuss any of this with *anyone*; do you understand?'

'We do,' said Winton. 'Come on Maggie, lunch; I'm starving.'

Joe ended the call. 'Shit.'

'Marshall found out where you are?'

'Worse than that,' Joe groaned. 'It seems that Melissa Davies's dental records have been *temporarily misplaced*; something to do with some dyslexic temp that the surgery used back in 2005. Harry informs me that the new dental nurse is currently hunting them down.'

'Well with a bit of luck the records will turn up soon,' said Richard. 'Listen, you can't stay in that awful B&B; Sally would never forgive me. Come and stay at ours for the weekend. I'll give her a call.'

Sitting at their table in the dining room, Maggie exclaimed, 'Jesus, Winton; Inspector Reed, skeletal remains: it's got to be Melissa.'

'Steady on, Maggie,' said Winton. 'Let's not jump to any conclusions.'

'But…'

'Good afternoon,' said their waitress, appearing as if from nowhere. 'Chef has prepared…'

Maggie reached out and grabbed hold of her arm. 'Do *you* know anything about these skeletal remains?'

The waitress leaned in closer. 'It's gruesome,' she whispered. 'Mrs Fletcher's daughter discovered them in her garden; buried underneath the pond in some sort of coffin affair, very macabre.'

'Mrs Fletcher's daughter?'

'Nicole Morgan, she lives at…'

'Black Sheep Cottage,' said Maggie.

'That's the place; do you know her then?'

'In a way; so, any idea who it was?'

'Mary Susan Tucker,' exclaimed Mrs Fletcher as she marched towards the table. 'I hope you're not indulging in idle chitter-chatter; you know what Inspector Soames said.'

Nodding, Mary scuttled away. 'Sorry Mrs Fletcher.'

'Nasty business,' said Mrs Fletcher. 'You'll be relieved to know that the worst of this weather is over, so at least you'll be alright for your journey back to London tomorrow. Now, what can I get you?'

Chapter 14

Harry's phone call arrived on Sunday evening as Sally was clearing the table after their meal.

'Harry; what news?'

'The dental records are on their way, sir.'

'Well done, lad.'

'Um, the thing is, Superintendent Marshall had been asking after you; he's concerned that he hasn't seen you about the station for a few days and um, well I'm afraid I panicked and told him that you were at home, suffering from food poisoning, sir.'

'And did he buy it?'

'I think so, sir; he said something about your dietary habits being a disgrace.'

'Well there you go; problem solved,' said Joe. 'Don't worry; I'll be back as soon as the remains have been identified.'

The weather had calmed down over the weekend and at 8:30 on Monday morning, Richard and Joe entered the autopsy lab. The walls and floor were fully tiled, spotlessly clean, and smelt surprisingly fresh. Filled with the bright early morning light and with the addition of four large halogen lights suspended over the four autopsy tables, it looked almost cheerful. On the right were two large sinks and up above, to the left, was an observation balcony.

'That can't be right,' said Joe glancing at an intact body laid out on the nearest table.

'Hah, that'd be a bloody miracle, that would,' said Richard. 'No, that's your Madeline's current case. Lawson will soon be able to determine the cause of death for that one. Unlike her previous case where they only had bone, fragments of tissue and succulent maggots to work with.'

'I thought you said her last case was child abduction.'

'It was but there was also…'

'Are you here to see these remains or what gentleman?'

'On our way, Hopkins—come on, Joe we don't want to keep the master waiting.'

'Bryan, this is Inspector Joe Reed from Peckham. Joe, this is Bryan Hopkins, our old bones man.'

Bryan raised his eyes towards the ceiling. 'Yes, thank you, Richard. Good to meet you, Joe.'

Joe nodded and glanced down at the skeletal remains laid out on the table.

'Sadly, this has proved to be a very straightforward case. I was hoping it was going to stretch my forensic skills a little further; I do like a challenge, but, as I said, this has been very straightforward. Good for you, I know, but…'

'Hopkins, just tell us what you've found,' said Richard.

'Right you are,' said Hopkins. 'Well, as you can both see, the skeletal remains are that of a female, mid to late 20's, of small stature, 5 foot 2 inches to be precise. We know this because…'

'Your findings Hopkins; spare us the forensics lecture.'

'Right you are,' he repeated. 'If you examine the skull you can clearly see it has suffered a severe blunt force trauma consistent with the back of the head either being struck by a heavy implement or falling back onto a sharp edged object. Given the evidence found by Meredith at the scene, I would suggest the latter, with the sharp edged object in question being the slate slab of the fireplace hearth. The small sample of blood retrieved from that slab is from the same individual whose bones are currently laid out here.'

Richard raised his eyes. 'And that individual is?'

'I'm coming to that. Now, look here, what can you see?' said Hopkins, pointing towards the chest area of the remains.

Joe looked. 'Um, well it's the ribs and the spine.'

'Good, good and what can you tell me about them? Look carefully.'

'Hopkins,' exclaimed Richard, 'we're not your bloody students; just tell us.'

Hopkins sighed. 'Alright, fine; I'll just spoon feed you.'

'That's the idea,' said Richard.

'The ribs, specifically ribs 6 and 7, the spine, specifically the 6th and 7th thoracic vertebrae and the xiphoid process, at the base of the sternum, have all been sliced through.' He picked up a folder from the steel cabinet situated at the head of the autopsy table. 'These photographs show the relevant areas magnified. Do you see the serrations?'

Joe nodded.

'Those serrations are consistent with the use of a chainsaw.'

'Jesus,' exclaimed Joe. 'Are you saying that the body was sawn in half?'

'Precisely; it makes sense: it wouldn't have fitted into the oak chest otherwise.'

Joe closed his eyes and clenched his fists; waiting for the wave of nausea to pass as Hopkins continued to expound. 'These chainsaw cuts are also present on the black plastic that the body was covered in. In other words, the body was wrapped in the black plastic *before* it was sliced in two; it implies a modicum of squeamishness on behalf of the perpetrator.'

'Can we get to the main point?' insisted Richard.

'The main point?'

'Yes, Hopkins, the main point; who the bloody hell is she?'

'Right you are; I've examined the dental records that were sent up from London…'

'And?' demanded Richard.

'And the ante-mortem and post-mortem data match in sufficient detail, with no unexplainable discrepancies, to allow me to say, with a fair degree of confidence, that they are from the same individual.'

'Jesus, Hopkins; get to the bloody point!'

'The skeletal remains on the table are those of Melissa Davies.'

'Thank you,' sighed Richard.

'You're welcome; the full report will be with you by the end of the day,' he replied, adding, as Richard and Joe made to leave, 'It would be useful if we could locate the chainsaw that was used. That way I could match the serrations on the blade with those on the body.'

Joe was on his phone before Hopkins had finished his sentence. 'Harry, Joe here; the remains that were buried beneath the pond have been identified; they're Melissa Davies. We've got him! He must have killed the woman, intentionally or unintentionally, and then buried her in her own bloody oak chest for Christ's sake. Take whoever you choose and arrest Dave Mardle (junior) for the murder of Melissa Davies. He should be at the Black Moon Bookshop. I'm leaving here in the next hour or so; should be back by about 3pm.'

Joe punched the air with his fists. 'Got the bastard; I knew it, I knew it,' he cried. 'A bloody chainsaw. Can you believe it? I take it your lot didn't find one at the scene?'

'Nope; we carried out a thorough search, including the out buildings, but we were looking for some sort of weapon that could have been used to cause the damage to the skull. We had no idea that the body had been hacked into two; essentially it was a box of bones. All we found in the shed were some bags of manure, a few garden tools, wheelbarrows and the like, nothing out of the ordinary. Hang on; I'll give Mr Morgan a ring.'

'Ah, Mr Morgan, sorry to bother you, Inspector Soames here; just a quick question; when you first moved into the property, I don't suppose you came across a chainsaw anywhere?'—'Right, yes, I see.'—'No, no; that's fine; most helpful.'

Richard shook his head. 'No chainsaw.'

'Shit,' exclaimed Joe. 'It's been dumped.'

On his return to London, Joe discovered that Dave Mardle was not sweating it out in one of the interview rooms.

'Where the fuck is he?' he yelled.

'Paris,' replied Harry.

'What?'

'He's in Paris, sir.'

'Yes, yes, I heard you; what's he doing in bloody Paris?'

'He's on holiday, sir, with Erica Woods.'

'Shit, shit and triple bloody shit!'

'They're travelling on the Orient Express; due to arrive back at London Victoria at noon the day after tomorrow. I've contacted the local Gendarmes; they're keeping a discrete eye on him.'

Joe took a deep breath. 'Right, OK; good work Harry. Get your coat; we'll pay a little visit to Mr and Mrs Mardle at The Retreat. I want to show them this,' He removed the evidence bag from his top pocket. 'There is no doubt in my mind that this necklace is the one that Melissa Davies inherited from her mother, but, to satisfy our dear leader, I need confirmation.'

As the pair raced out of the station they bumped into Marshall. 'Ah, Inspector Reed; feeling better are we?'

'Sir?'

'Your food poisoning?'

'Oh, that, yes, no, fine; sterling constitution.'

'And where are you both off to in such a screaming rush?'

Harry, who'd just finished buttoning up his coat, nudged his glasses up a little further. 'We're just off to follow up on a lead pertaining to those car thefts.'

'Excellent,' said Marshall. 'Well, off you go then; we need to close as many cases as we can in order to meet our target for this month. I don't want a repeat of last month's lamentable figures.'

Driving across London, Harry remarked, 'Sir, I've been thinking.'

'Dangerous occupation that,' said Joe.

Harry adjusted his glasses and cleared his throat.

'Come on, lad; spit it out.'

'It's just, well, once the family know we've found Melissa's remains, won't they alert Dave?'

'That's a distinct possibility, Harry, but you've informed the gendarmes so, if he does attempt to flee, they'll pick him up.'

Phyllis answered the door. 'Inspector Reed,' she cried. 'Gracious me, whatever are you doing back here?'

'Good afternoon; may we come in?'

Phyllis stood back. 'Yes, yes; come in. Have you got some news about Melissa?'

'There are just a few more questions.'

Phyllis frowned. 'More questions? Surely we've told you everything,' she said. 'And, if you're hoping to speak with my grandson then I'm afraid you're out of luck; he's in Paris, with the lovely Erica.'

'Yes, so Sergeant Carter tells me.'

One side of Phyllis's mouth twitched upwards and, with eyes that did not blink, she skewered Harry with an intense stare.

'Um, yes,' mumbled Harry. 'I spoke with a Mr Philip White at the bookshop this morning.'

'I see,' replied Phyllis. 'Well, come on then, my daughter and her husband are in the living room.'

'Jesus, Inspector; what is it now?' exclaimed Dave.

'Dave; don't be so rude,' said Deborah. 'It's lovely to see you again; have you found Melissa?'

Dave stood stock still and held onto the back of the settee.

'In a way; I'm afraid we've got some bad news,' said Joe. 'Skeletal remains have been found at Black Sheep Cottage. These have now been identified as the remains of Melissa Davies.'

Deborah clutched at her chest. 'No!'

Phyllis rushed to her daughter's side.

'I don't understand,' said Deborah. 'How could that be? My son has explained to you that she walked out on him soon after they arrived at the cottage all those years ago, and so how, how could her remains be there now?'

'That's what we need to find out,' said Joe.

'Surely you don't believe my son had anything to do with it. He *loved* her, Inspector; he would never harm her.'

'We're following several lines of enquiry, Mrs Mardle,' he said glancing sideways at Mr Mardle, who remained silent and impassive. 'We'll need to speak to your son again when he returns from Paris. In the meantime,' he said, withdrawing the evidence bag, 'could you take a look at this?'

Deborah identified the necklace as the one belonging to Melissa as soon as Joe revealed it. 'Where did you find it? Was it, um, was it with the remains?'

'I'm afraid I can't discuss details of the case at…'

'But she never took it off, Inspector, did she, Dave.'

'Not as far as I remember,' said Dave.

'Mrs Mardle, are you positive that this is Melissa's necklace?'

'Positive,' she replied.

Joe took a moment to glance at his notes. 'I wonder, can you remember when you installed the modern fireplace at the cottage in Yorkshire, Mr Mardle?'

'When I installed the—what the hell has that got to do with anything?'

'If you could just answer the question.'

'I can't bloody remember; it was years ago.'

Deborah reached across to take his hand. 'Calm down, Dave, the Inspector is only doing his job.'

'I remember,' said Phyllis.

Dave turned on her. 'How the hell would you know?' he snapped.

'Dave,' chided Deborah.

'Sorry, sorry; it's just seeing that necklace again and everything, sorry.'

'So, Mrs Adams; the fireplace?'

Phyllis glanced nervously at her son-in-law. 'It was soon after my grandson came back from Yorkshire; don't you remember, dear? You had a conference or something, up in York I think it was, and you said that you'd stay at the cottage. You, rather reluctantly if I recall, agreed to drop me off in Oxford on your way up.' She smiled at Joe. 'I visit Martha, an old school friend, regular as clockwork every year for her birthday. We have such fun; she's a real hoot, unlike dear Gertrude, whom you've met, Inspector. She and I…'

'Mum, I don't think the Inspector is particularly interested in your social calendar.'

'No, of course not, sorry.'

'So, when was this conference?' asked Joe.

Dave shrugged his shoulders.

'My son-in-law drove up to Yorkshire on the 20th of August,' said Phyllis. 'I remember because Martha and I were booked to go and see a performance of Wagner's *Tristan und Isolda* on Martha's birthday, the 21st; it was a marvellous performance, the best I'd ever seen.'

'Is that correct, Mr Mardle?'

'I've no idea; I'd have to check my diary.'

'Anyway I think my son-in-law was a little concerned about the work my grandson had done if truth be told. He was convinced that he wouldn't have made a good job of the pond that's for sure.'

Deborah smiled at Phyllis. 'Oh, that's right, Mum, I remember now; Dave rang to let me know that the conference was a waste of time. He said he needed to fix the pond because it was leaking and making a frightful mess of the garden.'

'So, I assume that you did the work on the pond and then turned your attention to the fireplace.'

'If you say so.'

'I'm asking you if that's correct, Mr Mardle.'

'We're talking years ago; I can't bloody remember.'

'I think that would be right, dear,' said Deborah. 'You said the pond was the priority and since you were at a loose end you said you might as well get on with blocking in the fireplace.' Deborah turned to Joe. 'We'd been talking about it for sometime, Inspector. It seemed a shame but needs must and all that.'

'Mr Mardle?'

'Um, actually yes, now that my wife has reminded me, yes that's right; pond first and then the fireplace, yes; makes sense.'

'When you did the work on the fireplace did you notice any problem with the hearth slabs at all?'

'What? No, what possible problem could there be with hearth slabs,' he barked.

'And you returned to London when?'

'I can't remember; a few days later I suppose.'

'No, no, it was at least a week,' added Phyllis helpfully. 'You were supposed to be collecting me from Martha's on the 27th. I always stay a week with my friend, you see, Inspector; we have so much to catch up on, you know, given that we only see each other once a year. Anyway that year it was my grandson who collected me. My son-in-law

234

didn't get back until, well, I'm not sure exactly, but it was certainly *after* the 27th of August.'

'I see,' said Joe. 'Mr Mardle, could you tell me what exactly you had to do to fix the pond leak.'

'Sorry, what?'

'The pond leak; what exactly did you…'

'Yes, I heard you,' exclaimed Dave. 'I'm just not quite sure how me explaining to you the mechanics of fixing a pond leak is going to help you discover who the bloody hell murdered Melissa.'

'I never actually said she'd been murdered, sir.'

'Oh, right I see,' said Dave. 'You're telling me that the woman walks out on my son and then returns to the empty property sometime later and somehow manages to drop dead in such a way that her body lies undiscovered for bloody years. Right, yes, I see, sorry.'

Deborah reached out to touch he husband's arm. 'Dave, just answer the Inspector's questions. I'm sure he knows what he's doing.'

'Fine! Right, well as it happens it wasn't a very complicated job; it was just that the silly boy had omitted to include an overflow, hence the leak. All I had to do was add an outlet pipe; I used hollow bamboo, more natural than those awful PVC pipe affairs that garden centres sell. Is that it?'

'So you didn't need to dig the whole thing out then?'

Deborah gave her husband a quizzical look and opened her mouth to speak.

Dave rushed on. 'No, Inspector, I've just explained that all I needed to do was add an outlet pipe.'

'And that would be added to the top of the pond then, would it?'

Dave gave Joe a pitying look. 'Yes, Inspector, obviously; it's simple physics.'

Just one more question, Mr Mardle. I wonder, do you own a chainsaw?'

'I beg your pardon?'

'I was wondering,' repeated Joe, 'if you own a chainsaw.'

'What in God's name has that got to do with anything?'

'As I just explained to your wife,' said Joe. 'I cannot discuss details of the case; if you would be good enough to answer the question.'

Dave opened, and then closed his mouth; he rubbed his forehead and glanced at his wife. Deborah remained silent.

'Fine,' he snapped. 'Yes, I own a chainsaw; so what?'

'Where is it?'

'Where you'd expect it to be, Inspector: in the bloody shed.'

'David, for goodness sake.'

'Well, what a bloody stupid question,' he retorted. 'I suppose you want me to go and get it.'

'That would be most helpful,' said Joe. 'Harry, if you could assist Mr Mardle.'

'I can manage, thank you!'

'Nevertheless, Sergeant Carter will accompany you.'

'Fine,' he snapped again. 'Follow me.'

Deborah watched her husband as he stomped out through the French windows.

'His slippers will get filthy.'

'Frightful weather we've been having, you know, for the time of year,' muttered Phyllis.

'Oh, Mum,' pleaded Deborah. 'What's happening?'

Phyllis scowled at Joe. 'I'm sure I don't know, dear, but try not to upset yourself.'

Dave stomped back into the living room, with Harry in hot pursuit, brandishing the chainsaw.

'Hateful things,' said Deborah, 'but needs must.'

'Needs must?' said Joe.

'Yes, frightening as they are, there is no denying their efficiency; you know, for clearing away dead trees and the like.'

'And this was at the cottage?'

236

'Yes,' said Deborah. 'The garden had been neglected for many years.'

'And who carried out that work?' asked Joe.

'I fail to see...' began Dave.

'Mostly, my son,' said Deborah. 'My husband has never been keen on the things; he did use it recently though, to tackle some trees at the back of this garden.' She paused and locked eyes with Joe. 'But you're not interested in trees are you, Inspector; I may have MS but I'm not stupid. You're saying, God, you're saying that a chainsaw, *this* chainsaw, might have been used to murder Melissa. Well, I'll tell you this,' she said, her voice trembling. 'There is no way, no way on this earth that my son could have done such a terrible thing.'

Dave rushed to her side. 'Of course he wouldn't; it's preposterous.' He whirled around to confront Joe, his face like thunder. 'That chainsaw was in the shed at the cottage until we sold it last year. *Anyone* could have used it; the shed was never bloody locked. We've told you before but I'll tell you again; the last time *any* of us saw Melissa, and that includes my son, she was fucking alive. You've got what you want, so I think you should leave now.'

'Right you are; I can only apologise. I in no way intended to cause upset to your wife, or anyone come to that,' said Joe as he stood to leave. 'Thank you for your help. I assume Sergeant Carter's explained that we need to keep hold of the chainsaw.'

'Take the bloody thing and get out,' yelled Dave.

Joe and Harry left.

Back at the station Harry arranged for the secure transportation of the chainsaw up to Northallerton while Joe braved a visit to Marshall's office to explain the new developments in the Melissa Davies case.

'So, let me get this straight,' said Marshall. 'You have not been suffering from food poisoning these last few days. You have been on a jaunt to Yorkshire.'

'Hardly a *jaunt* sir; I had reason to believe that the skeletal remains discovered in the garden of Black Sheep Cottage were those of Melissa Davies.'

'Based on what exactly?'

Jesus Christ Almighty, thought Joe.

'Based mainly on the location, sir,' said Joe through clenched teeth. 'As you know from my earlier report, according to Dave Mardle, Black Sheep Cottage was the location of the last known sighting of Melissa Davies and...'

'That was seven bloody years ago! My understanding is that the cottage has stood empty for most of those years; *anyone* could have dumped her body there.'

'While that is indeed true,' conceded Joe, 'my gut...'

'What, playing up now is it?'

'No sir; my *instinct*...'

'I'm not interested in your *instinct*, Inspector; the body was in Yorkshire, a tad out of your area wouldn't you say?'

'Again, sir, while that is indeed true, it related to a case that I'd been investigating, and my visit to the cottage turned out to be very worthwhile. As I have just explained, the necklace around Nicole Morgan's neck bore a striking similarity to the one worn by Melissa Davies and again, as I have just explained, Deborah Mardle positively identified it as such. Blood was found at the scene and the remains in the garden have now been positively identified as Melissa Davies; according to the forensic anthropologist they've been there for several years.'

'So, you have immediately decided that she was murdered by her boyfriend, this Dave Mardle.'

Clenching his fists, Joe replied, 'It seems the most likely scenario, sir.'

'But you cannot assume that; she could have been murdered some time *after* she left the cottage and then buried there at a later date.'

'By whom and for what reason, sir?'

'Well, *I* don't know do I; that's the point of an investigation, but it can't be ruled out.'

'There have been no sightings of the girl since the day she allegedly walked out of that cottage. It is my belief that she never left at all. I believe that she was killed and systematically dismembered by Dave Mardle, and then buried beneath the pond that he freely admits to building in the weeks following the woman's disappearance for God's sake!'

'Nevertheless, I have no recollection of giving you permission to travel up to bloody Yorkshire,' yelled Marshal. 'And as for Carter's misguided loyalty in lying about your whereabouts well, well...'

'He didn't lie, sir,' said Joe. 'I told him I was ill at home.'

Marshall's face was turning an alarming shade. 'Listen to me, *Inspector* Reed, and listen carefully. I will not tolerate insubordination. You think this station couldn't cope without you? Think again. One more incident, one more, and you're finished. Do I make myself clear?'

'Crystal.'

'I expect to be kept fully briefed on developments from now on; now, get out of my sight.'

'Yes sir,' replied Joe, resisting an overwhelming desire to click his heels together and extend his right arm in salute.

'You are on very thin ice here, Inspector,' said Marshall. 'Very thin ice indeed.'

Joe sauntered down the corridor unable to wipe the smug expression from his face. 'Right you lot,' he said on entering the control room. 'Anyone seen Carter?'

'I'm here sir,' he said, popping up from behind his desk. 'You've got a couple of visitors.'

'Where? Under your desk'

'Um, no, sir; waiting in reception.'

'And they would be…?'

'Maggie Hunter-Lopez and Winton Dacosta; they've been trying to get hold of you since Saturday.'

'Right, show them into my office,' said Joe. 'Any problems with the chainsaw?'

'None; I spoke with Inspector Soames; he's confident that the results will be with us sometime tomorrow.'

Maggie and Winton were shown into Joe's office. 'Ah, excellent,' said Joe. 'I'm glad you've popped in; it saves me a journey. Has Sergeant Carter offered you a coffee?'

'We're fine,' said Maggie. 'And what do you mean, it's saved you a journey? What's going on?' she gripped Winton's hand. 'The remains, Inspector, its Melissa isn't it; oh, God.'

'The Yorkshire police made a statement this afternoon,' said Joe. 'The skeletal remains discovered on Thursday, 22nd August at Black Sheep Cottage have been identified as Melissa Davies, last seen in the area in July 2006. Now the important…'

'But, but, oh shit!' exclaimed Maggie. 'Erica's with him, with Dave I mean, they're in Paris, Jesus! She's with a bloody murderer!'

'Let the Inspector finish, Maggie,' said Winton.

'Right, yes, sorry.'

'Yes, well, as I was saying; the important thing is not to spook any possible suspects.'

'Dave you mean.'

'I am not at liberty…'

'Oh, come on, Inspector.'

'He will be helping us with our enquiries on his return,' said Joe. 'What I need to know from you is, has Erica Woods been in touch with you, or you with her, since they left for Paris?'

Maggie shook her head.

'Excellent; and that's the way it must stay,' said Joe. '*Do not* contact Erica Woods; we don't want to cause unnecessary panic; do you understand?'

'Perfectly,' said Maggie. She gripped Winton's hand and gave Joe a brief nod.

Chapter 15

It had all happened yesterday, on the last day of their holiday. Wandering along the Quai de Conti, holding hands, Erica had glanced up at Dave. 'You're up to something,' she said.

'I don't know what you mean,' he declared. 'Me? Up to something? Perish the thought.'

'Where are we going?'

'Going? We're not *going* anywhere; we're simply two lovers strolling along the left bank.'

'Right; I believe you, thousands wouldn't.'

Dave gave her an angelic smile.

'You *are* up to something!'

As they crossed the junction at Boulevard St. Michael, Dave pointed across to the island in the middle of the river. 'Look there,' he said, 'its Notre Dame; magnificent isn't it?'

'Stunning,' she replied.

Arriving at the next junction, Erica expected to turn left and was startled to be yanked off to the right. 'What? I thought we were going across to the cathedral.'

Dave smiled again but said nothing.

Holding her hand tightly, he guided her along for a short while before turning left onto Rue de la Bucherie, and there it was in all its glory, the iconic 17th century Shakespeare and Co bookshop.

'Oh, Dave; I, I, wow, I...' She stood on tiptoes and kissed him. 'I've dreamed of visiting this place for as long as I can remember.'

'Given where we first met, I thought, well I thought, anyway; here we are.'

The sun glinted on the Seine; an old Parisian played the accordion just outside; inside, literary types from all walks of life wandered amongst the crowded shelves, chatting and laughing together. She was in heaven.

After a couple of happy hours they sat at one of the small tables outside for a lunch of steak, frites and green beans. Dave lifted his glass of cabernet Sauvignon. 'To you, Erica, with love.'

She smiled and toasted him back.

'Oh, Erica; you've always been frank and honest with me and I so wish I'd been the same with you, you know, right from the beginning. I'm so lucky that you stuck with me through all this recent mess. No matter what has happened in the past, know this, Erica Woods: I will always love you, and nothing can stop us from being together, not now, not ever.'

He removed a small antique box from his jacket pocket and placed in on the table in front of her. 'Marry me, Erica; I will love you, protect you and treasure you forever.'

Sitting on the Orient Express, Erica couldn't remember the last time she'd felt so happy. She knew she had a grin plastered across her face that probably made her look insane, but she didn't care. Holding her left hand in front of her, she rocked it slowly from left to right. The light filtering through the tinted train window danced off her ring, sending rainbow patterns across the carriage.

Dave reached across and took hold of her hand. 'We're home.'

Ten minutes later they were strolling, hand in hand, along the platform at Victoria, suitcases bumping along behind them, towards the exit. 'Are you happy?' Dave asked.

'More than I can say,' replied Erica.

'I can't wait to see the expression on Mum's face,' said Dave. 'She'll be thrilled, and Gran, well she'll just say, 'about bloody time!' or words to that effect.'

'And your dad?'

'Who cares?' he growled. 'I just hope *your* parents will be pleased,' he added as a small frown appeared on his previously relaxed and happy face. 'After all, this will be the first time that I've met them, and what if they don't like me?'

'Don't be ridiculous; what's not to like?' said Erica. 'Anyway Mum will be like putty in your hands and Dad, well Dad, he'll be fine as long as he knows that I'm happy, and I *am* happy, Dave, so happy.'

Dave stopped walking; he let go of his suitcase and pulled Erica towards him. The people walking behind tut-tutted as they manoeuvred around them. Neither Erica nor Dave seemed to be aware that they were causing an obstruction. The tap on Dave's shoulder caused him to pull away from Erica. His eyes were still partly closed; he was about to laugh and explain that he just couldn't help himself; he was with the woman he loved, and she'd agreed to marry him; he was going to apologise and beg their indulgence when his eyes focused on the scene. He and Erica were surrounded by five police officers. The hand on his shoulder belonged to Inspector Joe Reed.

The hustle and noise of the station faded. Erica was acutely aware of the hot smell of train brakes as the words *arresting, murder, Melissa Davies, say anything* and *given in evidence* drifted through her head. Darkness began to creep across her field of vision; she heard a whistle blow. *Do they still use whistles?* she thought idly. *Have I slipped into another dimension?* Someone was calling her name; they sounded a long way away.

'Miss Woods, Miss Woods,' said the officer gently. 'You need to come with me now.'

She found herself moving along the platform again. There was no sign of Dave. She wanted to ask questions, she just wasn't sure she wanted to know the answers.

'Miss Woods, is there anyone that you'd like me to contact?'

Erica stared at the police officer. She was decked out in full uniform; jaunty little bowler hat; thick padded waistcoat with radio attached to her left shoulder; thick trousers with baton and handcuffs hanging from the belt, and Erica worried that she must be feeling incredibly hot in this muggy August weather. Erica looked down at her own attire; a simple summer dress and sandals.

'Miss Woods,' the officer repeated. 'Is there anyone you want to contact?'

'Sorry, what?'

'We need to get you home, Miss Woods,' explained the officer. 'My vehicle is parked just outside…'

'No, no,' Erica replied hastily. 'I'll ring my friend; she'll come and get me.'

Erica sat, silent and ashen-faced, a wet handkerchief balled up in her hands. Maggie set three mugs of coffee on the table and sat down beside her. She glanced across at Winton; he gave an imperceptible shrug of his shoulders. Maggie put her arms around Erica. She felt tiny and vulnerable. Still no one spoke. The only sound Maggie could hear was the ticking of the bloody awful clock that Dave had bought. She wanted to smash it into a thousand pieces; she wanted to smash Dave into a thousand pieces; she wanted to make it all better for her friend; she felt helpless. She glanced at Winton again. He opened his mouth to speak, thought better of it and closed it again. Erica, with her head down, slowly raised her left hand. She held it up in front of Maggie's face.

Maggie grabbed hold of the hand and gasped. 'Oh, bloody hell, Erica.'

'Not quite the reaction I'd imagined,' said Erica in a small, quiet voice.

'No,' said Maggie. 'It's just, well it's just; oh, shit, Erica, I just don't know what to say to you.'

'What can you say,' said Erica. 'What can anybody say? But I'll tell you this, Maggie; there is no way, no way that Dave murdered Melissa. I refuse to believe it.'

At the police station Dave, insisting that he was innocent, declined the offer of a solicitor. Shaking and pale, he was led once again into Interview room A, where he was left alone with an officer who stood, silent and rigid, by the door. Joe and Harry observed Dave's demeanour through the two-way mirror. After a few minutes Harry cleared his throat.

'Out with it, lad,' said Joe. 'What are your thoughts?'

Harry resited his glasses to sit a little higher on his nose. 'He looks, well he looks anxious and nervous obviously, but he also looks confused and that seems strange. Assuming that he murdered Melissa Davies, dismembered her and stuffed her into the oak chest prior to burying it beneath the pond, why would he be confused at this point? He must know that we discovered the remains, otherwise why would we have arrested him?'

'Let's ask him, shall we?'

Dave looked up as Joe and Harry entered the room, but said nothing. Joe placed several files onto the table and sat down; he checked the tape machine, gave the date, time and persons present before launching into the interview. He opened the latest file and slid a photograph, taken on August 22nd, across the table towards Dave. The photograph showed an oak chest jutting out through mud that had once been the base of the pond.

'Do you recognise this?'

Dave's hand shook as he retrieved his glasses from his hair. He stared at the photograph. He swallowed. 'Yes.'

'Could you explain to me how it is that you come to recognise this oak chest?'

'It was the chest that Melissa inherited from her parents.'

'And are you able to explain to me how it ended up buried beneath the pond?'

Dave pushed the photograph away. 'I put it there.'

Joe nodded and extracted a second photograph from the file. He examined it for a moment and then, as before, slowly pushed it across the table towards Dave.

'And I wonder if you could explain how it was that these remains came to be in that chest.'

Without glancing at the photograph, Dave sneered. 'Remains? That's a bit of a stretch, Inspector, even for you.'

'Look at the photograph.'

Dave sighed deeply and looked. The blood drained from his face; he started to shake, his mouth dropped open, he squeezed his eyes shut and beads of sweat appeared on his forehead. 'I, I, I just, what? I, I don't understand.'

'What is it that you don't understand?' said Joe in a calm clear voice. 'These are the remains of Melissa Davies, remember her?'

'Of course I bloody remember her,' Dave thundered. 'And, as I have repeatedly told you, Melissa stormed out of the cottage back in 2006 and the last time I saw her she was alive.'

'Interesting; so how do we explain these remains inside this oak chest? An oak chest that you have just admitted belonged to Melissa; an oak chest buried beneath a pond that you freely admitted to building in the weeks following Melissa Davies's disappearance?'

'I don't bloody know; I just know that I didn't put her into the chest; I put…' He clamped his mouth shut.

'I'm sorry,' said Joe. 'You put?'

Dave gave Joe a thunderous look. 'You've already decided that I murdered her; you decided that bloody months ago, and so whatever I say now you won't believe.'

'I work on evidence, and the evidence so far is not looking good for you. I think you will agree that you've done a lot of lying and changing of stories since we first had our little chat, so forgive me if I seem a little sceptical.'

'May I make a suggestion,' said Harry.

'Please do,' said Joe.

Harry gave Dave a kindly smile.

'Oh, give me a fucking break,' yelled Dave. 'What are we now; good cop bad cop?'

'My suggestion,' persevered Harry, 'is that you simply take us through the events from the time that you arrived at Black Sheep Cottage with Melissa until you returned to London. Leave nothing out and tell us everything, no matter how embarrassing. All we seek is the truth, Mr Mardle.'

With a defiant look at Joe, Dave launched in. 'When I first put the idea to Melissa of a few days away at my gran's cottage she flatly refused but, miraculously, after a chat with Dad, she was suddenly up for it. We argued for most of the journey; I simply couldn't reason with her; she kept wittering on about her complicated feelings for my father and how I didn't understand, and when I suggested that she try to explain how she was feeling, in words of one syllable so that my simple brain could process it, she laughed in my face and said I was being ridiculous and what part of 'complicated' did I not understand.

'I told her that I loved her and I apologised for my infantile behaviour towards her. I tried to explain to her that my father had a bit of a reputation with young women, always had done. How my mother puts up with it I shall never understand. Anyway, she was having none of it. She said that even though that may be the case it didn't apply to her; returning the favour, I laughed in *her* face and told her she was being naïve in the extreme. I also said I understood, although I didn't, not really, but I wanted to at least *seem* to be sympathetic.'

'Big of you,' remarked Joe.

'Anyway, when we arrived at the cottage Melissa excused herself on the grounds of having a severe headache. She marched up the stairs with me in hot pursuit; she went into the spare bloody bedroom, slammed and locked the door.'

Dave glared at Joe. 'I've told you all this before, for God's sake!'

Joe opened up another file. 'At your first interview, Mr Mardle, you simply informed me that you and Melissa slept in separate bedrooms, and the following day she stormed out.' He looked across at Dave. 'What I need you to do now is fill in the details; what happened after Melissa Davies locked herself in the spare bedroom?'

'Jesus Christ; right, fine,' he closed his eyes momentarily. 'I um, I banged on the door for several minutes, telling her that she was behaving like a spoilt child, and she yelled back that that was rich coming from me.' Dave hesitated and gave a little smile. 'I could see her point. Anyway, I gave up; I think I had a drink or two, or maybe more, because the next thing I remember is waking up downstairs on the settee feeling rather worse for wear.'

'So, you didn't sleep in the other bedroom as you originally claimed, and you were drunk?' suggested Joe.

'The point is, *Mr* Inspector, I didn't spend the night with Melissa; I was on the settee, so fucking what! And, no, I wasn't bloody drunk; I wasn't in the right frame of mind to get drunk. I simply wanted to numb my brain. I wanted everything to be as it had been before she'd moved in with us, before my father got his fucking claws into her and corrupted her feelings towards me.'

'So, what happened the next day?'

'Melissa banging around in the kitchen woke me up. She was opening every bloody cupboard and slamming it shut again as far as I could make out, and when I staggered into the kitchen she gave me a filthy look and told me I looked like some tramp who'd been dragged in from the gutter. That didn't improve my mood.'

'So you were hung-over and angry?' suggested Joe.

'Yes, Inspector, I was hung-over and angry, but I wasn't feeling murderous, if that's what you're implying.'

'I wasn't implying anything; I am simply trying to get the facts straight. Carry on.'

'I pushed her...' Dave noted Joe's expression and started again. 'I pushed her *gently* out of the way and made a pot of coffee. We sat outside on the patio and drank it. I tried to talk to her, to reason with her, but she just sat there fiddling with that fucking bauble round her neck.'

'Just for clarification,' said Joe. 'Are you referring to the necklace with the silver butterfly pendant?'

'Yes, Inspector; the one I've already told you about. For Christ's sake, don't you ever listen?'

Joe sorted through his files and removed the small plastic evidence bag. 'For the sake of the tape,' he said. 'I am now showing the suspect exhibit A.' He handed the bag to Dave. 'Do you recognise this?'

'Of course I recognise it,' Dave yelled. 'It's her cheap, crappy necklace.'

'The one she wore all the time?'

'Yes.'

'So how is it, do you think, that we found it lodged between the slabs surrounding the fireplace?'

'You found it there, *Inspector*, because that's where I threw it.'

'And how did that come about?'

Dave clenched his hands. 'I, um, well; I ripped it off her neck. It was later on, evening time, not sure what time, but it was dark outside. I'm not proud of my actions. We were still alternating between silences and screaming; during one screaming row she started on about her trauma and everything again and I just lost it; I grabbed hold of the thing and yanked it. The bloody chain, some cheap crap as I was saying, simply snapped and I hurled it over her head towards the fireplace. I assumed it'd gone into the fire. Anyway, she lashed out at me, threw herself onto the hearth and started jabbing away at the burning wood and coal with the poker trying to find the stupid thing, but it'd vanished. She was beyond reason with anger and that's when she stormed out into the night, never to be seen again.'

'Again, just for clarification,' said Joe. 'This would have been on the evening of the 25th of July, the day after you arrived.'

'Yes!'

'And you're saying that's the last time you saw her?'

'That *is* the last time I saw her, and she was very much alive at the time. I did not kill her, I didn't. I'm many things Inspector, a spoilt, selfish individual and a liar even, but I am *not* a murderer.'

Joe consulted his notes. 'You then telephoned your parents and drove back to London to collect Melissa's things, correct?'

'Yep.'

'You returned to the cottage and, sometime later, you burnt these possessions and also, we now discover, you buried the oak chest beneath the pond that you constructed, correct?'

'Yep.'

'I'm sure you can see my confusion,' said Joe. 'You saw Melissa leave the cottage; you later bury the oak chest that you have collected from London. We find this very same oak chest seven years later and, in that chest, we find the remains of Melissa.'

'But I didn't kill her and I certainly didn't put her body inside the bloody chest. I did, however, put, oh shit, I put…'

'In your own time,' said Harry.

Dave took a deep breath in and held it for several seconds. Slowly he released it. 'It was Wednesday I think, the day after I got back from London, that I started to dig out the pond. It was bloody hard work and so I drove into Northallerton to hire a digger. They delivered it that afternoon and after a couple of hours I'd dug an enormous

251

hole. I threw everything that I thought would burn into the centre and then dragged the oak chest over. I stood staring down at the hole and thought it looked like a grave and something snapped in my head. I dashed around the garden like a demented idiot, collecting twigs and branches; I got some twine from the shed and I constructed what I can only describe as a fucking effigy of Melissa. I even dressed it in some of her clothes. *That* was what I stuffed into the chest. I set light to all the stuff that was at the bottom of the hole and watched it burn and when it had died down I lowered the chest down and covered it with earth. It was, as I think you mentioned, Inspector, a ceremony.' He looked down at his hands. 'I realise how bizarre and ridiculous it sounds but I swear to you it's the truth.'

'And when was it that you returned to London?' asked Joe.

'Um, it must have been about a month later,' Dave replied.

'That's a long time to stay,' remarked Joe. 'Why so long?'

'Because I did a lot of bloody work in the cottage, that's why. I built a couple of ramps, installed a French window, *and* I built a pond. Have you ever built a pond, Inspector?'

'Can't say that I have.'

'Well, let me tell you it isn't easy, not on your own anyway; oh, no doubt Dad would tell you that he could have done it in a day or two; considers himself to be the bloody world expert on pond building. Anyway, dear Daddy had some conference to attend or something, so I had to get back for Mum and of course I had the bookshop to run; life goes on and all that.'

'Well, for some anyway,' remarked Joe.

Dave slammed his fist onto the table. 'For the last fucking time; I did not kill Melissa and frankly, if I had, I certainly wouldn't have buried her at the scene of the crime for Christ's sake!'

'Did you need to use the chainsaw at anytime when you were building the pond?'

'What? Why the hell would I need a chainsaw to build a pond? Christ Almighty. I've just told you Inspector, I used a digger; I think you'll find that such a machine is much better at digging big holes than a chainsaw.'

'Yes, of course; silly of me,' said Joe. 'So, I wonder what else you might have used the chainsaw for.'

'What else? Oh, I don't know. How about cutting down trees? Jesus!'

A young female officer entered and, without speaking, handed a folded sheet of paper to Joe. Frowning, he unfolded the sheet. Having read the note, he checked the time, announced that the interview was suspended and switched off the tape machine.

'We'll take a break now and resume the interview in an hour. I'll arrange for some coffee to be sent in.'

Dave said nothing.

Outside Joe thrust the sheet into Harry's hand. 'Read this.'

'Shit,' said Harry.

'Quite.'

Back in his office Joe rang Richard.

'What the hell is all this about?'

'And hello to you too,' replied Richard. 'I thought I'd better let you know; have you arrested your suspect yet?'

'We were in the middle of the interview when your bombshell arrived.'

'Right well, first things first. Hopkins has confirmed that the cuts on the bones are consistent with being caused by the blade of the chainsaw that your Harry sent up here on the...'

'Yes, yes,' said Joe. 'But what about this bloody sighting of Melissa Davies?'

'Steady on mate; don't shoot the messenger and all that.'

Joe took a deep breath. 'Sorry. Carry on.'

'There was a report about the murder in the Yorkshire Herald a couple of days ago. Included with the report was the photograph of Melissa Davies that you sent to me back in May, helpfully supplied to the paper by our press office guys. Anyway, late yesterday a Barbara Wallis rang in to say that she recognised the woman in the photograph but she said it wasn't Melissa Davies. She explained that she knew her as Penny Fisher, who'd stayed at the Holiday Inn just outside York where this Barbara works; and get this: she said that *Penny Fisher,* aka Melissa Davies, stayed at the Inn from 25th July 2006 to the 21st August 2006. She remembers her because, firstly, it's very unusual for guests to stay for such extended periods, and secondly, because she hardly ever went out. I've checked the hotel records and spoken with the manager, and her story checks out.'

'Fuck. That means Dave's story, his latest one anyway, checks out.'

'Sorry, old chap.'

'Do you know if she had any visitors while she was there?'

'One of the first things I asked, as it happens,' said Richard. 'And the answer is no, none. But I did establish that when she left on the 21st August she left by taxi; my team are checking with the taxi firm as we speak and I should be able to tell you where she went within the hour.'

Joe replaced the receiver. Harry kept quiet. The tick of the wall clock filled the room. Joe flicked through his notes. 'Right,' he said. 'Dave maintains that Melissa walked out, alive and well, on the evening of the 25th July and that was the last he ever saw of her. We now find that she booked into the Holiday Inn, just outside York, on that very evening, staying there until the 21st August. Which is about a month, correct?'

Harry nodded. 'That's the same length of time that Dave told us that he stayed at the cottage.'

'We need to know exactly when Dave returned to London. Maybe Melissa was in contact with him, you know, during a cooling off period or something, and then, when they got back together, *that's* when he bumped her off.'

Harry checked his notebook. 'Actually, sir, we know when Dave returned to London.'

Joe frowned.

'When we called in at the Retreat on Monday, sir, Phyllis Adams told us that her son-in-law drove up to Yorkshire the day after her grandson returned from Yorkshire, on the 20th August, dropping her off in Oxford on the way up.'

'Shit, that's right,' said Joe. 'So that means that Melissa was still at the hotel...'

'Alive.'

'Yes, thank you, Harry; so, she was still alive when Dave Mardle (junior) returned to London. Do we know how long Mr Mardle (senior) stayed up in Yorkshire?'

Harry checked his notebook again. 'He said he couldn't remember, but Mrs Adams said he didn't return to London until *after* the 27th August.'

Joe dragged his hand through his hair. 'Meaning that it was Dave's father in Yorkshire; shit.'

'So it would seem sir.'

'Bloody hell, Harry; Mr Mardle's laptop! We need to find out about those emails that were password protected.' With a look of desperation, he pleaded, 'Please tell me you've got the results and you simply forgot all about them.'

Harry studied the ground carefully as he muttered, 'Um, no, sorry.'

'Not your fault, lad, not your fault; I'll give them a call.'

A few moments later Joe was yelling down the phone, telling the technical staff to get their act together. He slammed down the phone. 'They haven't even started yet. Unbelievable; get down there and point out to them the urgency of the matter, there's a good lad.'

'I wonder why Mr Mardle didn't remind us that we still had his laptop when we collected the chainsaw,' remarked Harry.

'Why indeed,' said Joe. 'Perhaps we'll find nothing important; just evidence of other assignations with young women. His mother-in-law is certainly under no illusions about the man's ability to keep his dick under control.'

At the door Harry turned. 'And another thing,' he said. 'How did Melissa pay for her stay at the hotel? Her bank hadn't been accessed since, when was it?'

Joe was frantically checking the files. 'Here it is; she withdrew £500 on Friday 21st July 2006; that's the Friday before she and Dave left for the cottage.'

'But that's not enough to cover a month's stay in a hotel; not even the Holiday Inn is that cheap,' said Harry.

'So how *did* she pay? Get onto them, Harry, and find out who paid for her room.'

'Before or after I speak to the tech boys?'

'After. We need to know what those emails are about.'

'Right.'

Richard's call came through twenty minutes later. 'Are you sitting down, mate?'

Joe swallowed. His knuckles became white as he clutched the receiver to his ear. 'Just tell me.'

'The taxi took Penny Fisher, aka Melissa Davies, to Black Sheep Cottage.'

Joe closed his eyes tight. 'And did the taxi driver see anyone else at the cottage?'

'Negative on that I'm afraid, but he did say that he remembers seeing a silver Rolls parked outside; not many of those in North Yorkshire.'

'A silver Rolls?'

'That's what the man said, why, is that significant?'

Joe hesitated. 'Richard I've, I've made a major cock-up here.'

'The car?'

'Yes, Richard, the bloody car,' said Joe.

'Because?'

'Because, Richard, our suspect's father owns a silver Rolls.'

'Ahh, right, I see; tricky.'

Joe replaced the receiver and buried his head in his hands. Had he been wrong all along? It didn't bear thinking about. He snatched up the phone and rang the desk sergeant. 'Stick Dave Mardle in a cell; tell him we'll resume the interview later.'

He gathered his files and started to go through them, cross checking dates and statements. He had a disturbing feeling that he'd been wrong. It seemed that Melissa Davies had, as Dave had maintained all along, left the cottage on the evening of the 25th July 2006, alive and well. She'd somehow managed to get herself to the Holiday Inn, where she'd registered herself as Penny Fisher, and then returned to Black Sheep Cottage two days *after* Dave Mardle (junior) left for London to allow his father to drive up to attend some conference in Yorkshire. More significantly, thought Joe, it meant that when Melissa Davies arrived at Black Sheep Cottage by taxi, it was to meet Mr Dave Mardle (senior).

Marshall's going to have a field day, he thought.

Chapter 16

The case files were strewn across Joe's desk. 'How the hell did you end up inside the oak chest, Melissa; tell me, how?'

A gentle knock on his door caused him to look up. 'Harry. What have you got for me?'

'I'm still working on the money thing, but the tech boys said they'd have Mr Mardle's password cracked within minutes.' He glanced at his watch. 'In fact they've probably already done it.'

Joe was about to call the technical lab when the phone rang. He snatched it up. 'What?' he yelled. 'I'm busy.'

'Um, it's me, Mark; it's about that laptop, but if…'

'No, no, don't hang up, sorry; what have you got?'

'We've managed to unlock all his emails. Didn't take long; the passwords used were infantile. It beggars belief, I mean, time and time again people use the most ridiculous…'

'I'm coming down.' He hung up and dashed downstairs.

'OK, Mark; let's have a look.'

Joe scrolled down the list and saw that the protected emails had been sent between 25th July and 21st August, and they'd been sent to Melissa Davies. 'Bloody hell,' he muttered.

'Useful?' asked Mark.

'Um, I'll say. Can you ascertain who sent them and…?'

'Already done,' replied Mark. 'They were sent from a residential address,' he flicked through his notes, 'Aynhoe Road, W14, to the Holiday Inn just outside York. Note the email address that they were sent to.'

Joe looked. 'And?'

'It's a different account,' said Mark. 'Not the same account that Melissa Davies had been using prior to 2006.'

'Well fuck me,' exclaimed Joe.

'I'd rather not if that's all the same with you.'

'Ha, ha; very funny,' retorted Joe. 'Can you print these off, quick as you can, I need…'

Mark handed Joe a small folder. 'Already done.'

'I take all insults back that I've directed towards your lot in the past and, for good measure, I'll apologise now for any future insults.'

'Very decent of you.'

Clutching the folder tightly to his chest, Joe shot along the corridor and up to his office; he took the stairs two at a time, grabbed Harry out of his chair and bustled him into his office. He slammed the door and thrust the file into Harry's hands. 'Read this.'

Harry read it. 'Shit!'

'Plus; I had a phone call from Richard while you were otherwise occupied.'

'Uh, uh; and?'

'And it seems that Melissa Davies was picked up by taxi from the Holiday Inn and taken to Black Sheep Cottage on the 21st August, and the taxi driver remembers seeing a silver Rolls parked outside.'

'Bloody hell, sir.'

'Take a couple of constables and get over to The Retreat right away, and bring Mr Dave Mardle in for questioning. Any problems just arrest him on suspicion of, oh, you know the bloody drill; move!'

Dave stood in front of Joe's desk, looking dazed. 'What's going on? The custody officer said I was free to go.'

Joe took a deep breath. 'Take a seat.'

Dave sat.

Joe looked him directly in the eye. 'You are, as the custody officer said, free to go,' he said.

'So, you actually believe me? Bloody hell; wonders will never cease.'

'It seems that I owe you an apology; evidence has just come to light confirming your statement that Melissa Davies was alive the last time you saw her on the 25th July. In fact she was alive until, at least, the 21st August.'

'The 21st *August*? So where the hell was she?'

'I'm not at liberty to…'

'Oh, don't give me all that twaddle,' yelled Dave. 'You've just put me through hell. I've told you all along that I never harmed Melissa but oh no, you'd already made your mind up, hadn't you, and don't lie, I could see it your eyes that day in the park.'

Joe loosened his collar. 'I wonder, could I ask you a couple more questions?'

Dave pushed his chair back, sending it crashing to the floor. 'No you bloody can't,' he snapped as he patted his pockets. 'I need to ring Erica; she'll be frantic with worry.'

'Your mobile will be locked away at the front desk; you can ring her from here.'

Dave snatched the phone from Joe's desk and stared at it. 'Fuck; I don't know her number; it's in my contact list.'

Joe opened the case file and dialled the number for Dave. 'It should be ringing now.'

'Erica, oh Erica it's me; listen, stop crying, Erica, Erica.'

'Dave? Is that you? It's me, Maggie, what's going on? Erica's in a dreadful state.'

Dave explained and, by the time it became clear that he was no longer suspected of murdering Melissa, Erica had calmed down and informed him that she was on her way down to the station. Dave handed the phone back to Joe and mumbled his thanks.

'I take it Erica's on her way?'

Dave nodded.

'For what it's worth,' said Joe. 'I'm pleased.'

'Pleased?'

'Yes, pleased; Erica's a lovely girl and well, I was a bit concerned, anyway…'

Dave burst out laughing. 'Ah; you were a bit concerned that she'd got herself romantically involved with some deranged murderer of small, blue eyed, pixie faced women.'

Joe smiled in spite of himself. 'Well, um, yes; anyway, you're free to go and once again, my apologies but...' he was interrupted by his mobile. He checked the caller ID. 'Excuse me a moment, it's my Sergeant,' he said, 'I need to take this.'

'He's gone, sir,' said Harry.

'Gone? What do you mean, gone? Gone where?'

Catching his breath, Harry replied, 'Well that's just it; I've spoken to his wife and she's not sure. She said he suddenly announced that he had an important meeting with a client and had to dash. He told her he'd forgotten all about it; he said it was because of the awful news about Melissa Davies. The thing is she was expecting him to ring her first thing this morning but he didn't; she's tried to contact him but his phone goes straight to voicemail.'

'When did he go?'

'Last night, sir.'

'Did he go in his car?'

'Yes.'

'Did he say where this meeting was?'

'No, sir.'

'OK; have another word with Mrs Mardle and Phyllis Adams and see if they can give you any more details. Mrs Mardle told me that her husband still did a bit of private consultancy work; find out what sort of consultancy work and see if she has access to his client list. Oh, and ask Mrs Mardle about the work that her husband said he'd done on the pond; I don't know about you, but I got the distinct impression that she wanted to say something when we were there last. I'll get a search out for the car. Get back here as soon as you can.' Joe hung up and made his way to the door.

'What the hell's going on *now?*' demanded Dave.

'Two seconds; I just need to organise a search for a missing vehicle.'

He returned moments later. 'I'm sorry to tell you, but it seems that your father has gone missing.'

'My father?'

'Yes; we wanted to have a chat with him about his movements following your return from Yorkshire, but, as you heard, it seems he's had to dash off to meet one of his clients; any ideas where that meeting might be?'

'My father and I rarely communicate. I'm aware that he has some private clients but as to who or where they are I'm afraid I haven't a clue.' He bent down to right his chair and sat back down. 'You asked your Sergeant to check on some work that my father had done on the pond; which pond exactly?'

'The pond at Black Sheep Cottage.'

'He didn't do any work on that pond. I told you, *I* constructed it.'

'I'm aware of that, but your father maintained that it was leaking; something to do with you forgetting to include an overflow pipe.'

'He said what?'

'He said that...'

'Yes, yes I heard you,' said Dave. 'But I can assure you, Inspector, I definitely installed an overflow pipe; even I'm not that stupid.'

'Nevertheless, when I spoke with your family on Monday, your father was adamant that he had worked on the pond, installing this vital overflow pipe; simple work he informed me. I did, however, get the impression that your mother didn't agree with your father's version and...'

'Hang on a minute; are you saying what I think you're saying?' said Dave

'It depends on what you think I'm saying,' replied Joe.

'Are you saying that you now suspect my father?'

262

'Let's just say that we think he can help us with our enquiries.'

'So, you *are* saying that you suspect my father,' said Dave. 'You think he dug up the pond and found the oak chest that I'd buried; well, so what? If he did it would simply have confirmed to him that I was a fool. Melissa was long gone; I *told* you, she walked out the evening after we arrived, never to be seen again.'

'Except that I have now been reliably informed that she *was* seen after that,' said Joe. 'As I said she was last seen, alive and well, on the 21st August.'

'I'll ask you again; *where* was she seen? Surely I have a right to know.'

Joe thought for a moment and decided that perhaps Dave was right; he did deserve to know, and the knowledge of where she was last seen might actually concentrate his mind. 'Fair enough; on the 21st August 2006, Melissa Davies was delivered by taxi to Black Sheep Cottage.'

Dave opened his mouth and immediately shut it again. He stared at Joe for a long moment.

Joe said nothing.

'But, sorry, she went *back* to the cottage?'

'She did.'

'But, but was that when Dad was there, no, surely not, he never said, surely he would have said. Are you certain?'

'Positive.'

'So I was right all along; they *were* having a bloody affair. Jesus! No wonder Dad wanted to accompany me back up to Yorkshire with Melissa's stuff. God, I've been slow.' He again pushed his chair back. He began pacing back and forth.

Joe watched and waited.

Dave exclaimed, 'It was him, wasn't it? You're saying that my father killed her, dug up the pond and stuffed her body into the chest. Dear God.' He slumped back down. 'How? Why?'

'I can't answer those questions, I'm afraid,' said Joe quietly. 'That's why we need to speak to your father.' He consulted the case file. 'Would it be alright if we go over a few points again, to clarify the time line?'

Dave gave Joe a resigned nod.

Joe extracted the interview notes from the file. 'When you first suggested the trip up to Yorkshire, you said that Melissa flatly refused but, after a chat with your father, she changed her mind. Is that right?'

Dave nodded.

'Any idea why?'

'Not a clue.'

Joe glanced at his notes again. 'Can you remember when your father left London for his conference in York?'

Dave looked to the ceiling and rubbed his forehead. 'Hold on; I stayed at the cottage for about a month and so, um, it must have been towards the end of August.'

'Did he leave London, before or after the 21st August?'

Dave screwed up his eyes. 'Shit, I can't; oh hang on, yes, I remember; Gran was due to visit her old friend, Martha, she goes every year, that's right, yes, so I must have driven back home on the 19th August, so that Gran could travel over to Oxford on the Sunday; Dad dropped her off on his way up to the cottage.'

'So, that would have been on the 20th August?'

'Yes, that's right. Oh, dear God.'

'And when did your father return to London?'

'Um, um, oh shit, um I can't think.'

'Take your time,' said Joe calmly. 'How long does your grandmother normally stay in Oxford?'

'She always stays for a week.'

'For a week, right; so, who was it that collected her?'

'Me; it was meant to be Dad but he was,' he took a deep breath, 'but he was still in Yorkshire.'

'So, when did you collect your grandmother from Oxford.'

'It must have been the 27th August, yes, that's right,' said Dave. 'I think Dad got back a few days later.'

'And how did he seem?'

Joe's mobile rang. He checked the caller. 'Sorry, I need to take this.'

'Harry, where are you?'

'Downstairs sir with a very frantic Erica Woods; she said the desk sergeant told her to wait in reception and…'

'Bring her up. Dave Mardle's in my office.'

After an emotional reunion, Erica turned to Joe. 'I *told* you; I *knew* he couldn't have hurt Melissa, but you wouldn't listen, you just wouldn't listen.'

'Mea culpa,' said Joe. 'I've obviously apologised to Mr Mardle here and I now apologise to you, but I hope you understand that in situations like these, we cannot afford to rule anybody out until we have evidence that they are innocent.'

'So do you have any idea, any at all, about who killed…?'

'It seems it was my father.'

'Your *father*,' cried Erica. She took hold of his hand. 'I, I don't know what to say.'

The desk phone trilled loudly. Harry picked up. 'Inspector Reed's phone.'

'Right, well, you're free to go,' said Joe. 'If you hear from your father then…'

'Sir,' said Harry as he hung up. 'That was traffic. They've located the car.'

'Dad's car?'

'Um, well…'

'It's alright, Sergeant,' said Joe. 'Where is it?'

'They found it abandoned in Highbury Hill, sir.'

Dave's eyes widened. 'We own a lock-up there, or rather Mum does; it's where we store stuff for the bookshop. Dad's never been interested in anything to do with Mum's

265

shop, so why the hell he drove out there I've no idea, and then to *abandon* his precious bloody car. Shit, Erica, what the hell is going on?'

'I've no idea,' said Erica. 'But I think we should leave the police to do their job.'

'Don't forget, if you hear from your father…'

'Oh, fear not; I'll be in touch.'

They went back to Erica's flat.

'And now they've found his dad's car, *abandoned* in Highbury Hill,' said Erica.

Maggie stared, open-mouthed.

'This is a rare event,' remarked Winton with a wry smile. 'My woman lost for words.'

'*Your* woman,' exclaimed Erica. 'Maggie Jane Hunter-Lopez, explain immediately. I leave you alone for a couple of weeks and I return to find that you and Winton are, well, what exactly *are* you and Winton?'

'Bloody hell, Erica, you can talk! You go off to Paris for a break and return *engaged* for goodness sake.'

'Fair enough, I'll give you that, but come on, tell all; what's been going on?'

Maggie glanced at Winton.

'I think it best if you tell Erica where we went and everything; better to be honest, don't you think?'

'Where you went?'

'Oh, Erica; promise me you won't be cross,' said Maggie. 'I was only thinking of you; I was worried and so we…'

Winton shot Maggie a warning glance.

'So *I* decided to do a bit of digging and Winton agreed to come with me.'

'You went up to Yorkshire, didn't you?' said Dave.

Maggie nodded.

'Why?' asked Erica.

'I think I can answer that,' said Dave. 'Maggie never really believed me about what happened to Melissa and …'

Maggie started to protest but Dave held up his hands. 'It's alright; I mean I wasn't exactly truthful and up front to start with, now was I? So, knowing you as I do now, I can see how that would have set your antenna twitching.'

'Sorry,' mumbled Maggie.

'Forgiven,' said Dave.

'Will you two stop twittering. I'm waiting for Maggie to explain about,' she looked at Winton and Maggie who were now holding hands, 'well, explain about *this*, for a start,' she said pointing at their clasped hands.

Maggie smiled and, in a rush, she told Erica and Dave about their trip. 'I'm truly sorry, Dave, but I was convinced you were lying and I thought Erica was in danger.'

'Honestly, Maggie,' said Erica.

'I know; it sounds ridiculous now, but, there you go; it's true.'

'We stayed at a small hotel, not far from Northallerton,' added Winton.

'The Moor-House,' said Maggie.

'That's where Dave and I stayed,' exclaimed Erica.

Maggie blushed. 'Yes, I know.'

'And?'

She explained about their visit to Black Sheep Cottage and the Green Man restaurant. 'And then we bumped into Inspector Reed at the hotel,' she exclaimed.

'It was a bit awkward actually,' admitted Winton. 'You see, we were on our way down the stairs, on our way to the dining room for lunch; we'd, um, we'd missed breakfast, you see.'

'Well, I'll be damned,' said Dave as a huge grin spread across his face. 'All I can say is watch out; your life will now be constantly under the eagle eye of detective Maggie Hunter-Lopez.'

Maggie and Erica thumped him simultaneously.

'Oh, and Erica,' exclaimed Maggie. 'You were right about Jay-Jay.'

'Sorry?'

'You thought that Penny was his new girlfriend and she is; well, she wasn't when you first saw them together obviously, but well, she is now. He's planning to accompany her back to Australia.'

'He's emigrating?' exclaimed Erica.

'No, no; Penny's moving back to Britain. Her Dad died, you see, and she wants to be near her Mum, you know, now that's she's all alone.'

'And she and Jay-Jay are tight,' added Winton.

'Just like you and Maggie, it would seem.'

Maggie smiled. 'Yes; brilliant isn't it?'

'Who'd have thought,' said Dave as they made their way across London towards The Retreat. 'Maggie and Winton.'

'I think they make a lovely couple,' said Erica. 'I'm not really surprised, not when I think about it. They seemed to hit it off from the moment that I introduced them. Yes, I don't know why I didn't see it earlier, most unlike me to miss something like that.'

Dave smiled. 'Your detective juices probably weren't in full flow at the time; you needed the infamous 'Dave hunt' to get them going I expect.'

Erica thumped him again.

'I say,' he said as he rubbed his arm. 'Have I made a terrible mistake here? Am I about to marry a tiny, feisty monster?'

Another thump.

'My God; should I be contacting Inspector Reed for protection?'

Erica's face became serious. 'Oh, Dave, your poor mum.'

'I know.'

'Do *you* think your father could have, well, you know.'

'What, murdered Melissa?'

Erica nodded.

'I can't see him *planning* to do her in, no,' said Dave. 'But maybe, you know, in the heat of the moment, oh, I don't know. I mean, who knows what anyone is capable of?'

Phyllis rushed down the steps of The Retreat as Dave and Erica came through the gate.

'Thank God,' she said. 'Maggie rang to say you were on your way. Are you alright? That nice Sergeant Carter was here asking questions; he said you'd been arrested and then released; he was asking about your father, who's gone off somewhere; what's going on?' She clasped Erica's hand. 'Lovely to see you again dear, how was, oh goodness me,' she exclaimed as she felt the ring. 'What's this?'

Erica held her hand up.

'Engaged? Oh, what wonderful news; come in, come in, tell your mother, she needs a bit of good news.'

Phyllis took them into the living room where Deborah was seated in her wheelchair by the French windows. 'I'll make us all a nice cup of tea,' announced Phyllis.

'Mum,' said Dave. 'Are you alright?'

'I am dear, yes, I'm fine, don't worry about me. What about you; arrested, gracious. How awful.'

'Yes, but it's all been sorted out now. The police are saying that they want to talk to Dad now.'

'I know, dear, I know,' said Deborah as she wheeled herself over towards her son. 'Now then, do sit down; you look like a couple of guests who've stumbled into the wrong party. Tell me, how was Paris?'

'It was wonderful,' said Erica.

Dave took hold of Erica's left hand and held it out towards his mother.

'Engaged; oh, many, many congratulations to you both.'

'Mum,' said Dave as he and Erica sat, 'have you any idea what meeting Dad was off to?'

'None at all, dear,' said Deborah. 'I actually doubt very much that he had a meeting. Much as I doubted that he

269

went to a conference in York all those years ago. I'm afraid your father was in the habit of inventing meetings and conferences as a means of, well, I'm sure you can imagine.'

'Bloody hell, Mum,' exclaimed Dave. 'Why did you put up with him for all these years?'

'For the simple reason that I loved him. I always have and I thought I always would, but now, well now, I just don't know. Ever since the police came asking questions about Melissa he's been very jumpy. And then, when they took away his chainsaw...'

Dave blanched. 'The police asked me about a chainsaw. Jesus, I feel sick.'

Phyllis clattered into the room, pushing a small hostess trolley. 'I thought some cupcakes would be nice; they're from Betty Blythe's café,' she said with a grin. 'I know Erica likes them.' She looked around at everyone.

'Is everything alright? Well, you know what I mean, I know everything isn't alright, obviously, but has something happened?'

'Everything's fine, Gran, and those cupcakes look delicious, don't they Erica?'

'They certainly do,' agreed Erica brightly. 'You sit down, Phyllis; I'll be mother.'

Waving a cupcake in the air, Dave said, 'Just before Erica and I left the police station a report came in saying that Dad's car had been found, abandoned in Highbury Hill of all places.'

'Where the lock-up is?' asked Deborah.

'Yep.'

'Whatever could he be doing there? He hasn't even got a key to it. Abandoned, you say?'

Mid chew, Dave nodded.

'Well I never. So, I was right, there was no meeting,' Deborah took a deep breath. 'It's not looking good, is it?'

'Not really, no,' said Dave.

'I've put up with many things from your father over the years. Mum tried very hard to dissuade me from marrying him but, as with all young people, I knew best. But never, never in a million years did I believe that he could actually hurt someone; it doesn't bear thinking about.'

Back at the station the police were scanning through the CCTV footage around Highbury Hill. A man fitting Dave Mardle's description had been seen entering the Underground at Arsenal. From there it had been relatively easy to follow his progress. He'd travelled on the Piccadilly Line to Leicester Square where he'd changed onto the Northern Line, and then changed onto the Jubilee Line, alighting at Canada Water. It was there that they lost sight of him.

'So, where's he going?' asked Joe. 'What's in Canada Water?'

'A lot of swanky flats for one thing,' said Harry.

Joe picked up the phone.

'This is Inspector Reed. Could I speak to Dave Mardle please.'

'Sorry, he and Erica have gone over to be with Dave's mum,' said Maggie. 'Can I help?'

'Not unless you know anything about Canada Water.'

'Sorry, never heard of it.'

'No problem; I'll ring The Retreat.'

Joe hung up and quickly redialled. 'Ah, Erica, excellent; Inspector Reed here, may I speak with Mr Mardle.'

'Assuming you mean *my* Mr Mardle and not the father who still hasn't turned up, or rung come to that, I'll go and get him; hold on a tick.'

'Inspector,' said Dave. 'Have you located my father?'

'Not as such,' replied Joe. 'Do you know of any reason why your father might be visiting Canada Water?'

'Canada Water,' said Dave. 'It rings a bell um, let me think.'

Joe drummed his fingers up and down on his desk as he waited.

'I think Philip White owns a flat out that way. Hold on, I'll ask Mum.'

Joe resumed his drumming.

'Yes, I was right. Philip owns a little pied-a-terre out that way, in the Royal Docks; Mum thinks it's somewhere on the Western Gateway. She said that Dad stayed there a few times; 'entertaining clients' was how she put it. Apparently Philip allows various friends use of the place. Do you think he might be hiding out there?'

'We shall see,' said Joe. 'Thank you very much; you've been most helpful. How's your mother holding up?'

'Remarkably well, actually,' replied Dave. 'Thanks for asking.'

'We'll be in touch.'

Joe replaced the receiver and immediately instructed Harry to find out where Philip White's property was. 'I think we've got him; quick as you can.'

They found Dave's father at Unit B, 20 Western Gateway some thirty minutes later. The door of the property was unlocked and Mr Mardle was sitting quietly on the settee beneath the mezzanine bedroom. He looked up as Joe and Harry entered; eyes devoid of emotion. 'Inspector Reed, I wondered how long it would take you to find me.' He looked at his watch. 'Not that long I see.'

Joe walked over to him. 'Mr David Mardle, I am arresting you for the murder of Melissa Davies in August 2006. You do not have to say anything. However it may harm your defence if you do not mention when questioned something which you later rely on in court. Anything you do say may be given in evidence. Do you understand?'

Dave hauled himself upright. He stood before Joe, closed his eyes momentarily and simply nodded. He offered no resistance, no argument.

Back at the station he refused the offer of a solicitor. 'Let's just get this done, shall we.'

Joe and Harry took Mr Mardle into Interview room A. Joe switched on the tape machine and identified the people present.

'It has recently come to our notice that Melissa Davies was alive and well, staying at the Holiday Inn just outside York, from the 25th July to the 21st August. Do you know anything about that?'

'Don't play games with me, Inspector. I assume you've broken my rather pathetic attempts at password protection and are therefore perfectly aware that I was in contact with Melissa for the entire time that she was staying at the Holiday Inn.'

Harry discreetly placed a small folded sheet of paper in front of Joe. A smile crossed Joe's face as he quickly glanced at it; he waited for Mr Mardle to continue.

Dave cleared his throat. 'There was no conference in York, so don't bother checking. I went up to the cottage with the sole intention of being with Melissa.'

'I see,' said Joe.

'I don't think you do, Inspector. I was in love with Melissa and I wanted very much to be with her. She was young, vibrant, and fun to be with, but, and this is very important, I also love my wife. I'm not sure why she loves me but she does, and for that I will be eternally grateful.'

'And you drove up to the cottage on the 20th August, is that correct?'

'Yes, as my mother-in-law informed you in detail, Inspector. My son returned on the Saturday and I left the following day, dropping Phyllis off in Oxford on the way up.'

'And what car did you use?'

'What car did I use?' asked Dave. 'I used my Rolls, Inspector. What car did you imagine I would use?'

'And how long did you stay at the cottage?'

'Until the 31ˢᵗ August.'

Joe again consulted his notes. 'So you rang your wife to tell her that the conference, the conference that didn't exist, was a waste of time and that you were going to stay on at the cottage to…'

'To get on with some building work, I've already told you that.'

'And when exactly did Melissa join you?'

'The day after I arrived.'

Joe consulted his notes. 'That would have been on the Monday, the 21ˢᵗ, correct?'

'Correct.'

Joe again consulted his notes. 'According to your son, Melissa wasn't very keen on travelling with him to the cottage, and it was only after she'd spoken with you that she agreed to go; have you any comment?'

'Melissa was very unhappy in her relationship with my son, Inspector. Quite frankly she preferred being with me, and the only reason she agreed to go with my son to the cottage was because I devised a plan for us to be together. I bought her a new laptop and set up a new email account for her.'

'Yes, so I discovered.'

Dave gave a small nod. 'I pre-booked the Holiday Inn. That way she could leave my son, go to the hotel, and then return to the cottage to be with me. I also organised a York taxi firm to pick her up.'

'So, her exit from the cottage on the 25ᵗʰ, the day after arriving with your son, had been planned in advance?'

'Yes; well done, Inspector.'

'And am I to assume that she had her own key to the cottage?'

'Yes, I gave her one before she left London. I assumed that my son would come back to London as soon as Melissa walked out. Then I was going to suggest to

Deborah that I might as well go up to the cottage early so that I could get on with the improvements that we'd discussed.'

'But he didn't come straight back,' said Joe.

'No, he stayed up there for a bloody month. Melissa was going insane. The Holiday Inn is not the most salubrious of places.'

Joe consulted the note that Harry had handed him. 'You paid by Visa I see.'

'Well done again, Inspector; yes that's right,' said Dave. He smiled and continued, 'As it happens, by saying that Melissa had left the country, my son was a great help. At one point my wife said that it was probably for the best. She's not a fool; she knows me very well, and was perfectly aware that I was besotted with Melissa, had been from the moment I first set eyes on the girl. Well, you've seen her photograph, and then, when I first saw Erica I nearly fainted. Still, beside the point I suppose. The point is, when my son told everyone that Melissa had run off to Australia I realised that I could meet her with impunity. I intended setting her up in her own flat in Yorkshire, and then we would be free to carry on our relationship.'

'So, what went wrong?'

Dave clutched on to the edge of Joe's desk. He closed his eyes as a shudder went through his body. 'It was an accident; an awful, tragic accident. I couldn't believe it; one minute she was screaming and shouting at me—she was like a wild animal, I'd never seen the like—and the next she was just laying there, blood oozing from the back of her head. The silence in the room was unbearable.'

'You're telling me that you killed her?'

'Yes Inspector! I'm telling you I killed her. It happened so quickly. Jesus, just so damn quickly.'

'And why was she shouting at you?'

'She was apoplectic with rage at the suggestion of becoming my permanent mistress. She made it clear that there was no way she was going to live like that; for her it was simple: I should leave Deborah to be with her. When I told her that that was impossible she just went for me.

'My son had told me that she had a violent temper, but I'd always dismissed that as nonsense; as far as I was concerned she was a sweet-natured young woman, not a mean bone in her body. How wrong I was. I tried to fend her off without hurting her. I held onto her arms but she struggled free and fell backwards. I scrabbled to try and catch hold of her but I was too slow. As she hit the hearth there was a sickening sound like some awful sound effect from a radio horror programme, a hammer sinking into a melon, that sort of thing; her head ricocheted once and then she was still.'

'So, why didn't you report the incident at once, if as you say it was an accident?'

'I don't know! I panicked; I couldn't think clearly, it was all so unreal. And then, and then I thought, no one knew she was here, as far as my family were concerned, well, apart from my son who didn't have a clue where'd she gone, she was in Australia. I picked her up, she felt so tiny, and I carried her out to the shed; it was as if I was observing the scene from a distance. I, I put her into our old chest freezer, and then I went back into the living room to clean the hearth. I scrubbed it over and over again. I kept thinking that it was all a terrible dream, I'd wake up and there she'd be, staring into my eyes, comforting me. I drank a bottle of whisky and passed out.' He turned to Harry. 'Would it be possible for me to have a coffee or something?'

Harry glanced at Joe who nodded.

'And when you woke up?'

'That's when I rang my wife. I told her that the conference was a complete and utter waste of time and that I was going to stay on at the cottage to get on with blocking in the fireplace. We'd already discussed how impractical the inglenook fireplace was. I also told her about the pond that Dave had constructed. I'd noticed when I'd first arrived that it was leaking; the ground around the perimeter was very soggy and I suspected that my son had forgotten to include a layer of sand; you need a good layer of sand, it acts as a cushion and prevents small rocks and the like from sticking into the plastic sheeting and damaging it. Essentially it needed rebuilding; it needed to be a bit smaller and much deeper.'

'So it wasn't just a matter of adding an overflow pipe?'

'No, my son had installed an overflow pipe, a horrid plastic one I might add, but an overflow pipe nevertheless.'

'Here you are, I've put two sugars in,' said Harry as he handed Dave some coffee.

'So you *did* need to dig up the pond,' said Joe.

'Thank you, Sergeant,' said Dave. He took a sip before continuing with his account. 'Yes, Inspector, you're quite right. It was all displacement activity, I realise that, but I was in such a state. I just didn't know what else to do. I kept getting flashes of Melissa's body, cold and lifeless, lying in the bloody freezer. Somehow the physical work allowed me to block it out. Anyway, I drained the whole bloody caboodle to check the plastic sheeting and sure enough there was a split in it. When I removed it I noticed something jutting out from the soil beneath; Melissa's oak chest. I hauled it out only to find that it contained a rather macabre human figure made out of twigs, sticks and twine. It even had one of Melissa's dresses on. I thought my son had really lost it and I actually burst out laughing, and then...' he swallowed. 'And then the terrible thought entered my head; I could put Melissa in the chest, rebury it, and rebuild the pond.

'I remember stuffing the split plastic sheeting into the chest and dragging it across to the shed. I retrieved Melissa's body and realised immediately that it wasn't going to fit. I yanked the sheeting out, covered Melissa's body and tied it in place with the twine. It looked like an innocuous black log. I remember grabbing the chainsaw and pulling the cord; it fired up immediately and, without thinking, I lowered the saw across the *log* and, may God forgive me, I sliced it in two. Still in some sort of manic trance, I put the two halves into the chest and wrapped the rest of the sheeting around it, dragged it back to the pond, buried it more deeply and then drove over to the builder's merchants to purchase sand and thick plastic sheeting. I finished the job in a couple of days. The fireplace took a bit longer. Normally I would have got a carpenter in but, well, um, well, I didn't want to risk it, given the awful circumstances.'

'You say you placed the body in a chest freezer that was in the shed?'

Dave swallowed and nodded slowly.

Joe consulted his notes. 'When I visited the cottage my colleagues never mentioned a chest freezer.'

'I dumped it. Never wanted to see the bloody thing again; hired a trailer and took it to the recycling centre. I drove back down to London a few days later.'

The tape machine was switched off. The custody sergeant accompanied Mr Mardle to the cells. Joe collected his notes and made his way along the dimly lit corridor to Marshall's office.